PRAISE FOR NERO BLA
The Crossword Mur...

"A puzzle lover's delight. With a touch of suspense, a pinch of romance, and a whole lot of clever word clues, Blanc has concocted a story sure to appeal to crossword addicts and mystery lovers alike. What's a three-letter word for this book? F-U-N."

—Earlene Fowler,
author of *Seven Sisters*

"Designed to delight both crossword puzzle enthusiasts and mystery readers . . . Adroit wordplay and high society intrigue . . . an enjoyable, complex solution and likable protagonists . . . Clever."

—*Publishers Weekly*

"An inventive, unique novel that shows there are still many creative ways to distribute clues to readers. The story line is clever, uncanny, and entertaining."

—Harriet Klausner

TWO DOWN

NERO BLANC

BERKLEY PRIME CRIME, NEW YORK

TWO DOWN

PRINTING HISTORY
Berkley Prime Crime trade paperback edition / July 2000

The Penguin Putnam Inc. World Wide Web site address is
http://www.penguinputnam.com

ISBN: 0-425-17510-3

Berkley Prime Crime Books are published by
The Berkley Publishing Group, a division of Penguin Putnam Inc.,
375 Hudson Street, New York, New York 10014.
The name BERKLEY PRIME CRIME and the
BERKLEY PRIME CRIME design are trademarks
belonging to Penguin Putnam Inc.

PRINTED IN THE UNITED STATES OF AMERICA

10 9 8 7 6 5 4 3 2 1

Dedicated to
Blake Hawkins
and
Bill Herndon
Friends and mentors of the highest order

ACKNOWLEDGMENTS

Two Down would not have been possible without the
generous contributions of
Lt. Matthew J. Gimple & C.W.O. Bob Booth of the
United States Coast Guard Cutter *Sturgeon Bay,*
and
Dick Hale of Pirate's Cove Marina, Fishers Island,
New York.

Two Down

CHAPTER

1

"Where's Jamaica?"

The question was posed by a self-confident male voice, and it raced upward to the second floor of the Pepper home by way of a curving staircase dominated by a spacious Palladian window. All the trappings of wealth and power appeared framed by this window: the manicured gardens grown dusky silver in autumn's evening light, the impeccable view of the Massachusetts coast, the sculpted trees and marble benches arranged artfully beside a reflecting pool. No lesser house, no distant light or neighborly noise disturbed this perfect scene.

The question was repeated. The male voice had become more insistent.

A woman responded from the second-floor master suite. "In the Caribbean where it's always been." There was an edginess to the tone that could have indicated either anxiety or anger, but it was quickly supplanted by a conciliatory: "Sorry, darling, I just couldn't resist. Jamaica must be still dressing . . . You know how we women are . . ."

"Indeed I do!" The first voice reverberated with smug robustness. "You wear half the clothes we males are forced to don for these events—and you still take twice as long."

"I thought you said we had plenty of time . . ." Although still attempting humor, the timbre had turned crisp.

"We did before you two started staring into your closets . . ."

"But cocktails don't begin until seven-thirty—"

"Do you want to arrive at the same moment as every other guest and wait in an interminable line at the entry gate? You know what it's like getting into the club for this party . . ."

"I'm not going to be rushed . . . And you know Jamaica won't be . . ."

The words continued to collide mid-landing and midstep caroming across the antique Persian carpet, the elegant English landscape paintings, the crystal sconces with their rose silk shades, and the chandelier that hung in their midst like a gigantic, multifaceted diamond.

In a chintz-swagged guest room, the person who had inspired this domestic unease smiled as she walked toward her half-open door. "I'll be down in five, dear ones," she sang out in a rich contralto, "ten minutes at the very most . . . Don't squabble now, darlings; you're my best friends in the entire universe, and we're going to have a perfectly glorious evening."

She smiled again, then caught her reflection in the mirror. For a split second the radiant expression froze, transforming itself into something neither pleasant nor happy. Then, as rapidly, the speaker resumed her buoyant facade and tone. "You don't know how much good it does me to be here with you both. I feel positively reborn. I'll never miss Los Angeles. Never. Never!"

"Say that after you experience one of our New England winters, Jamaica," the man's voice called back.

"Nothing you say can scare me. I'm here to stay. A new life. A new me!"

Jamaica Nevisson—or Cassandra Lovett, as she was better known to a legion of adoring fans addicted to the daytime drama *Crescent Heights*—had spent thirteen years in the City of Angels creating, inhabiting, and eventually becoming the raven-haired, emerald-eyed, conniving *femme fatale* of the show. Jamaica had been wearing Cassandra's jet-black wig and emerald-tinted contact lenses so long she'd almost forgotten what she looked like without them.

"I really should thank my lucky stars for that odious photographer," she continued. "I needed a catalyst. I needed to reexamine my priorities!"

"No more disembodied chat, Jamaica." The man called up the stairs again. "I have some very good champagne sitting in ice down here. Two more minutes alone, and I'll be forced to pop the cork."

"Aye aye, sir," was Jamaica's amused response. No sound came from the master suite.

Jamaica finished dressing by pushing a strand of her own short, sandy-brown locks beneath "Cassandra's" black wig. She shook her head slightly, giving the false hair a totally natural appearance, then strolled to a Louis XV dressing table surmounted by a matching mirror. "Forty-five," she murmured. "Almost forty-six." It wasn't a joyful sound.

She smoothed the flesh-colored lines of a skintight, floor-length sheath that had been constructed to appear as if only the random pattern of sequins concealed her body's secrets. From five feet away, Jamaica Nevisson might have been wearing nothing more than a sparse and shiny bouquet. Then she applied a final coat of black mascara to her pale brown lashes, outlined her lips in the dense, carmine color for which "Cassandra Lovett" was famed. While working, she tossed around the words she'd heard moments before: "Where's Jamaica?", and her serene expression darkened into an angry glare.

How many times had some wandering-palmed director or overweight stage manager mangled the same phrase? How many predawn hours had she endured, dragging herself to that wretched studio in the godforsaken San Fernando Valley only to be greeted by a bevy of backbiting scriptwriters armed with *clever* quips about the stupidity of actors and the brilliance of their own art? And how many evenings had she finished taping at eight, or even nine o'clock at night—only to find twenty pages of new dialogue shoved toward her weary chest with a dismissive: "Let's try to get it right tomorrow, huh, babe? For a change—*Cassie, babe?*"

Jamaica glowered at the mirror, shook her raven hair again, and attempted a more winsome pose, but her wrathful expression seemed permanently stuck. Embittered, middle-aged female, it all but shrieked. Stalled career, no permanent relationship, no true and loving home.

Jamaica's shoulders sagged, and her back, always held so proud and straight—and youthful—drooped in despair. Forty-five, she thought again, with all the wrinkles, lines, and blotchy skin to show it. Forty-five in an industry where twenty was considered "seasoned."

When had her age begun to betray her? she wondered, although she already knew the answer. It had been when one particular *paparazzo* had decided to make her his moving target. Catching "Cassandra Lovett" with her proverbial pants down had become his obsession. Jamaica hadn't been able to shop at Neiman's or dine in a Santa Monica bistro without encountering this demon with a Leica. She hadn't been able to approach her home in Holmby Hills without finding him encamped by the gates—or lurking in the neighbor's bougainvillea—waiting for her to take her daily swim, then squeezing off a roll that had ended up as CASSANDRA BARES ALL according to *The Hollywood Globe*'s salacious headline.

Reggie Flack was the cretin's name. On retainer with *The Hollywood Globe,* his main assignment was to photograph Jamaica Nevisson in poses as revealing—and unkind—as possible. He'd stalked her obsessively, taking perverse pleasure in affixing bitingly sarcastic theatrical quotations to each published photo.

The last straw had come several weeks earlier. Jamaica had sailed to Catalina Island on her Oceanis 352 with an "unidentified male friend"—as *The Hollywood Globe* later trumpeted—and had opted to take advantage of a supposedly secluded cove for a topless frolic. How Flack had discovered the outing, she didn't know, but he'd followed the pair to the island, scaled a cactus-infested hillside, and managed to snap a good many unflattering photos, all of which appeared in a full-color center spread under the caption: *The Island of Jamaica—"the Bounded Waters Should Lift Their Bosoms Higher Than the Shores."*

On the day the photo spread had appeared, Jamaica had marched bravely into the studio. She'd been determined to ignore the wretched press, but Phil Carney, the foulmouthed actor who played the show's patriarch, had goaded her unmercifully. "Philly" took delight in torturing the female performers, extras and leads alike, with a daily

torrent of off-color comments—behavior the studio
greeted with deaf ears.

His lewd remarks about Flack's photographs had
pushed Jamaica over the edge. She'd slapped him across
the face, stormed into the production office, told the head
honcho to "take this job and shove it up your expletive
deleted!", and slammed back to her dressing room. From
there, she'd placed a call to her longtime friend Genevieve
Pepper in Newcastle, Massachusetts.

"Come back east!" Genie had laughed in response to her
friend's woeful phone call. "We have plenty of room, and
you know Tom adores having you visit . . . Besides, there's
the Commodores' dinner dance at the Yacht Club on October first. You can shake up the musty old place, and find
some fabulous guy with scads of money! . . . After that,
you and I can charter a boat . . . sail to Nantucket . . .
You'll forget California ever existed . . . And, yes,
Jamaica, the guest rooms *are* equipped with Jacuzzis and
steam showers . . . We're not as primitive in Massachusetts
as you might imagine . . ."

Now, as she sat safely in one of those peaceful guest
suites, there was no question in Jamaica's mind that leaving *Crescent Heights* was the smartest thing she'd ever
done.

Jamaica gave herself another wink, unconsciously repli-
cating Cassandra's come-hither look, then scooped up her
ermine stole from the settee, sailed down the stairway, and
stepped into the Peppers' baronial living room.

"Ahhh . . . There she is. And, looking as luscious as
ever . . . You're going to knock their socks off, Jamaica!"

Compliments came easily to Edison Pepper, or "Tom,"
as he was known to both the elite and humble of the city of
Newcastle. Late forties with an athletic six-foot-four

frame, eyes the color of sun-spattered steel, and perfectly tousled graying hair, Pepper had risen from humble origins to become a phenomenally successful investment banker whose newest venture, Global Outreach and Lender Development Fund, was proving an extraordinary boon to Newcastle's not-for-profit institutions.

Investing their endowment capital with the G.O.L.D. Fund permitted the organizations an enormous return on their money. Everyone from the local historical society to the hospital's new multimillion-dollar children's wing was benefiting handily. With his easy charm and manicured good looks—accentuated this evening by a hand-tailored dinner jacket, watered-silk bow tie, and hefty diamond studs—Edison "Tom" Pepper, was Newcastle's hero.

"It's hard to believe you could look more lovely in person than you did on the set of *Crescent Heights,* but it's true. You're making my knees knock." Tom gave Jamaica a light kiss on the cheek and again called upstairs to his wife, "Genie, Jamaica won the battle . . . I'm off to the conservatory to fetch that bottle of champagne." He glanced at Jamaica. The smile he gave her was dazzling. "Why not? My driver is chauffeuring us tonight."

Genie entered the living room at the precise moment Tom was exiting. Although she was easily five years younger than Jamaica, it took only one glance at Tom to make her realize how potent were her friend's charms. "Two Peppers and one Nevisson, as per your request, sire," Genie said as she tossed her lithe body on a Sheraton sofa whose gold satin upholstery matched the color of her ball gown. Then she raised her voice and called toward the conservatory: "And I defy you to say I'm late."

"I didn't want us to miss the champagne," her husband's distant words replied.

"Thanks to your careful advance planning, we won't."

"Let's make this a festive affair, Genie," he called back. "Please."

The tone had a finality that made Genie grimace—a reaction she tried to hide by adding a quick, dismissive laugh. "I was going to say that if you don't walk away with a husband tonight, the men in this city need to have their heads examined . . . but now I'm not so certain a stuffy Yankee spouse is what you need."

"Who said I was in the market for a mate?"

"Ah, 'my dear Lady Disdain, are you yet living?' " Genie laughed more freely, all tension suddenly gone. "You were marvelous as Beatrice in *Much Ado* . . . When was that? Three years ago? Four?"

Jamaica sidestepped the issue of years, instead answering with an airy: " 'Done to death by slanderous tongues . . . ' "

"That's not true! You got fabulous reviews. Even in New York."

"And you, Genevieve, should never have left the stage."

"Thanks for the compliment, but that was a long, long time ago."

Jamaica forced a smile. "Don't remind me . . . A youthful summer playing everything from Shakespeare to O'Neill—"

"And who was always cast as a lead?"

"Supporting players are just as important as the show's star."

Genie grinned. "But they don't get offers from Hollywood studios . . . Anyway, you look absolutely stunning. I wish I could get away with wearing risqué evening gowns, but Tom is always harping about 'appropriate dress' . . . I'm afraid I'm in serious danger of becoming a dowdy old wife."

Jamaica managed another thin smile. "You, old? Never."

"Next year, I'll be pushing forty."

"My heart bleeds."

The explosive sound of the champagne cork interrupted them.

"The dowdy woman's husband doth call," Jamaica said.

"I'm so glad you decided to leave L.A.," Genie answered as they crossed the marble foyer to join Tom. Their high satin heels clicked over the polished stone. ". . . happy you called us . . ."

"I didn't realize how much I needed to escape until Tom picked me up at the airport yesterday. I feel as if I've been granted a reprieve . . . And I'm so looking forward to leaving for Nantucket tomorrow . . . A week of total privacy . . . Promise me you'll never mention Hollywood."

"I promise."

"Or Beverly Hills . . . or Wilshire Boulevard—or Catalina Island!"

"I swear!" Genie was beaming. "Scout's honor." Then she changed tack by focusing on the planned cruise. Her demeanor became all business. "Of course, I would have preferred to take my own boat, but it's been stripped to the bones for racing . . . However, the yacht broker assured me the *Orion* is brand-new, besides being 'extremely manageable for two gals'—his words." Genie began imitating the broker's condescending delivery. " 'No backstay, Mrs. Pepper . . . a walk-through transom . . . nice taffrail seats. You two gals should have a blast out there . . .' However, I'm still concerned we're—"

"Are you two yammering about spinnakers and tidal charts again?" Tom handed each woman a flute of champagne. "Cheers! Here's to good friends." He raised his glass, then draped a long arm over his wife's shoulders. "Stop worrying, Genie. It's the first of October. Don't most of the experienced sailors hereabouts continue to ply these waters until Thanksgiving?"

"Of course they do," was Jamaica's pleasant rejoinder. "Nantucket's a piece of cake. Thirty miles from Hyannis . . . And an extra thirty or so from here—"

"I still feel we should practice on a day sail before attempting a longer cruise," Genie continued. "Just to get a feel for the way the boat handles—"

"Genie . . . Genie . . . listen to your old pal . . . 'piece of cake' like the lady says." His tone had become perceptibly less patient.

Genie's body stiffened immediately. "Perhaps Jamaica's a better sailor than I, Tom."

"Maybe she's just got bigger—"

"Hey, hey, you two! Break it up! I didn't come east to witness marital feuds. Besides, you'd better not get on this lady's bad side, Tom. Remember what the Bard said: a 'tiger's heart wrapped in a woman's hide.' "

Pepper drained his glass. "That's my little wife, all right. She's quite a determined package—although you might not know it to look at her." He bent down to kiss her, and for a moment they were so consumed with each other, their guest might not have existed. "Listen, darling," Tom finally murmured, "if you get bored with your cruise, you can always head home. Or, hey, ditch the damn boat in Nantucket, and you and your buddy can hole up in that spa they have . . . I'll hire someone to sail the *Orion* back to Newcastle. This is your holiday, remember."

"Why don't you join our little trip, Mistah Peppah, honey?" Jamaica's voice had been transformed by an accent as soft and creamy as magnolia flowers. "Fo'get about the elk or moose or whatevah it is you gonna be shootin' up theah in the no'thlands of Maine."

Tom laughed heartily. "You know I wouldn't set foot on

a boat if it was Noah's Ark and I was the last man on the planet! I'll spend my mini-vacation in a warm cabin on dry land rather that heaving my cookies on the high seas, thank you very much."

"Come with us, Tom darling," Genie added, continuing to nestle close to her husband.

She exuded such wedded bliss that Jamaica found herself sighing in envy. "You're a fortunate woman, Genie. And you're right. I have to find one of these for myself." Then she shook her black mane and raised her glass in homage. "To Tom and Genie Pepper, who saved my life . . . Don't laugh, you two; I mean that! . . . No more *Crescent Heights* . . . no more Reggie Flack . . . no more pea-brained ingenues . . . Here's to good friends, and the glories of life in Newcastle."

CHAPTER

2

Rosco Polycrates had not been placed in this world to wear dinner jackets, frilly white shirts, cummerbunds, mother-of-pearl cuff links and studs, patent-leather shoes, and do-it-yourself bow ties. But when Sara Crane Briephs, the reigning dowager empress of Newcastle's social set, had asked him to attend the Commodores' dinner dance at the city's exclusive Patriot Yacht Club, the invitation had come with one simple request: "Please, Rosco, don't be so *déclassé* as to wear a clip-on bow tie."

A third-generation Greek American and former Newcastle police detective turned private investigator, Rosco's time on earth had made him more than savvy enough to know that a situation involving "self-tie bow ties" required a good deal of advanced planning—even though the salesman at Best Man Tuxedo Rentals had assured him that tying a formal necktie was no more difficult than lacing one's shoes. "Once you get the hang of it," the man had said.

Rosco had opted to allocate a full hour to accomplish the complicated task. It was an activity that made him regret his lack of a fancy Ivy League education. U. Mass. grads just couldn't compete with Harvard alums when it came to this kind of elaborate getup. Those rarefied types could probably tie bow ties in their sleep—and they'd probably inherited the neckties from their fathers' fathers. On the other hand, Rosco's dad had been a commercial fisherman; he'd passed away when Rosco was a kid. Patent-leather shoes and puckery shirts requiring little gold buttons hadn't been among his possessions. Neither had self-tie bow ties.

"Okay, just like shoes," Rosco muttered as he stood before his bathroom mirror, fiddling with a few fractious inches of glossy black satin. As he struggled, his mind skimmed over the events that had garnered this coveted invitation and resultant necktie battle. Two and a half months earlier, Mrs. Briephs' son, the much-lauded cross-word editor at the *Newcastle Herald,* had been murdered. It had been a complex case, involving more than a few prime suspects and a series of bizarre crossword puzzles.

Rosco had finally apprehended the culprit; in doing so, he'd endeared himself to the elderly Mrs. Briephs. All spit and polish, with a personality that defied her eighty-some years, she'd found Rosco's youthful vitality, casual demeanor, and rugged good looks welcomely refreshing in her otherwise constrained world.

"Dang it." Rosco tugged at the ends of the tie and started from the beginning. "Okay . . . just like shoes . . . but backward."

For all the ugliness of the Briephs' case, there had been three very positive outcomes. One, Rosco had formed a lasting friendship with the redoubtable Sara. Two, the killer had been brought to justice. Three—and possibly the most important—Rosco had met Annabella Graham, the young crossword editor of Newcastle's other daily newspaper, the *Evening Crier*.

With an expertise in cryptics and a stubborn streak that had *insisted* the puzzles were connected to the crime, Belle had not only identified Briephs' killer, she'd also snared Rosco's respect, admiration, and deep affection. Fighting their mutual attraction had proven difficult from the beginning. Now most of Newcastle was of the opinion that Rosco and Belle had become "an item."

"Aghhh." He yanked the tie loose once more and pressed the ends flat to his chest. "All right, bucko, concentrate. It's the same as tying . . ." He looked down at his shoes as if to gain inspiration from their knotted laces, but realized he'd already slipped into a pair of rented patent-leather dancing pumps with tidy grosgrain bows. His feet looked as if they'd been clad in an oversized version of a little girl's party shoes. He sighed again and continued to grapple with the tie, thinking of Belle as a sappy smile spread across his face.

The Yacht Club dinner dance would be the first opportunity for Sara and Belle to meet. And although Rosco didn't particularly relish the idea of spending an evening dressed like a gigantic penguin, he was eager to ensure that the women's relationship developed well. Belle was more than capable of holding her own, but Sara could intimidate a striking cobra if she put her mind to it. If the *grande dame* took it upon herself to be *displeased* with a person, it could take that individual a lifetime to elicit even the frostiest smile. Rosco's fondness for both ladies made him acutely aware of the pressure he was facing. He had to make this dinner dance a success.

He glanced at his watch: six-thirty. The hour he'd set aside for tie tying had somehow managed to evaporate.

He'd told Belle he'd pick her up at six forty-five, then Sara at seven, and deliver everyone to the Yacht Club by seven-thirty for cocktails and chitchat and whatever else they did in the halls of power, prestige, and nautical lore. He looked back into the mirror one last time and decided that although not *perfect,* the bow tie was *acceptable.* He grabbed his keys, ducked out of his apartment, and trotted over to his waiting chariot: a canvas-topped, four-wheel-drive red Jeep that predated the Sahara and Laredo models designed to attract the urban cowboys.

October 1 in Massachusetts was often heralded by the crisp signs of a New England autumn: scarlet-hued leaves, the cold blue of the bay, and scudding whitecaps that looked as clean and frothy as fresh snow. But this evening was unseasonably mild, and the sinking sun had left a mellow pink-orange streak in the sky. The bigwigs at the Patriot Yacht Club party couldn't have asked for a better night.

Rosco seriously considered removing the Jeep's canvas top for one final summery ride, but decided against it. Instead, he slipped a cassette of an early Ella Fitzgerald recording into his antiquated tape player and eased into traffic. He arrived at Belle's front door fifteen minutes later.

Annabella Graham lived on Captain's Walk in the oldest section of Newcastle north of the original piers along the river that bore the city's name. The tiny houses were first built and owned by seafarers in the early eighteenth century. Two centuries of Massachusetts' snow and ice, and an increasing exodus of city dwellers had left the places vacant and in gross disrepair, but a dozen years prior, a number of adventurous souls had purchased the derelict properties and returned them to their original charm. Belle's former husband, Garet Burke, had been part of this vanguard group. Garet was an Egyptologist who'd discovered he had more interest in tombs and mummies than he had in his wife—a concept Rosco found hard to fathom.

Rosco, the semitough ex-cop, had fallen for the erudite (and often quixotic) Belle hook, line, and sinker. He considered her the best thing that had ever happened to him—a thought that had lodged in his mind at the exact moment she opened the door in greeting.

"Rosco, look at you!" Her beaming smile indicated she was as stuck on him as he on her. "You're absolutely gorgeous!"

"Me . . . ? What about . . . you?"

Tall and slim with vibrant, dark gray eyes, and hair as pale and fine as corn silk, Belle looked as if she'd just stepped out of a 1920s Pierce-Arrow advertisement. Her floor-length gown was midnight-blue satin, exposing her shoulders and slender arms, while the narrow skirt seemed molded to her hips. When the fabric met the floor, it flared out as though her feet were dancing. Again, Rosco was reminded of a picture from another era.

"John Singer Sargent," she said as if in answer to an unspoken question. "What do you think?" She spun around in an excited circle. *"Madame X."*

Rosco grinned; he'd grown accustomed to Belle's rarefied references, and a brain in perpetual motion. "I take it that's not the name of the designer—or the dress style."

"What a guy." Belle laughed indulgently; her eyes flickered with delight. "Sargent's portrait of one of his patronesses is entitled *Madame X* . . . I couldn't resist buying this dress; it's almost identical to the one in the painting. It makes me feel like the queen of the world."

"I'll bet the lady in the picture didn't look as nifty as you."

"In Sargent's interpretation she did . . . but then most of

his women subjects look downright lascivious . . . I think John Singer did a good deal more than simply *paint* his ladies—or if he didn't, he wanted to . . ." Belle suddenly furrowed her brow with a quizzical expression Rosco had learned to recognize as a sign that reality had entered her lofty realm. "What happened to your necktie?"

"What do you mean?" He patted the black satin with nervous fingertips. "Is something wrong?"

"It's a little . . . off. Gives you a kind of raffish, Wile E. Coyote look."

"I'll take that as a compliment."

Belle laughed. "You shouldn't . . . Here, let me fix it."

She stepped up to Rosco, and loosened the tie. As she worked, he placed his hands on her waist and attempted to kiss her.

"Ah, ah, ah . . . I just put on my lipstick. Besides, we have to leave. I don't want to be late for my first meeting with Sara. Not after the grim stories you've prepped me with."

"Hey, tonight'll be easy as pie compared to a Polycrates 'Third Tuesday' family shoot-out. Which, I'll remind you, is a gauntlet you have yet to run."

"Personally, I think your big sisters sound like fun."

"That's because you don't have any . . . And don't forget the Polycrates dinners come with two overbearing brothers-in-law, a handful of clamorous nieces and nephews, assorted aging and opinionated cousins—some of whom still speak Greek exclusively—one younger brother with a revolving assortment of jobs and lady friends, and one sister's *ex*-husband, who's always invited because Mom likes him much better than her present mate, 'The Troll.' "

"Uh-oh." Belle chuckled. "Does that mean I have to compete with the ghosts of your past?"

"Only with one . . . and my mother didn't like her."

Belle cocked an amused eyebrow. "Thus your quick two-year stint into married life?"

"I make my own decisions about domestic relationships," he answered a little stiffly.

She smiled again. "I wouldn't be so boastful, if I were you. It sounds as if you get a lot of help."

"Greek women are pros when it comes to dispensing advice."

Belle finished looping Rosco's tie into a perfect bow. "You're right, an evening with Sara Crane Briephs is beginning to sound like child's play. At least she speaks a language I can understand."

"That's what you think."

"And on your next 'Third Tuesday,' I vow to positively resist all temptation to say, 'It's Greek to me.' "

"Smart choice."

They strolled toward the Jeep hand in hand. But when Rosco opened the door for Belle, she suddenly balked. "I don't know, Rosco . . . Do you think you should have rented a car for this evening?"

"This is a car."

She sighed. "Well, yes, if you want to get picky about definitions, it is . . . What I meant was . . . would it have been advisable to consider renting something a bit more . . . more—"

"Upscale? I asked Sara that very question. She knows about the Jeep, but insisted it's *nouveau* to *rent* limousines." Rosco attempted a Sara Crane Briephs voice: "If you don't own one, my dear boy, you have no business riding *around* in one."

Belle laughed, then turned serious. "I hope I pass muster. She sounds dreadfully overbearing."

"You'll do fine, Belle. She's very 'fond' of me. She'll be just as crazy about you."

Belle groaned. "Is that the type of specious reasoning they spout at the police academy? That women who share affection for the same man are the best of friends? I would imagine the idea would raise the hackles of any criminal investigator."

"I'm talking about Sara. Not an ax murderer."

"What's that line about a jealous woman from Shakespeare's *The Comedy of Errors*? 'Poison more deadly than a mad dog's tooth . . . '?"

Pride spread across Rosco's face. "I'll never understand how you *know* all this peculiar stuff. You're basically a walking encyclopedia, aren't you?"

In the rosy darkness, Belle's bare neck and shoulders blushed a shining crimson while her lips formed a small, self-deprecating smile. "I told you, I had an eccentric childhood . . . Just don't ask me to quote Nancy Drew."

"How about the Hardy Boys?"

"Don't tell me you read the Hardy Boys?"

Rosco chortled. "Hey, just because I have relatives who don't speak English doesn't mean I didn't have a normal American childhood."

They pulled into White Caps' sweeping circular gravel drive at five minutes before seven. The Briephs estate sat high on Liberty Hill, overlooking Newcastle and the harbor beyond. Sara's brother, Hal Crane, a United States senator, owned the adjacent property. Both pieces of land had been in the Crane family for over three hundred years and were a dominant feature on the city's landscape. The exterior of the homes, their manicured gardens, and brick outbuildings had been only slightly altered since they'd been built in the mid-1700s, creating the impression that the Federal era in a prosperous Massachusetts whaling city was still at hand.

Emma, Sara's faithful maid, opened the door for Rosco and Belle, then led them toward the parlor where the great lady was waiting. Over the years, Emma had assumed many of her mistress's mannerisms, making her a shorter, squarer, slightly younger version of the home's *doyenne*.

Walking behind the maid's starchy form and listening to the taffeta rustle of her black uniform, Belle experienced the same unease Rosco had encountered during his initial visit to White Caps, although to Belle the engendered memories were of sojourns to the unconventional homes of her professor parents' friends. She recalled similar dimly lit and foreboding hallways, the slow tock of a grandfather clock, paneled doors that hid unseen rooms— and a sense of dread that she was about to endure another excruciating interview: What Has Little Annabella Graham Learned at School This Week?

Emma turned a polished brass handle and opened a heavy door revealing a surprisingly cheery room that boasted a pleasant fire burning beneath a marble mantel alive with cupids, swagged ivy, and carved bouquets. Bunches of late-blooming roses dotted the many tabletops.

"Mr. Polycrates has arrived, ma'am. And Miss Graham."

Sara stood. Imperious, ice-blue eyes swept over Belle, registered the faintest whiff of approval, then moved to the man of the evening. "Well, well, well, Rosco. I knew you were a handsome devil, but you have certainly outdone yourself. I do so admire a man who handles a necktie to perfection."

"Right . . . Something I picked up at the police academy." He cleared his throat and turned to Belle. "Sara, this is Annabella Graham."

Sara extended a regal hand and waited for Belle to approach. "So nice to make your acquaintance, Miss Graham . . . I am assuming it is Miss . . ." The great lady wore an evening dress almost as antiquated as her home. Jet beads glimmered on black chiffon while over her shoulders was a tippet of ancient brown mink.

"Call me, Belle, please, Mrs. Briephs."

"If you wish, Miss Graham. I'm so pleased Rosco has been able to add a little . . . distraction . . . to his life."

Belle attempted a winning smile. "I try not to distract him too much."

"You are a very lovely young woman, and I'm sure you distract him to no end. Although you should add some weight to your frame. In my day, a man would hardly waste a glance on someone as waiflike." She turned her attention to Rosco. "Well, dear prince, I believe our public awaits. Shall we be off?"

She marched toward him, took his arm, and they paraded to the front door with Belle dutifully trailing behind. When she eventually caught Rosco's glance, she rolled her eyes in such an exaggerated fashion, he almost choked to keep from laughing aloud.

CHAPTER

3

In honor of the dinner dance, the Patriot Yacht Club's security guards had been outfitted in replicas of uniforms worn by Revolutionary War marines. Matching the Colonial-era theme, all exterior electric lighting had been reconfigured into oil lanterns and bayberry candles that illuminated only a few figures at a time while leaving the rest in darkness: women in silk evening dresses hurrying in and out of the light, their escorts half-hidden in timeless black, and the gaitered, brass-buttoned marines who stood at attention as if awaiting General Washington and his entourage.

Approaching the long brick building along a cobble-stoned drive, Belle took it all in. If it weren't for the fact that she'd been crammed into the backseat of an antiquated, slightly rusted, red Jeep, and that the two cars arriving immediately prior to Rosco's were glossy black Lincoln Town Cars, she would have sworn she'd slipped into an earlier era.

Belle had remained quiet for the ride from Sara's house, opting for a speak-when-spoken-to attitude that only compounded the absurd, little-girl sensation of being stuck in the back of Rosco's car. It was like acting a part in a movie, she decided; tonight she was no longer Belle Graham, once married, now divorced, a woman who had a successful job, owned a house, voted, paid taxes, and was romantically involved with one Rosco Polycrates. Tonight she'd been thrust backward through the decades to a time when young women were "girls" and older women their superiors—and despotic chaperons.

Sara had seemed content to spend the trip complimenting Rosco on everything from how exhilarating it was to "travel in such a manly vehicle" to his "choice of haberdashery." Belle practiced smiling to herself, although sometimes the expression turned grim; it wasn't easy to compete with a woman of eighty-plus—especially on that lady's uneven playing field.

As a uniformed valet opened the passenger-seat door, Sara suddenly seemed to remember Belle's presence. "Rosco must be quite smitten with you, Miss Graham," she murmured in a stage whisper. "He usually doesn't wear socks, you know."

Belle forced a smile. "Call me Belle . . . please . . ." then added a determined: "I'm sure Rosco's choice of footwear is your influence, Mrs. Briephs."

Sara laughed as she took Rosco's arm. "We must have tea one of these afternoons, dear girl . . ." She paused for a moment to consider the invitation. Belle could see years of female machinations spinning across a seemingly serene face. "On second thought, I'm free Monday. Shall we say four o'clock?"

Belle groaned inwardly, but a glance at Rosco revealed the importance he placed on her friendship with this fierce old woman. "That will be very nice, Mrs. Briephs."

"Good. Now, Rosco, let us brave the beasts . . . one of them being my brother, Hal."

"I didn't know the senator would be here this evening," Rosco answered while giving Belle a clandestine nod of gratitude and encouragement. "I'll make it up to you," he mouthed. "I promise."

"Oh, my dear! He wouldn't miss this party on a dare! There are more votes in this building than you can shake a stick at—to say nothing of campaign funding in this *all-important* year. I may insist that my brother is a traitor to his class, but, *liberal* though he may be, he remains a Crane in a city where ancestry counts."

With that, Sara swept through the club's entrance as two doormen snapped to attention. Naturally, Sara knew their names—and the names of their offspring. And, naturally, her brief queries on everyone's health were treated like pearls of wisdom.

"Quite a performance," Belle whispered to Rosco.

"She's all right," Rosco answered. "It just takes her a while to warm up."

"Are we talking geological ages? Or human years?"

The club's foyer was awash with people and noise. The multicolored marble floor inlaid with a polished brass compass rose did nothing to diminish the clamor; neither did the domed ceiling, which Belle decided resembled a smaller version of the Capitol's rotunda in Washington. Men in full evening regalia and women with meticulously coiffed and lacquered hair were everywhere; all seemed to be talking at once. Those who weren't already in animated conversation were busy greeting friends; the air was full of ancient, prep-school nicknames and kisses that brushed past powdered cheeks.

"We'll head for the club room," Sara commanded in a stentorian tone. "It's a mostly male enclave, and Hal will be working the crowd. I want him to meet you, Rosco . . . at long last." She smiled glowingly, although the expression was not intended for her brother.

As the three pushed their way through the jostling throng, a voice with a curiously mannered British accent assailed them: "Mrs. Briephs! Such an *inestimable* pleasure! An event such as this would never be complete without your *gilded* presence!" The speaker was a diminutive man with a nearly bald head across which a few wispy strands of parchment-colored hair drifted in the breeze. Everything about him was small, almost preposterously frail, but the most outstanding feature of his appearance was a pair of horn-rim glasses so large and prominent they made his eyes look like those of a mutant insect. Six weeks prior, amid great hoopla—and a lucrative new contract—Bartholomew Kerr had been lured from his position as society-page editor of the *Newcastle Herald* to create a gossip column at the *Evening Crier*: a column known as *Biz-y Buzz* that was already the rage of the city's socialites.

A notepad seemed permanently affixed to Kerr's tiny left hand while a pencil paused doggedly in his right and a battered camera drooped from a strap around his neck. "You know who's rumored to be coming tonight, don't you?" Bartholomew's bug eyes glinted upward. He nodded briefly but magnanimously to fellow *Crier* employee Belle, while nearly ignoring Rosco—all the while affixing a rapturous expression on Sara. Kerr was a man who knew where his bread was buttered. "A photo, dear lady, if I may be so bold?"

Her picture was snapped before the *grande dame* had

time to protest. "I have not been apprised of the guest list, Bartholomew," she said. "But I imagine it comprises the usual suspects." Sara extended icy fingers and moved on before Bartholomew had further opportunity to speak. "Dreadful snoop," she whispered to Rosco. "When he worked at the *Herald,* my son had the most terrible things to say about him." Then memory stopped her. "But, of course, you know that—"

A communal gush of "It's Jamaica Nevisson!" interrupted Sara as the actress made a dazzlingly theatrical entrance. She paused mid-stride as if overwhelmed by the throng before her, then cast down bashful eyes that finally rose in hopeful exultation. In the space of a nanosecond she transformed herself from lowly walk-on to glamorous diva; every inch of her sculpted body reverberated with pride in her well-honed powers of persuasion.

With Jamaica, of course, were the Peppers. Genie shrank back with a gentle murmur of "Good evening all," but Tom quickly captured a sizable piece of the limelight. A crowd of pedigreed, Ivy-Leagued, moneyed, and socially superior citizens surged slavishly toward the trio, calling out an excited round of "Tom! Good to see you, old man!"; "Genie! Looking marvelous as ever!"; "And this must be your intriguing houseguest . . . ?"

"Well." Sara sniffed. "So, it's come to this! Actresses and *arrivistes* ruling the Patriot Yacht Club! And look at that scandalous frock! What is this city coming to?"

"Here's to the suspension of reality," Rosco whispered to Belle.

"The last of the great Greek philosophers, I see." She smiled in return, then looked at Jamaica again. Envy and curiosity filled her brain. While those thoughts careened around her head, Bartholomew Kerr snapped a photo.

"Very nice, Annabella," he purred. "*Stage Struck?*, I think I'll call it."

"I'd say you were definitely a fish out of water." The husky female voice was closer to Rosco's ear than the crowd lining the dance floor seemed to warrant. He took his eyes from Belle and a rather cumbrous and sweaty partner to find Jamaica Nevisson beside him.

"Watch out, boy, this lady's big trouble for single guys." Tom materialized at her back. Close up, they looked larger than life. Rosco had a sense of something like electrical energy emanating from their bodies; his reaction was to inch forward as if these two people had created their own magnetic field.

"Let me guess," Pepper's voice boomed out. "Navigational aids?"

"What?" Rosco's mind was blank.

"No, no, wait . . . You look like a guy who sees more action than someone who owns a manufacturing company . . . Yacht Club . . . Yacht Club . . . Don't give me any hints; I'm good at this . . . Wait, I've got it! . . . You're a member of the America's Cup team, right?"

Rosco almost turned around to see if Pepper was addressing a person other than himself, but Tom's powerful gaze held him—as did the hearty smile, the perfect white teeth, the knot in the formal tie that Rosco couldn't have replicated in a hundred years. No doubt about it, Tom Pepper was a charismatic guy. "I'm not a sailor, sir—and never will be. My name's Rosco Polycrates . . . I'm a private investigator."

Tom's infectious laughter pealed forth again. "A private eye! What do you know! . . . And with a name like Rosco!

I like it . . . Strong product recognition . . . That's good . . . That's good . . . Marketing is everything these days . . . a private eye . . ."

Then he turned quietly earnest. "Forget the 'sir' business, Rosco. I'm Tom, and this is my wife's longtime friend Jamaica Nevisson. The two gals were actresses together, if you can believe it . . . That's before I snagged my little Genie away from the boards." Tom looked at Jamaica with an expression Rosco could only interpret as that of a benevolent relative ignoring a youthful indiscretion.

"I saw your photo in *The Globe*," Rosco stammered, and immediately regretted the remark. When Tom's face clouded in anger, Rosco felt decidedly worse.

"Ahhh, then you've seen quite a bit of me." Jamaica drew out the words; although her expression had turned stony, her tone was disturbingly flirtatious.

"Well, it was in the supermarket . . . I only saw the cover. I didn't open up the magazine."

"You must be the only man in America who didn't." A tight smile played across Jamaica's wide lips.

"It was an outrageous invasion of privacy," Tom fumed. His healthy pink skin had turned a mottled red. "Jamaica's been hounded by that lunatic photographer for years. Coming out here was the only way she could lose him."

Jamaica kept her sultry gaze on Rosco. "Maybe I should get myself a private dick . . . What do you think, Tom? Get rid of that damned Flack once and for all?"

But Pepper ignored the question, giving Rosco the impression that the investor already had a plan for dealing with Jamaica's pesky *paparazzo*—a plan, Rosco imagined, involving a phalanx of highly paid lawyers. "So, Rosco, I take it you and I are the only men here who aren't mad for water sports?"

"I'm happier on dry land." Rosco started to insert another deferential "sir," but stopped himself in time.

"Put 'er there, pardner! I can't put my feet on anything that rocks or rolls or pitches or tosses, without worrying I'll lose my lunch . . . I leave nautical pursuits to the distaff side."

"I still wish you'd agree to come to Nantucket with Genie and me tomorrow, Tom," Jamaica cooed, although her green eyes remained fastened to Rosco. "It would be such fun!"

"Not for me, it wouldn't! . . . So, Rosco, how does a landlubber like you find yourself at a shindig like this? Or are you here on business?"

Tom's broad wink made Rosco relax, and he began to explain his connection to Sara—and then to Belle—while Pepper nodded enthusiastic approval, concluding with a noisy "I like this guy!" that seemed loud enough for half the room to hear.

But before conversation could continue, Pepper and Jamaica were lured away with enthusiastic cries of "Tom! The mayor needs to talk with you about . . ." and "Miss Nevisson, may I introduce . . . ?" In parting, Jamaica gave Rosco's arm a gentle but provocative squeeze. "Come for supper with your little lady sometime. Genie and I are off on a weeklong cruise tomorrow . . . but after that . . . I plan to be around Newcastle for a while . . . a long while . . ." The way Jamaica said "a long while" made Rosco blush all the way down to his patent-leather shoes.

"I saw that." Belle had stepped off the dance floor, deserting her sweating partner with a polite but unencouraging smile.

"Who was Mr. Twinkle Toes?" was Rosco's hurried rejoinder.

"Don't try to change the subject . . . an *associate* of Garet's. I don't remember meeting the man, but he insisted we were introduced five years ago at some museum function . . . Well, what's up with La Nevisson? Quite a dress, isn't it?"

But Rosco wasn't about to be hoodwinked into discussing the actress's attire—or lack thereof. "She was inviting us for supper."

Belle cocked her head and gave Rosco a quizzical stare. "Us? As in you and I?"

The term "your little lady" bombarded Rosco's brain, but he managed a seemingly nonchalant, "Sure, why not?"

"Watch out for her, Rosco. She spells trouble with a capital *T*."

"Funny, that's just what Pepper said."

"Well, maybe you should heed his warning."

The "powder room" was rose pink and dove gray, and festooned with so many orchids in baskets and cachepots that Belle almost wondered whether she'd wandered into a florist's shop. The two rooms were also chockablock with seriously primping party goers. She watched a rainbow of lipsticks, lip pencils, lip glosses, eye shadows, blush, foundation, and powder flash from jeweled, beaded, and embroidered evening bags. Perfume spritzes clouded the air, while frothy conversation and a good deal of purposeful gossip continued amid a patter of "Fabulous color!"; "I don't know *what* he did with my hair, this time"; "Do you really like it?"; "I thought I'd resurrect it for the night"; and a bevy of "Great party!"; "Isn't it a gorgeous party?"; "Glorious evening." In typical fashion, the women glanced only at the faces reflected in the mirror.

No dialogue, either serious or otherwise, was conducted face-to-face.

Belle smiled at the frivolity of the atmosphere and flicked a comb quickly through her hair as Genie and Jamaica suddenly joined the throng. No one turned to look at the newcomers, although every pair of eyes swiveled toward their mirror images. Belle sensed that Jamaica was keenly aware of the reaction, but also recognized that the actress was feigning indifference. Her voice became louder than necessary.

"Darling, it's simply too divine," she said to Genie. "Something out of a play by A. R. Gurney. All these marvelous WASPs buzzing around their natural habitat. An endangered species, I'd say . . ."

Genie appeared slightly unnerved by her friend's remarks, but she also seemed to be feeling the effects of champagne and a full orchestra. There was something giddy and reckless in her demeanor. She grinned mischievously into the mirror, catching curious glances from the other women gathered at the long dressing table while Jamaica continued her languid speech.

". . . It almost makes me regret my decision to become an entertainer. I should have followed your example, Genevieve, and snagged a domesticated male . . ."

The powder room had hushed to near silence.

". . . According to my dear mama, however, a career on the stage was an excellent first step in capturing a wealthy man. She was from the Marion Davies School."

Teasing her hair, Genie answered her friend in a stagy tone. "But surely there are wealthy men in Los Angeles, Jamaica."

"Too many secrets out there, darling. One never knows for certain whether a partner is gay or straight or in between—even after marriage . . ."

A gasp from an elderly matron seemed to pass Jamaica unnoticed.

". . . And that goes for the young men as well as the old. Ah, me, what's a working girl to do?" Then the actress suddenly noticed Belle standing there. "Your husband's quite a dish," she said without taking her eyes off her own reflection.

At first Belle was unaware she was being addressed, then she stammered, "He's not my husband." The words sounded hideously loud in her ears. She realized she'd become an additional focal point for the women primping at the mirror.

"No? I assumed everyone in this charming little ville was respectably wed."

Belle found herself growing irritated at Jamaica's patronizing assumptions. "Not all of us, no." The terse reply was intended to denote not only an autonomous state but also Belle's career, education, and proud self-reliance. The actress batted aside the response as if it were a mere ball of fluff.

"You're a pretty girl. I can't imagine you've been lacking in marriage proposals."

Whether it was the term "girl" or the actress's snooty tone, Belle flushed angrily. "I *was* married," she answered.

"Ah . . ." Jamaica calmly replied. "So, you tested the waters and found them tepid . . . or possibly too hot?"

In answer, Belle jammed her comb into her purse and snapped it shut. She was not about to discuss romance with a woman for whom the word had no meaning. Jamaica, however, had other ideas.

"And now you're on the rebound with a private dick—"

"That's not how I would categorize our relationship,"

Belle interrupted hotly, but Jamaica hadn't finished her performance.

"And this *ex-husband* you are so loath to discuss . . . I assume he's the spitting image of your parents?"

Belle's jaw dropped. She wanted to contradict the statement, but couldn't. Jamaica was correct. Garet had manifested many traits of the elder Grahams—and not the better ones, either.

"You see, Genie?" Jamaica continued. "There is the psychology of true drama . . . the inner life of the mind . . . That's what made *you* a good performer. You were able to enter your characters' brains and inhabit the murky unconscious. Subliminally, we all want Mummy and Daddy; we want to be carefree babies again." Then she turned toward Belle, adding a seemingly benevolent: "Following the end of a permanent relationship, you must always beware of 'transitional' situations, darling. I've had a number of such impermanent types in my life. It's important to know that some lovers are not intended to linger. Many, in fact."

"Oh, really, Jamaica," Genie said with a wry shake of her head. "What a wicked thing to say to this poor woman. To say nothing of presumptuous!" Genie extended her hand. "I'm Tom Pepper's wife," she said with a genuine smile. "We haven't met, although I know you by reputation."

"Belle Graham." The look Belle gave Genie was full of gratitude—as well as a core recognition that Jamaica with her clever verbiage and facile innuendo would continue to spin circles around them all.

The actress intruded upon the incipient friendship. "A word to the wise never hurt anyone, Genie darling. 'Transitional' doesn't mean impossible."

Genie turned away from Belle and studied her friend. "You're a vicious person, Jamaica," she said with a bemused chuckle. "And I disagree with your previous statement. Words can do a great deal of harm."

CHAPTER

4

T ry as she might, the term "transitional" had stuck in Belle's brain. Jamaica's obnoxious warning had nearly ruined the remainder of the dinner dance. Sunday had also seen Belle laboring under its gloomy shadow; she'd had a difficult time thinking about Rosco without the epithet sneakily inserting itself into the picture. He was so very different from Garet, so very different from the aloof and bookwormish people with whom she'd been raised.

Involuntarily, she began questioning her decision, wondering whether Rosco was merely a passing fancy, someone she'd "get over" when she "came to her senses." It bothered her horribly that she could hear parental disapproval whispering in her ears—especially since her mother was long dead and her father almost incommunicado from his distant home in the Florida Keys. I'm thirty-two years old, Belle reminded herself repeatedly. I don't have to please anyone but myself. Gentrified Garet was the aberration, not Rosco. It's normal to have a big, tumultuous family rather than the other way around. But Rosco's descriptions of the Polycrates clan kept clanking ominously through her thoughts.

For these reasons—and maybe a hundred others—having tea on Monday with Sara Crane Briephs was the last thing Belle wanted to do. But she'd agreed, and she never reneged on her word. If she happened to catch pneumonia or break her leg in a freak fall down the stairs, well, that would be another thing . . .

Disconcertingly whole and healthy, Belle rang the bell at White Caps precisely at four o'clock Monday afternoon. As before, Emma led the way through the austere foyer, conducting her to the house's mistress as if delivering a sacrificial lamb.

After a few murmured pleasantries, Belle found herself seated with her ankles demurely crossed and her back barely touching the rigid frame of an antique chair. An inquisition conducted by a grade-school headmistress could not have begun more forbiddingly. The great lady poured; Emma proffered the filled cup; Belle sipped and then sipped again; the weather was mentioned, likewise the "journey from Captain's Walk" (all of fourteen minutes away). Belle began counting the seconds until she could reasonably take her leave. Rosco was going to have to face this grueling friendship alone.

"More tea, Belle?" The hostess sat rigidly erect in a crimson-backed chair so stiff and imposing it resembled a medieval throne. She can't possibly be comfortable, Belle thought, but inadvertently sat straighter in her own high-backed chair.

"Thank you, Mrs. Briephs."

Emma removed Belle's gold-rimmed porcelain cup and relayed it to her mistress, who then lifted both cup and saucer in one hand while raising the teapot in the other. Steaming, golden liquid cascaded unhesitatingly through the air in a ritual so practiced it looked faintly religious.

"Another slice of lemon?"

"Please." Belle very nearly added, "ma'am." Instead, she uncrossed and recrossed her ankles in an involuntary replication of childhood.

"So, both of your parents were professors?"

"Yes . . ."

"Up until your mother's untimely demise, I should say?"

"Yes, that's correct." Again, a traitorous voice almost inserted a squeaky "ma'am."

"And your father no longer teaches?"

"He lives in Florida." The answer struck both Belle and Sara as odd—as if the entire state contained no institutions of higher learning. Sara raised a quizzical eyebrow while Belle hastened to amend the statement. "He has a house in the Keys . . . in Marathon. We rarely see each other."

Sara paused as if considering an appropriate response, then silently passed the refilled cup to Emma, who returned it to Belle before withdrawing noiselessly to the tea cart.

Belle fidgeted with the cup, picked up her teaspoon, and stabbed the lemon slice floating on the surface of the hot liquid, an activity her hostess regarded with a quick, basilisk stare. Repressing a sigh, Belle placed the dainty silver spoon on her saucer. What, she wondered, would a person do with a sugar lump or two?

"Marathon," Sara mused. "Part of a *tetrapolis* in ancient Attica . . . the sight of the famous battle in which the Greeks defeated the Persians in 490 B.C. . . . Did your father choose his domicile because of the name association?"

"I don't know, Mrs. Briephs."

The answer seemed to take Sara by surprise. "But surely you must have discussed the historical reference? It's so very obvious."

"My father and I seldom . . ." Belle began, then changed tack, opting for the simpler: "No, we didn't talk about it."

"The relationship between parent and child is a vital one, young lady. My son and I were very close. We were not only family, we were best of friends."

Belle's determined lack of response made Sara pause. She studied the younger woman, then redirected her conversation. ". . . So, your cerebral upbringing inspired you with an appreciation for learning and the mastery of language, which facility enabled you to establish a career as a word maven—similar to my son's chosen profession?"

"Well, no . . . not precisely in that order," Belle said.

A round crystal plate containing minute cucumber sandwiches arrayed on a lace doily was passed by the mute Emma. Mrs. Briephs declined the comestible with a slight but gracious smile, then turned to Belle with a dictatorial: "From our garden. The seeds were brought from England by my forebears. No one else grows cucumbers like these."

Belle juggled her cup in one hand to select a tiny sandwich, then wondered where to put it. "Thank you, Emma," she murmured, repressing a groan. She imagined the phone ringing to announce a disaster, the kitchen catching fire, the furnace exploding: anything that would curtail this hideous conversation.

" 'Not precisely' like my son's vocation, do you mean?" Sara demanded. "Or are you referring to your own career path?"

Belle felt her hackles rise. Sara's questions had become far too intrusive. Life wasn't precise; how could anyone suggest that work—or relationships—have an orderly flow? If routine and safety were prerequisites to living, she wouldn't have met Rosco. In fact, she'd probably still be married to the lordly Garet. Or—and here, Belle's imagination began taking giddy flight—she would have waltzed away from college, decamped to Paris, where she'd currently be living in bohemian splendor on the infamous Left Bank.

Then, before she knew it, the damnable word "transitional" roared into her head. Belle clutched the saucer tighter. She was very tempted to heave it onto the table and run hollering from the room.

Instead, reason and a grudging respect for Sara's age took charge. "I used the term 'not precisely,' Mrs. Briephs, because I didn't set out to write crossword puzzles. I intended to become a poet."

"Who stopped you?"

"No one. I stopped myself . . . I wasn't very good."

The response brought another quick smile to the old lady's face. "Good answer," she said. "I like honesty in people and architecture."

While Belle, in order to subdue her ire, took another cucumber sandwich, and gave Emma a decidedly pointed: "Thank you."

A conspiratorial glance passed between Sara Crane Briephs and her minion; and Emma withdrew, leaving the tea cart behind. Belle was strongly tempted to follow in her trail, but she stuck to her guns and chomped the last bite of wafer-thin bread.

"Your parents raised you properly, I'm happy to see," Sara observed placidly. "Well-bred people are always courteous and considerate to those who serve them. Only upstarts need to display their self-importance by humbling others."

Belle imagined she was about to undergo additional queries on her history, but Sara apparently had dispensed with the past. "What is your impression of Edison Pepper?"

"We weren't introduced," Belle responded warily.

"Lucky for you!"

Belle was about to retort that Rosco had thoroughly enjoyed his conversation with Pepper, when the true cause of Sara's wrath was revealed.

"That awful woman in that absurd dress! Did you see how she was trying to bamboozle Rosco?"

The archaic colloquialism made Belle's bright eyes flash with humor—a mistake as she quickly realized.

"I see nothing funny about it, young lady! A woman of obvious artifice employing what was clearly a dearth of art. And nearly naked, to boot! In my day—"

"Rosco's a grown man, Mrs. Briephs; he can take care of himself."

"I'd be more careful if I were you. When a woman is that obvious in her flirtation, she will stop at nothing."

Belle frowned, then began wondering whether Jamaica's conversation in the powder room had been a ruse, an attempt to create a wedge between Rosco and herself. "We've been invited to dine at the Peppers' home in a week or so," she admitted slowly.

"Just so," Sara growled. "Just so . . . Well, mind your p's and q's."

Unbidden, a plethora of words beginning with *p* and *q* zoomed into Belle's brain. *Potentate*, she thought. *Purpose, Pluck, Philanderer . . . Quail, Quell, Quisling . . .* Then Genie's pronouncement "words can do a great deal of harm" rushed forward. It seemed like a warning, as if Genie were well aware of Jamaica's predatory nature.

"Genie seems pleasant," Belle finally ventured.

Sara stared, perplexed.

"Genevieve . . . Mrs. Pepper . . . I met her in the loo . . . the ladies' room—"

"I know what a 'loo' is, young lady. I'm not asking for an explanation of vulgarisms, I am seeking your opinion of this social climber Edison Pepper."

Belle's face turned fiery red. She opened her mouth to speak when the grand old woman suddenly slammed her teacup on the table. The vigor of her action nearly shattered the saucer.

"I'm sorry, Belle. Forgive me, please . . . I've gotten off to an exceedingly poor start with you. I've made myself seem like a cantankerous old cow . . . My son would not have been proud." Tears swam into Sara's eyes and down her powdered cheeks. She didn't bother to dab them away. "In fact, he would have been appalled."

Belle stared slack-jawed, then half rose from her seat. The sudden display of emotion had affected her more than she knew. She fumbled in her purse for a handkerchief, but found only a crumpled tissue. "I don't seem to have a handkerchief, Mrs. Briephs—"

"Sara. Call me Sara." The old lady swiped at her glistening cheeks with fingers bony and rigid with a lifetime's worth of self-discipline. For the first time Belle understood the effort required to create such an indomitable facade.

"Yes, I will . . ." Belle was about to walk to the old woman's side when the door flew open and a breathless Emma rushed in.

"Oh, madam, I just heard it on the radio in the butler's pantry . . . Those Pepper people who bought the old

Drexel estate on the point . . . The Coast Guard says the missus's boat caught fire in Buzzards Bay . . . a tragedy for all of Newcastle, the radio is saying . . . Both women are reported lost at sea. . . ."

CHAPTER

5

R osco was leaving his office when the phone rang. He decided to let his answering machine take the call, but when he recognized Belle's shaky voice, he grabbed the receiver.

"Hi. I'm here. Are you all right?"

"Did you hear the news?"

"Two hours ago. Tom Pepper called me right after the Coast Guard notified him. He was already on board his plane, flying back from his hunting cabin. He asked me to meet him at his home."

"It's horrible, Rosco, I . . . I just talked to those women Saturday . . . Genie seemed so . . . She seemed so nice . . ."

"And she probably still is, Belle. Let's not assume the worst. The boat was badly burned but afloat, and the Coast Guard hasn't located the *Orion*'s inflatable tender yet. Besides, the women were known to be excellent sailors; they should have been able to handle almost any situation."

"But what if the tender tore loose in the blaze and they couldn't escape?"

"Then the Coast Guard would have found two bodies aboard the *Orion*—which they did not, meaning the women and the dinghy have to be somewhere . . . There's a full search-and-rescue operation under way, Belle. We have to give it a little time."

Belle remained quiet for a long moment. "Why does Pepper want to see you?"

"He's very upset . . . which is natural. And he's a guy who's accustomed to getting things done quickly—and calling all the shots. Obviously, the Coast Guard has no answers presently. So . . . he's not a happy man."

"You mean he's *hiring* you? To investigate this?"

"Like I said, he's upset. I'll just have to talk to him. See what he has in mind. I've investigated maritime loss in the past. He knows that."

"Well, he must be thinking the fire's a result of foul play." Rosco could almost hear Belle's brain whirring with this new piece of information.

"I doubt that. Most likely, he just wants to make sure the Coast Guard is giving the situation one hundred percent . . . Which you can bet they are; they don't go into these things halfheartedly."

"You really believe Genie and Jamaica are all right?"

"Absolutely."

Another unhappy pause. "I'd been thinking some terrible things about Jamaica . . . I wish I hadn't . . . It makes me feel so guilty . . ." Then Belle's practical side kicked in; she was a person addicted to finding solutions. Ambiguity and doubt were two sensations she abhorred. "Why didn't the women radio for help—or even phone? I can't imagine Jamaica going *anywhere* without a cell phone."

"I'll check with Pepper. Maybe he knows." Rosco

glanced at his watch. "Look, I should be going. I told him I'd be there by five-thirty. Are you all right?"

". . . Yes."

"You're sure? You don't sound it."

"I'm okay . . ."

"I'll stop by after I leave Pepper's, how's that?"

"Thanks."

"I almost forgot . . . How was tea?"

"We're still having it . . . Sara says hello . . ."

Rosco smiled into the receiver. "Sara?"

"I'll be home at six," Belle said in answer. "Get there when you can."

The drive from Rosco's office to the Pepper home took about twenty minutes. It was five or six miles south of the Yacht Club on a high bluff. On a clear day the property would have had a commanding view of the coastline and the sea beyond, but a thick bank of burly gray clouds had suddenly swept in from the east, bringing with it a squally rain that stung Rosco's face as he stepped from his Jeep. He turned up his coat collar, trotted over to a broad entry portico, and rapped three swift times with the polished brass knocker. The door was opened by a short, beefy man in his sixties. He was dressed in the formal black suit of a butler, but his build was more like that of an aging bodyguard.

"You must be Mr. Polycrates." The accent was vaguely British, although Rosco guessed England wasn't the man's country of origin.

"Yes."

"Come in, please. Mr. Pepper is expecting you."

From over the butler's shoulder Rosco heard Pepper call out an irritable: "That's all, Anson. No . . . Wait! Take the man's coat. Hang it up."

After Rosco had shed his soggy coat, Pepper approached. A rocks glass filled with Scotch was in his left hand. He offered his right to Rosco. "I appreciate the hell out of you coming here on such short notice . . . The weather's certainly turned foul . . . Scotch?"

"I think I'll pass. Thanks."

Tom stared down at the glass. "Yeah, you're right. It's early . . . Sorry, I just needed to calm myself down. I'm a wreck . . . Why don't we step into my office. I've set up a command post there."

Rosco followed Pepper down a corridor whose walls were covered with oil paintings and hunting prints, and they entered a spacious corner room lined, floor to ceiling, with bookcases. A pair of wide bay windows overlooked the bluffs, and the two men stood watching as six-foot swells pounded the rocky coast. The storm was definitely building.

"I can sit in this room and stare at the sea for hours at a time. It fascinates me. I wouldn't go out on it on a dare, mind you, but it's something to look at." As if suddenly aware of the significance of this speech, Pepper sighed heavily.

Rosco turned to face him. "I'm like you . . . I don't do well on the water."

"It just drives me crazy thinking that my Genie could be floating around lost somewhere . . . I mean, look at this stuff . . . How long do you think it would take before—"

"I have a lot of confidence in the Coast Guard, Mr. Pepper," Rosco interrupted gently. "I've seen them handle similar situations in the past. If your wife is out there, they'll find her."

Pepper's response was close to explosive. "I don't want to hear about the damn Coast Guard! I tried to maintain an open line to those SOBs and some 'chief petty officer' cut me off. Told me he'd call when he got something. That's why I phoned you. I don't know where to turn at this point."

"These rescue situations can be a communications nightmare for the Guard. They need every phone line they have."

"What the hell good does that do me?"

"Well, sir—"

"Cut the 'sir' bunk, Rosco. I want my wife back. And I want the man who rented her that damn boat drawn and quartered . . ." He finished his drink and glanced down at the shrunken ice cubes. "You know, she had a premonition . . . And I . . . I laughed at it . . . Laughed at her! . . . My little Genie . . . !" His voice cracked with emotion while he struggled to pull himself together. "She's an excellent sailor, you know . . . She and Jamaica both are . . ." Pepper poured himself another hefty Scotch and dropped his tall frame into a dark green leather club chair. His eyes were bloodshot, and his jaw so tightly clenched his face muscles popped dramatically from under his skin.

"What should I do, Rosco?"

"Do you mind if I sit?" Rosco asked.

"Do whatever you want. Get a drink if you'd like it . . ."

Rosco sat on a couch covered in the same dark leather as the chair. The hide creaked, giving off the luxuriant aroma of an expensive car's interior or of matched luggage in an upscale shop. "I'm not sure there's anything I can do to push the Coast Guard, Mr. Pepper," Rosco said as he pulled a small pad of paper and a pen from his breast pocket. "But why don't you fill me in on this trip your wife planned. I'll see what I can find out."

"What do you want to know?"

"You're a member of the Yacht Club . . . I take it you own a boat?"

"Genie does."

"Why did she charter one, then?"

Pepper sighed deeply. "Hers is a racing sloop. It's stripped for speed. The barest galley, boards for berths . . . It's not for pleasure cruising . . . Not Jamaica's style."

"Who did your wife charter it from?"

"Mystic Isle Yachts." Pepper sat up straight in his chair, his eyes fiery and hot. "That's where I want you to start. I want blood from Mystic's owner. I want him to rot! He set my wife up in a death trap, and I want him to pay big time."

"What exactly happened, do you know?"

"How could I . . . ? All I know is that some fishermen found the *Orion* somewhere in Buzzards Bay. They towed what was left of the boat back to Mystic Isle Yachts . . . Then someone phoned the Coast Guard. The Coast Guard called me. Apparently the *Orion*'s inflatable tender hasn't been found."

"I know this is tough, Mr. Pepper, but I wouldn't give up hope. Until they find that tender, there's a very strong, *very strong* possibility that the women are still alive."

Pepper stood and pointed at the bay window. "Look at those swells, Rosco. The water temperature's already down to fifty degrees. Could you hang on in a four-foot rubber boat? Huh? Could you? Look at the size of those damn waves! Look at them!"

The telephone rang, and Pepper jumped like a jack-rabbit.

"Yes . . . Pepper here," he bellowed into the mouthpiece.

Rosco watched as Tom listened for thirty seconds. He didn't say a word, and finally slammed the receiver down into its cradle.

"That was the damn Coast Guard. They've suspended the air portion of their search because of the weather.

They'll pick it up again when this thing blows out. Visibility's down to nothing."

Pepper drained what remained of his Scotch while Rosco pondered the news and allowed the frightened husband a moment of silence. Rosco avoided glancing at the bay windows and growing surf.

"What about a cell phone?" he finally asked. "Does your wife carry one? Did she have it with her?"

Sitting behind his desk, Tom angled the chair to face the wall of bookcases. He lowered his head, brought his hands to his face, and rubbed hard at his eye sockets. Rosco wasn't certain if he'd been heard or not, but as he opened his mouth to repeat he questions, Pepper spoke in a strangely subdued tone. "Her cell phone . . . that's right . . . she should have had it with her. Yes . . . Yes . . . !"

"I can check transmissions for you." Rosco walked to the desk. He felt such empathy for Pepper, it was hard to remain detached and professional. "I'm afraid this is a waiting game, Mr. Pepper. But I'm an optimist. I only met your wife and Jamaica the other night, but I have a strong feeling they'll come out of this alive. They're survivors." He cleared his throat slightly. "There is another problem that's bound to come up . . . If it hasn't already . . ."

"What's that?"

"The press. Have they called?"

"Not yet."

"They will . . . Jamaica Nevisson's an international celebrity. They'll be camped out in front of your house by tomorrow morning. Do you have any staff? Someone to handle your phone? Someone who can keep them at least out of your drive?"

Pepper gritted his teeth. "Dammit! I didn't consider those miserable bloodsuckers . . . Jamaica . . . Dammit! Those creeps will stop at nothing!" Both men were obviously conjuring up Jamaica's unfortunate coverage in *The Hollywood Globe*. "I'll bring my secretary here for a few days."

"What about out front?" Rosco continued. "I know a guy. He's big; he can handle just about anything . . . And be professional about it. I work with him all the time."

Tom considered the suggestion for what seemed an excruciatingly long time. Eventually he answered with an even: "No. I'll get an acquaintance of mine to do the job. He knows his way around the house . . . And he's *persuasive*—if you get my drift." Pepper whipped open the desk's center drawer, removed a checkbook, and scribbled furiously in it. "I assume three thousand dollars will cover things for now?"

"I usually don't expect to get paid if I don't produce, Mr. Pepper . . . Why don't we wait and see what's out there?"

"Just get me something on Mystic Isle Yachts. Get my wife back. I don't give a damn what you do with that check . . . You don't want to cash it, don't."

The temperature had lowered markedly by the time Rosco left, and the air had a raw, cruel feel. As soon as the Jeep's engine warmed up, he turned on the heater, then set the wipers at their highest speed while he navigated the long, deserted drive. Water descended in torrential sheets, making visibility difficult. Then, true to form, the windshield's interior steamed up, forcing Rosco to rub at it with the cuff of his coat. He drove with a single circle of clear glass, like a ship's porthole.

Another person might have been put off by Tom Pepper's abrasive behavior, but Rosco had recognized that the man's reaction was due to raw emotion. He desperately wanted to take control of a situation over which he had no

power, and was exercising the only option he could find—
go after the individual who had chartered the boat to his
wife. The disaster had to be *somebody's* fault.

Rosco picked up his car phone, punched in star-1, and
waited for Belle to answer.

"It's me," he said. "Can I come over?"

"Of course . . . What did Pepper want?"

"I'll fill you in. See you in twenty minutes or so . . .
Maybe a little longer . . . The weather's filthy."

Concern tinged Belle's voice. "Drive carefully."

"Thanks for reminding me."

"I mean it, Rosco."

"I know."

Rain descended diagonally onto Belle's front porch, streak-
ing the lower halves of the windows and pounding the
white-painted clapboard siding. By the time Rosco rang the
bell, daylight had vanished totally, leaving the stormy
evening black and desolate. He scraped his feet on the sodden mat, but a squelch of water merely resaturated his soles.

"Hi," Belle said, opening the door and then immediately
slamming it shut when Rosco hurried in. Her worried
smile and anxious demeanor exuded domestic peace. For a
moment he felt as if he were returning home rather than
paying a visit. The sensation engendered a complex reaction that was partly happiness and partly concern that he
and Belle might be moving too fast. To mask his thoughts
Rosco studied the floor; his shoes had made puddles on the
bare wood.

"Don't you think a carpet might be a nice touch, Belle?"
he said in an attempted jest. He couldn't bring himself to
verbalize his feelings, while immediately embarking on a
discussion of his interview with Pepper seemed absurdly
businesslike.

Sharing Rosco's mixture of emotions, Belle followed his bantering vein. "I don't know . . . I think I'm getting fond of the bare-bones look . . . It reminds me of my foot-loose college days. Besides, the house used to look so . . . well, you know, *decorated* . . . I'm glad Garet took all the stuff." Then she grew pensive. "What did Pepper say?"

Rosco sighed. He didn't answer for a moment, then finally said, "It's a tough situation, Belle . . . The man's frantic with worry."

"I would be, too."

Both were silent while around them the little house creaked and groaned under the violent attack of the wind-driven rain. The fact that the entry and living room had been nearly denuded of furniture following Belle's divorce made each sound echo dolefully. Her eyes drifted across her new thrift-shop decor: an overstuffed chair covered in green cretonne printed with cabbage roses, a standing lamp, and a good-sized hinged wooden box she'd snagged from a local junk hauler transporting it to the dump. Faded block letters claimed the box to have once belonged to CRUZ BROS. DAIRIES, SANTA ROSARIO, CALIF; how it had arrived in Newcastle, Mass., remained a mystery that Belle found intriguing. At the moment, however, none of these objects brought pleasure or solace.

"Has Pepper heard anything?" she asked at length.

Again, Rosco sidestepped the question with a noncom-mittal: "Is there anything to eat?"

"Besides my famous deviled eggs, you mean?" Belle matched his mood, and forced a bemused smile.

"That's what I was hoping."

Belle thought for a second. Deviled eggs were her one and only culinary specialty—as well as being a food she treated with both reverence and relish. Her other staple was licorice—which fortunately needed no cooking.

"There might be a can of soup . . . cream of something . . . broccoli, maybe?"

This time Rosco smiled genuinely; he found Belle's quirky view of nutrition endearing. "I'll pass, thanks."

"It might have cheese in it . . . or something exotic like that."

"Most people don't consider cheese in the 'exotic' category, Belle."

"Anything you don't have to cook yourself is extra special," she countered, before turning serious again. "So, tell me about your conversation with Pepper."

Rosco didn't respond for a long minute. "The Coast Guard has suspended the air portion of their search until the weather improves."

Belle shut her eyes, then opened them wide and stared at the rain-drenched windows. "I was afraid they might." Then she looked at Rosco; her gray eyes swam with concern. "Could anyone survive in an open boat in a squall like this?"

Rosco didn't answer. After a moment, he pulled her into his arms. "Look at you and me, Belle . . . Anything's possible . . ."

CHAPTER

6

The storm had moved off about three A.M., and the morning revealed crystal-clear weather, warmed to a comfortable sixty degrees. Shafts of reflected sunlight ricocheted wildly through the black-tarred harbor pilings as Rosco angled his Jeep into Mystic Isle Yachts' gravel parking lot and studied the picturesque scene. The marina water was cobalt blue, and the seas still running high and fresh in the storm's wake. Whitecaps sent feathery plumes of salt spray spiraling into the air or jouncing against the sun-spattered pilings and wood-decked walkway. The tang of ocean, wet teak, and hot tar pervaded the air. A perfect day for anyone who loved the sea.

Rosco eyed the waves with nervous distaste, then stepped out of the car and chugged toward the docks. He hadn't set foot in the marina or seen the owner, Ed Colberg, in over two years. The occasion had not been a happy one; Rosco had been investigating a suspected insurance fraud.

Colberg had been a professional surfer, "until the knees went." Rail thin, mid-fifties, six-foot-five or a little more, his height was disguised by the slouch of a man trying to hide himself from the world. He moved with a jerky, spasmodic energy, and kept his long, sandy hair pulled into a haphazard ponytail because he believed time was money; barbershops, "stylists," even combs were a waste of his precious minutes. In Colberg's book, everything, and everyone, had a price. His failure to achieve megabuck status was due to poor timing, ill luck, the weather, fate—anything other than his own bad judgment.

On two previous instances Rosco had been hired to investigate Mystic Isle Yachts. Shore Line Mutual, the largest maritime insurance carrier in Newcastle, had paid for his services. In each case, Colberg had reported boats stolen from his marina. Valued at eighty thousand dollars apiece, the yachts were never recovered. There'd been no doubt in Rosco's mind that Colberg had scuttled them, but the detective hadn't been able to assemble conclusive evidence to support the theory. Shore Line had been forced to pay Colberg's claim.

Because he was downwind, Rosco smelled the *Orion* before he saw her. The combination of burned fiberglass, plastic, nylon rope, and melted Styrofoam had combined to create a grim, distinctive stench. It forced Rosco to snap his head in the direction of the boat that was moored at the end of a short dock. He walked down the pier and stopped. A boat burned to the waterline is a troubling sight.

The *Orion*'s hull appeared scooped out as if gutted by some huge and ravening beast. Fragments of molten metal shone through the sodden ashes; everything else had been charred brown black while the aluminum mast had collapsed onto the stern and baked within the intense heat. A few seat cushions made from "fireproof" material had retained their shape, giving them the look of gigantic char-coal briquettes.

"You didn't see the sign over there, Polycrates? This is a private dock. Owners only." Ed Colberg's voice was a snarl as he stepped up behind Rosco.

Rosco didn't bother to turn. "This is a mess, Eddie. What can you tell me?"

"I can tell you she wasn't insured by Shore Line, thanks to you, buddy-boy. They dropped me like a hot potato after your report on those 'stolen' boats." Ed put a meaningful spin on the word "stolen."

"Yeah . . . well, speaking of hot potatoes . . ." Rosco glanced at Colberg, and cocked his head back toward the *Orion*. "What gives on this one?"

"You working for those ambulance chasers at A.M.I. now, or what? What happened to Mr. High-and-Mighty? Shore Line dump you? Can't blame 'em much."

Rosco had never worked for American Marine Insurance, but if it would get Colberg to talk, he saw no point in relinquishing the truth. "You know me, Ed, I'm not picky when it comes to employers. Get 'em where you can, that's my motto."

"What you see is what you get with this one, buddy." Colberg spat into the *Orion*'s charred remains.

"Any idea what caused it?"

"Couldn't tell ya. The Coast Guard's sending investigators. So it's 'lookie but no touchie' . . . got it?"

"Right. Who pulled her in?"

"Sport fishermen on their way back from a tuna run. They chartered that Hatteras over there for three days." Colberg jabbed a grease-streaked thumb toward a forty-three-foot fishing trawler berthed at a neighboring dock. The name *Dixie-Jack* streaked across the stern in red-and-gold letters. "The bums brought it back a mess . . . Beer cans and tuna blood all over the place . . . Not to mention them towing this piece of bad news home for me." Once again, Colberg spat into the *Orion*.

"These fishermen have names?"

"They might . . ."

Rosco chuckled. "Look, Eddie, you know how these insurance companies are; if they think you're hiding something, they'll put on the full-court press. You don't have to like me—or what I do—but I suggest you play ball. If those women turn up dead, things are going to get nasty."

Colberg seemed to ponder this. Then he shrugged and said, "The guy who chartered it's named Vic Fogram. I don't know the other two."

"Does he have a number—this Fogram?"

"He owns a bar called the Red Admiral. Down on Water Street near the old docks . . . It's a place for regulars. No tourists. Know what I mean?"

Rosco eyed the *Orion* from stem to stern. "What else can you tell me that might interest an insurance company?"

"Look, Polycrates, this boat was clean . . . damn near brand-new . . . no oily rags lyin' around . . . no loose wires . . . no nothin' that wouldn't pass the white glove test . . . The engine had less than twenty hours on it. I've chartered to Mrs. Pepper before—not this vessel, but others . . . She's a better sailor than ninety percent of those bozos at the Yacht Club. Why do you think she comes back here? She knows what she's getting, that's why . . . So, what happened? I don't know." Colberg pointed at the base of the mast, his hand trembling noticeably. "See the way that mast is buckled? The propane tank from the galley stove did that when it blew. But it was a good unit. I checked it myself. All connections were solid."

"It could have blown after the fire started."

"Yeah . . . I suppose." He studied the *Orion* a little

longer, then said, "Look, I got work to do. Don't touch anything."

Colberg started to walk off, but Rosco stopped him. "What about communication gear? What kind of stuff did she have?"

"Hey, Mrs. Pepper pays top dollar, she gets a top-dollar boat. The *Orion* was loaded. You name it, she had it. Radar, depth finder, weather fax, SSB, VHF, and shortwave."

"What about one of those emergency beacons?"

"An EPRIB? Every boat in this yard has an EPRIB. Check 'em out if you want. But people have to activate them or they don't do much good."

"Aren't they activated as soon as they hit water?"

"Yeah . . . But they gotta be turned on. There's a switch."

"Would she have known to do that? Turn it on?"

"I don't know. Why don't you ask her? Hey, Polycrates, all EPRIBs are on when a boat leaves my marina. The question you gotta ask those babes is, why did they turn it *off*—not on."

Rosco could feel his jaw tighten. "What about the dinghy?" He corrected himself in an attempt to sound more professional: "The inflatable tender?"

"Yep, that was insured, too . . . A 290 VS . . . nice little unit . . . eight-horsepower outboard, too . . . Damn! I don't think I insured the motor separately."

Rosco found himself fighting a strong temptation to belt Colberg. The man seemed to have little regard for the fact that two women had been aboard the *Orion*—two women who were now missing. "All right," Rosco said after taking a long breath, "what I want to know is, could the dingy have carried Mrs. Pepper and her friend to landfall?"

"Where's that concern A.M.I.? They doin' life insurance now?"

Rosco shook his head. "It doesn't concern A.M.I. It's *my* question. Call me softhearted. I just wondered if they might still be alive . . . If you think about it, a witness could make your claim go a lot quicker . . . On the other hand, a witness might also blow your claim right out of the water . . ."

"Give it up, Polycrates," Colberg snapped. "If they haven't found those babes by now, they ain't gonna . . . Sorry, but that's the law of the sea . . . If it makes you feel any better, though, the inflatable's motor was gassed up. I'd say they could have got two hours from it . . . It depends how far out they were . . . The clowns who towed in the *Orion* were so boozed when they hooked up the boat they didn't take a bearing. That's why the Coast Guard's having such a tough time—"

"Doesn't procedure call for a rescue craft to remain with a wreck? Radio the Coast Guard, and wait for their arrival?"

Colberg let out a short, mean laugh. "Go look at the *Dixie-Jack,* buddy. Then tell me what those three turkeys knew about 'procedure.' "

Rosco glanced across to the next dock and the fishing boat rocking in the waves. "You don't mind if I inspect it, then?"

"Suit yourself. I haven't touched her. I got a gal who cleans these charters for me, but she didn't come in yesterday. Her kid's sick or something. Good thing it rained last night. Kept the fish blood from drying up on her." Colberg pulled a cigarette from his breast pocket, struck a match, and lit it. His hands shook almost uncontrollably, and his eyes darted around the marina as if unwilling to rest on a single object. He tossed the match into the water, then turned and loped toward his office with his too-tall, bent-kneed, awkward gait.

Rosco watched him leave, then walked to the *Dixie-Jack*.

Ed Colberg had been correct. The aft deck was a disaster, awash in a dark pinkish liquid that sloshed back and forth with sickening speed. Fifteen or twenty empty Budweiser cans floated in the bloody muck, tapping against the bases of two aluminum sport-fishing chairs anchored to the deck. Scattered among the cans were empty potato-chip packages, plastic sandwich bags, cigarette wrappers, and stubbed-out butts. Four seagulls perched on the gunwales fighting over hotdog shards and unidentifiable tuna entrails. The smell of rotting fish was undeniable.

Forward, the captain's seat and helm were protected from the elements by a large overhanging blue canvas Bimini top. Although the decking there was also deep in garbage, the chair and nautical gauges had been shielded from the rain, and had remained dry.

Not caring to ruin his shoes, Rosco stood on the gunwales, supporting himself by holding the Bimini top. He studied the array of gauges. The tachometer, fuel indicator, oil-pressure gauge, and throttle handle were caked with a brownish substance he identified as dried blood. Upon closer examination, he noticed there was a slight differentiation in the shades of brown. The dried blood on the gauges was a hint lighter than the blood on the throttle.

He swung himself forward to sit in the captain's chair, then removed two small Ziploc plastic bags from his coat, took samples of the blood types, marking one bag *throttle* and the other *gauges*. After that, he leaned down and attempted to open the Plexiglas hatch leading to the cabin. It had been locked. Rosco shielded the sun's reflection with his hand and peered in.

Although the interior of the boat was dry, it was also littered with the beer cans, food wrappers, and cigarettes. A dirty towel lay near the entrance to the head. It had clearly been used to clean blood. Rosco jumped off of the *Dixie-Jack* and headed toward Colberg's office.

"There's an awful lot of blood on that boat," he said as he entered.

Colberg jerked his head up from his newspaper. He'd been working the *Crier*'s daily crossword puzzle, and he tossed his pencil onto the desk. "The guys were out for tuna . . . Don't make it into a federal case . . . Happens all the time . . . Fishermen don't want to bring back heads, bones, and guts, so they fillet their catch at sea . . . They only have room in their coolers for meat."

"What did these guys haul?"

"A couple of two-hundred-and fifty-pounders . . . that's what they said . . ."

"Fogram and company . . . You remember those names yet, Ed?"

Colberg only shrugged. The hand holding the newspaper shivered wildly.

"Come on, Ed, you let someone take a hundred and fifty thousand dollars' worth of your property all the way to the trench, and you don't get their names?"

Ed sat stony-faced.

"Okay," Rosco continued, "it's your insurance claim . . . not mine." He turned to leave.

"Hold on, Polycrates." Colberg turned in his chair, removed two cards from a file drawer, and placed them on his desk. "Stingo and Quick . . . Home addresses are all I got."

"Thanks, *buddy*." Rosco copied the information into his notepad. "Any idea where they work?"

"Nah."

Rosco smiled thinly, but didn't speak.

"I'm dead serious . . . I've never seen these two guys

before in my life. And I'll be a happy man if I never see them again."

Before leaving the marina, Rosco made one last visit to the *Orion*. He stared at the burned-out hulk as if waiting for the silent shell to speak. Then his glance traveled to the *Dixie-Jack* and slowly returned to the *Orion*. He found himself wondering not only how a fire of that magnitude had started, but how it had been extinguished—and by whom.

CHAPTER

7

Rosco glanced at his pad of paper, double-checking the address. Fifty-five Duxbury Court was the last in a straggling line of permanently affixed mobile homes in the seedy enclave of Warren, at Newcastle's westernmost edge. He flipped the pad shut, looked at his watch, automatically noting that one in the afternoon was probably an optimal hour for exploring Duxbury Court. Later on, the weary residents would be coping with hungry kids and hard-worked tempers; earlier, those without steady employment would be staring blearily at another dismal day.

He knocked on the trailer's screen door. The latch had been broken, and the door rattled in its frame, making more noise than he'd anticipated. After a few seconds the main door was cautiously opened by a wiry woman in her forties with wheat-colored hair and deep-set eyes. Although her features seemed harsh initially, she was solid New England and not unattractive—the type of person given to few, but genuine smiles. Instinctively, she drew back into her home's dark interior. She seemed uneasy at finding a stranger on her front steps.

"Yes?" The accent was blue-collar Boston, the tone defensive and hostile.

"Good afternoon, ma'am." Rosco tried for a reassuring smile. "I'm looking for Moe Quick. Do I have the right address?"

"Who wants him?"

Rosco pulled his identification from his jacket as he spoke. "My name's Rosco Polycrates, ma'am. I'm a private investigator looking into the fire on that sailboat Sunday night . . . the one with those women aboard . . . I just wanted to ask Mr. Quick a few questions. Apparently, he towed the boat in . . . Are you his wife?"

"I don't know anything about no women."

"Yes, ma'am . . . Are you his wife?"

"I—I shouldn't be answering questions like this."

"No, ma'am, you're right. It's good policy to be careful with strangers. If I could talk to Mr. Quick . . ."

"He's not here."

"I see. When do you expect him home?"

"Don't know."

"You are his wife? Am I correct?"

"Yep." The word came out like a short, barked *Yip*.

"Well, Mrs. Quick—"

"Doris. Call me Doris, I don't like Missus. It makes me feel old." She smiled suddenly, and the expression shed years from her face and stern demeanor. Rosco could almost see her as a twenty-year-old facing a hope-filled future.

"All right, Doris. Maybe you could tell me where your husband's place of work is—"

"Can't do that."

"Why is that, ma'am?" Rosco could feel his reasonable manner deserting him.

"He works all over. That's why I never know when he'll be home. He doesn't like to check in . . ." Something troublesome momentarily weighted the words, but Doris dispensed with the emotion with a determined shake of her head.

Rosco's voice turned gentler. "He works all over?"

"Yep. [*Yip.*] Him and Bob . . . They're truckers. Long distance."

"Bob? Would that be Bob *Stingo*? The man your husband went fishing with this past weekend?"

"Yep. And Vic. Vic Fogram . . . Owns the Red Admiral down near the docks . . . He went, too . . . Got some nice tuna."

"I see. So, Mr. Stingo and your husband are off on a run, is that what you're telling me?"

"Yep. They're partners in the rig. Left this morning. St. Pete."

"Florida? They're on a run to St. Petersburg?"

Doris took a small step backward. "Look, mister, I don't think I should be talking anymore. I don't know nothin' about that boat business. Moe Quick's who you want to talk to, not me. I don't answer for him; he don't answer for me. We're one of them 'modern couples' you hear about." She laughed briefly as if this term were a wry private joke, then started to close the door.

Rosco stopped her. "Fine . . . that's fine, Doris, but how can I contact your husband?"

"You can't." Again, the door edged shut.

Rosco gritted his teeth and tried again. "When do you expect him . . . Doris?"

"No telling . . . four, five days . . . 'I expect him when I see him'—that's what they say." Doris smiled at this second witticism, and again, her stony image was transformed. The metamorphosis was so rapid and so eerie that Rosco found himself wondering if there were more to this woman than the underprivileged, undereducated person she presented.

He retrieved a business card from his wallet. "See that your husband gets this, Mrs. Quick."

"*When* I see him . . . And *if* I remember," she announced regally. "And the name is *Doris* . . . as in Doris Day." Then she slammed the door without another word.

Arriving at his office, Rosco called the Coast Guard. Their full search-and-rescue operation had resumed, but, as yet, they could supply no updated report on the missing women. Lieutenant Evans, the "on-scene commander" in charge of the operation, was as abrupt with Rosco as his CPO had been with Tom Pepper; clearly, his level of frustration was also rising. "We'll contact Pepper the moment we spot anything," he said, and Rosco got the message. *Don't call us; we'll call you.*

He hung up with a polite, "Thank you, sir," then checked his contact at the phone company, who informed him that Genie's cell phone had not been activated since the day of the dinner dance. Finally, Rosco punched in Tom Pepper's number, and brought him up to speed, summing up his report with an earnest:

"I know it's not much, Mr. Pepper, but until they locate that dinghy, you can't give up hope. Survivors have lasted weeks in open boats . . . As far as instigating a lawsuit against Mystic Isle Yachts, there may be possibilities of negligence, but it's too early to tell . . . We'll have to wait for forensics to issue a report on the cause of the fire . . ."

The monologue was received in total silence. At its

conclusion, Rosco wondered if the line had gone dead, and said so. A strangled "I'm still here," was Pepper's pained reply, after which Rosco heard a heavy breath that meant the man was finally marshaling his forces. It was the sound of a person accustomed to fighting numerous battles.

Pepper began asking pointed, intelligent questions, and repeating the responses as if writing rapid notes on a legal pad. He requested the name and manufacturer of the inflatable tender, the type of outboard motor with which it was equipped, the fire-extinguishing system aboard the *Orion,* and the maker of the vessel's propane stove. Some of these facts Rosco supplied; others he promised to deliver.

Pepper ended the conversation with a falsely robust: "Keep up the good work, Rosco . . . Oh, and by the way, you were right about the press. It looks like World War Three is being assembled in my drive . . . steadi-cams, satellite trucks, the works; they sure do love a disaster . . . There are a lot of sick people out there in TV land."

"Let me know if you need additional help," Rosco said as the line went dead. Then he sat pondering the situation for several moody minutes. The deeper he delved into the case, the more complex it seemed to become. He couldn't help feeling as if he'd been handed a bucketful of eels. *Stingo*, he doodled on a pad, *Quick, Fogram, Colberg, Dixie-Jack, blood . . . St. Pete.*

Then he grabbed the phone again, called star-1, and gave Belle an abbreviated version of the day's events. His recitation was finally broken by a gentle:

"You're doing everything you can, Rosco . . . If Genie and Jamaica are still alive, the Coast Guard will find them . . . We have to *believe* that . . ." Then she assumed a brighter mood. "What are you doing now?"

Rosco recognized the question as an invitation to come
to her home. It was one of the many things he liked about
her: the ability to say one thing and mean something else.

"I can't, Belle, I've still got work to do."

"Can't what?"

"Come over."

"Who asked you to?"

He smiled into the phone. "Never mind."

"Besides, why can't you come over? We could have an
early dinner."

"I have to check out the Red Admiral, and this Vic
Fogram character."

"I could meet you there—"

"I don't think so, Belle. The place doesn't really cater to
women."

"It's a gay bar?"

Rosco laughed. "No . . . It's on Water Street, across
from the fishing docks . . . Obviously, women do patronize
it . . . just not your type of female, that's all."

Rosco heard a sigh; it meant Belle's brain was racing to
come up with a retort.

"Look . . . it's a tough, shot-and-a-beer-chaser fisherman's bar . . . a place for regulars . . . Women don't go
there unless they can beat guys at arm wrestling and har-
poon slinging."

Again, Belle sighed. "Take care of yourself," she finally
said.

The closet in Rosco's office contained a smattering of dis-
guises: a navy-blue suit (poorly fitting enough to resemble
an unsuccessful accountant or an undertaker's assistant), a
green windbreaker that looked vaguely DEA, torn jeans,
scuffed work boots, a hooded black sweatshirt faded to a
mottled gray, and a variety of baseball caps. For the Red

Admiral, Rosco opted for a "commercial-fisherman look": jeans, sweatshirt, boots; the hat he chose was orange and black, and sported the Baltimore Orioles logo. It made him look like a definite out-of-towner. Dressed in this outfit, he studied himself in the mirror. He hadn't shaved all day, and an appropriate amount of stubble appeared on his chin. He passed his left hand across his face, nodded approval, then checked the time.

"Four-thirty . . . Must be nearing happy hour down at the docks."

On the way to the Red Admiral, he made one detour to drop off the blood samples for analysis at TX Bio-Lab. "Thursday's the best we can do," he was told. "Wednesday night, maybe, but I wouldn't count on it."

Although Rosco had never entered the Red Admiral, he'd driven past it, and had had the opportunity to observe the arrivals and exits of its clientele. Almost all appeared to be commercial fishermen: men accustomed to spending a month chasing cod on the outer banks, running through their earnings in a weekend, and then shipping back out, broke and hungover. Their brief hours on land were dedicated to consuming the tavern's inventory of alcohol. Lacking any permanent home, some men even used the Admiral as a mailing address; for them, it was all they knew of stability. There were, of course, fishermen in Newcastle with families, houses with mortgages, kids in school, and wives holding regular jobs. However, these men did not frequent the bars on Water Street.

From the sidewalk, it was impossible to see into the Admiral. The door was solid if battered; the two small, grimy windows bracketing it were curtained with dense beige cloth. Displayed in the left window was a neon Miller Lite sign; the right held a blinking Budweiser sign.

When Rosco stepped through the door, all conversation ceased; the eight customers—all of whom were men— swiveled their eyes, although not their heads and bar stools, in his direction.

Rosco opted to sit on the right side of the horseshoe-shaped bar. He noticed that no one sat with their back to the door, and followed suit, leaving two empty stools between himself and the next customer. Then he spun around slowly on the stool, appearing to study a collection of neon domestic beer signs littering the walls while he waited for the bartender to amble over—an event that took a good five minutes.

The man was balding, in his late forties or early fifties with a hefty build, bulging gut, and arms that were preter-naturally long, giving him a decidedly apelike appearance. He hadn't shaved for several days; suspicion was etched in his scruffy face. "Are you from down Baltimore way, or just looking to get your neck broke? This is Red Sox coun-try, pal."

Rosco removed his hat and pretended to ponder the black-and-orange oriole. "I work out of Maryland a lot. Don't pay much attention to baseball. It's functional." He placed the hat back on his head.

"What kind of work."

"Chesapeake stuff. Stripers and blues, mostly. Crabs when those slack off."

"What brings you to Newcastle?"

"On my way to Maine."

"Yeah? What's in Maine?"

Rosco shook his head slightly. "Death in the family . . . Not that it's any of your damn business."

They exchanged an icy stare that lasted until the man to Rosco's right tossed a five-dollar bill toward the bartender.

"Hell, Vic," he said, "give the Oriole a beer on me. Closest I'm ever gonna get to Cal Ripkin."

With a show of dismissal, Vic reached below the bar, uncapped a Budweiser long neck, and slid it toward Rosco. No glass was offered. As he turned to the cash drawer, the front door of the Red Admiral flew open and a huge man strode in. He was thick-shouldered, bullnecked, ham-fisted, and padded with as much fat and muscle as a prime steer; he was also probably only twenty-one years old. A toothy smile was pasted to his blubbery face, and a wad of cash stuck in his upraised left hand. He slammed the money down on the bar. "The *Sally-B* is back, and Charlie Yarnell's buying the beers."

For the next two hours the atmosphere resembled that of a stag party. It took Rosco that long to get the patrons to accept him—without noticing he wasn't keeping pace with their alcohol consumption—and another hour before the subject of the *Orion* was introduced. Naturally, it was the newly returned Charlie who instigated the discussion; despite being a regular customer, Yarnell's questions elicited only the most evasive answers from Vic Fogram. "I don't know more than they're saying on TV," the tavern owner kept repeating.

"Was she burning when you found her?" Rosco finally interrupted, making the question sound as disinterested as possible.

"Nah . . . We hit a surprise squall that night. Short and sweet . . . Happens all the time out in Buzzards Bay. Could be that's what doused the fire. Who knows? Hell, we almost ran smack-dab into her. If the moon hadn't come out, we would have."

"Well, you're a better man than me," Rosco said, hoisting his beer, and attempting to slur his words. "Me . . . ? I would have just radioed the Guard and left the tub right where I found her."

Vic gave Rosco another cold stare. "Yeah, well, that's you, pal. We do things different in Massachusetts."

"Come on, Vic." Charlie laughed. "What'd you three geezers do with them two babes? I seen that show on TV . . . The one with the black hair was a real looker. Too old for me . . . but you guys . . ."

"Didn't see 'em."

"Ahhh, get off it . . ."

Charlie's laughter was infectious; another patron joined in to tease Fogram. "Tell me another one, Vic. I'll bet you old fogies have them cuties stashed away for a rainy day."

Vic's simian face suddenly flushed; he spun toward the man in anger. "I'm telling you I didn't see those broads. And I'll tell you another thing. If I'd known it was Tom Pepper's wife who'd chartered that boat, I would have done just like Baltimore here said." He pointed at Rosco. "Except I would've gone one better. I wouldn't've just left that wreck out there . . . I would have blown it clear out of the water!"

CHAPTER

8

On Wednesday morning, Belle stood in a sunny window of the converted rear porch that served as her home office. Her eyes drifted across the small patch of greenery that composed her garden. Broken twigs and branches—the detritus of Monday night's storm—made the area look as though giants had been playing pick-up sticks and become bored with the game. Sparrows hopped exuberantly among the wreckage, discovering tasty new sources of sustenance, but Belle shuddered as if chilled. The sunlight, the lingering green of the grass, the gilding of the autumnal leaves did nothing to dispel an ominous sense of doom.

Her brow furrowed and her wide eyes narrowed. She'd felt the same palpable fear ever since her conversation with Rosco the evening before. Something was amiss, and it wasn't simply poor nautical "procedure," or an accident that could have befallen any unlucky sailor. Without intending to, her mind conjured a litany of maritime disasters: shipwrecks, collisions, winter gales, freak waves. *Why didn't Genie and Jamaica use that cell phone?* her brain demanded. *Where could the inflatable tender have gone? Why disengage the locator beacon?*

Belle sighed aloud and returned to her desk—a hodge-podge of graph paper, open dictionaries, empty coffee mugs, and one conspicuously denuded platter upon which three deviled eggs had recently rested. The plate had a crossword design—as did the mugs, and a seriously tilting lamp shade. In fact, the entire room was a symphony—perhaps, a cacophony—of black and white: curtain fabric with bold, black letters on a white ground, two deck chairs in white-and-black canvas, a wood floor painted to resemble a crossword grid. Belle had lived with this unusual decor so long, she assumed it was normal. Besides, as she liked to boast, her bathroom was worse; there, the cryptics theme had run seriously amok: black-and-white ceramic tiles running up, down, and across.

Belle stared at the empty plate, muttered a quiet, "Darn. I don't remember finishing them," then opened her "bible," the *Oxford English Dictionary,* her much-thumbed *O.E.D.* She'd been attempting to create a crossword on a garden theme—thus her stroll to the window—but her fascination with botany rivaled her love of cooking. If it was green and survived without human care, a plant was her friend. If it required nurturing, it would need another home.

Suddenly she glanced up. She had a horrible sense of being watched by sinister eyes. She looked through the windows. No one. Captain's Walk with its row of tidy homes and quaint, secluded gardens was as silent and peaceable as ever. She turned toward the door leading into the near-naked living room. Nothing. No sound. No stir of air. Belle's eyes spun over the shelves of research books: the *Larousse, Harrap's Italian Dictionary, Roget's Inter-*

national Thesaurus, the atlas, her treasured *Encyclopaedia Britannica*—the famous eleventh edition. The books stared dumbly back.

She returned to her crossword, a work combining horticulture and women's names. *Whither Flora?* was the puzzle's name. *Black-eyed* SUSAN, she scribbled on a pad, LADY'S *slipper,* VENUS *flytrap, Queen* ANNE'S *lace, Christmas* ROSE. Belle's mind began making double and triple connections, then her head jerked up again. She was certain someone was prowling around outside.

"Okay," she announced. "Enough is enough!"

She marched through the living room and yanked open the front door, intending to storm outside and berate this unseen and unnerving presence. But a piece of paper stopped her in her tracks. Tucked under a corner of the doormat was a hand-drawn crossword puzzle. Still standing in the entry, Belle quickly scanned several of the clues: *Hunter . . . Call to Aladdin's lamp? . . . "Evil in the Deep" . . .*

ORION, she silently ticked off, GENIE . . . She was in her office with her trusty red Bic pen in hand before she knew it.

Across

1. Mississippi——
6. "Show——"
10. "Star——"
14. Hunter
15. Tale Starter
16. Jai——
17. ". . . Lady Disdain,——" Shak.
20. Trip starter?
21. Under, to Burns
22. 1-Across P.O. addresses
26. Govt. lender
29. JFK arrival
30. Coral island
31. Belief
32. Du Maurier novel
34. Scrap
37. "Men were——," Shak.
39. Annoy
40. Call to Aladdin's lamp?
42. Hemp refuse
43. Tatum or Ryan
44. Cranberry patch
47. Directional suffixes
48. ". . . thou art the thing——,"Shak.
49. "The——Suspects"
51. GA neighbor
52. "Bait the hook well,——,"
    Shak., var.
60. This is only a——
61. Two-masted vessel
62. Passes bad paper
63. Lip
64. Sink or——
65. "Deadly Blessing" actress Sharon

Down

1. Edmond O'Brien classic
2. "To——is human . . ."
3. Falsehood
4. Type of boy?
5. Fish story, e.g.
6. "Evil in the Deep" actor Stephen
7. Single
8. 1/5 of *Henry V*
9. ATT part
10. Short——radio
11. Name game?
12. Overacts?
13. Out of——, out of mind
18. Ship prefix
19. Naut. engine type
22. Mil. rank
23. Rocket parts, Ital.
24. Speed of light discoverer
25. Antiaircraft fire, var.
26. Pals
27. Matisse & others
28. Eye part, var.
31. Grotto
33. Stogie
34. Oasts
35. ——Adorée
36. 57-Down venue
38. Shrink conversations?
41. Sprite
42. Port lead-in
44. Rams
45. Milo——
46. ——who?
48. Sick
50. Sterns
51. 1-Down, e.g.
53. Part of CBS
54. Gee &——
55. It ended at 11 A.M. on 11/11
56. ——part; walk-on
57. Lance——
58. "——Little Indians"
59. Wind dir.

PUZZLE 1

CHAPTER

9

B elle's pen almost flew from her hand as she inked in the puzzle's final clue. To her mind, the cryptic screamed complicity in the mystery surrounding the *Orion*'s fire. JAMAICA, she recited silently, BOAT; YAWL; WAVE. Who wouldn't immediately recognize the value of this piece of evidence? Her hand was on the phone and punching in Rosco's number before another second had passed.

"They've been murdered," she announced the moment he answered. ". . . Or maybe kidnapped."

"Whoa . . . whoa . . . I take it you're referring to Genie Pepper and Jamaica Nevisson?"

Belle, in her office, stared dumbfounded into space. "Of course I am."

"And, what might you be basing this theory on, if I may be so bold as to ask?" Amusement crackled through the telephone line.

"Very funny, Rosco . . . Obviously, I'm talking about the puzzle in my hand." Belle waved the cryptic in the air, although Rosco, of course, didn't observe the gesture. "14-Across: the answer is ORION; the clue is *Hunter*. That was the type of boat the women chartered, wasn't it? A Hunter 380, or something? And named *Orion*? Could anything be more plain—"

"Mind if I interrupt for a moment?"

"Be my guest."

Rosco heard more than a hint of irritation in Belle's tone. It was difficult for her to understand thought processes more methodical than her own. "Can we go back to the beginning?"

A brief but tolerant sigh greeted the suggestion. "There was a puzzle on my front porch . . . under the doormat . . . No, wait . . . There's more to the story . . . I was working on *Whither Flora?*"

"*Whither Flora?*"

"Never mind . . . And I thought I was being watched . . . But when I went to the door to chase whoever it was away, I found the puzzle."

This time it was Rosco's turn to groan. "Belle, if you believe you have a prowler, you don't *personally* try to scare that individual away . . . I think we discussed this situation a couple of months ago?"

"But that was a *murder* case—"

"Didn't you just use that term in reference to the *Orion* fire?"

Rosco heard a mumbled, "Well, yes, but—" Belle hated to admit that she was often a rash and reckless human being.

"Look, Belle, I'm not saying the disappearance of two women is analogous to the Briephs murder—"

"But it might be, Rosco. That's just the point. This puzzle has *crime* written all over it—and Jamaica's and Genie's names!"

A mechanical click interrupted them. Rosco said, "Hold on a sec. I've got another call," then disappeared while Belle thrummed impatient fingers on her desktop. When his voice returned, she opened her mouth to resume her tirade, but Rosco beat her to the punch. "It's the Coast Guard," he stated. "They have a 'priority situation' . . . Look, let's have supper tonight . . . We'll discuss your theory then. In the meantime I want you to be careful, okay?"

"I *am* careful."

"I'm serious about this, Belle."

"I'll see you tonight," was all she answered before ringing off.

Rosco tapped his phone pad, putting the Coast Guard on speaker. "Rosco Polycrates," he said.

"Sir, this is Chief Warrant Officer Osborne, assigned with Lieutenant Evans. I'm over at the Green Point Station . . ."

"Yes?" Rosco shuffled some papers on his desk, and found a note he'd scribbled on Monday. "Right, I spoke with Lieutenant Evans earlier."

"Yes, sir, the lieutenant is absent from the op center at the moment. I'm presently directing portions of the SAR-Op." Osborne spoke with the standard unmodulated drone that the military liked to affect when speaking with civilians.

"SAR-Op?" Rosco asked.

"Search and rescue, sir."

"Right . . . How do things look? Any sign of the women?"

"I'm not calling about that phase of our operation, sir. Although I can assure you that we have all available personnel dedicated to the SAR." Osborne took a beat and added, "I'm calling in reference to Mr. Pepper."

"*Mister* Pepper?"

"You are an employee of Mr. Pepper, am I correct?"

"In a manner of speaking, yes . . ."

"Well, sir, we have Mr. Pepper in the lieutenant's office here at Green Point. He's being confined for security reasons. I was hoping that you might be able to conduct him home. I don't believe he's in the proper frame of mind to operate his own vehicle."

"W-w-what's going on?" Rosco stuttered.

"Mr. Pepper drove through our gate half an hour ago. We were encouraged to restrain him. His behavior is not advancing our efforts here, sir. Now, I could call the Newcastle police, but the lieutenant would prefer not get into that kind of paperwork at this point in time."

Rosco glanced at his watch and said, "I can be at Green Point in ten minutes."

"Thank you, sir. Inform the gate that you're here to see me. They'll direct you to building six."

CWO Osborne took a few minutes to brief Rosco on the "situation," then walked him down a tan-colored interior corridor to Lieutenant Evans's office, where the door was unlocked by a chief petty officer. Tom Pepper sat on an aluminum chair with his wrists handcuffed to a filing-cabinet drawer. Not a word or smile was exchanged. Rosco resisted the temptation to chide his employer for being so stupid as to storm a Coast Guard installation single-handedly. Instead, he held up one hand in a gesture intended to keep Pepper from speaking. It didn't work.

"Dammit, Polycrates, I want a list of everybody in this damn base before we leave. I want every last one of them court-martialed."

"Mr. Pepper, I think the best plan would be for us to leave quietly. I'm sure they can supply a personnel duty roster if we need to reference it for names—"

"That's the one." Pepper suddenly jutted his chin in CWO Osborne's direction. "He's been withholding information from the git-go. When I phoned the station earlier, he hung up on me—twice. Him and that Evans character . . . It's my Genie we're talking about, not some goddamned weather buoy." With that, Pepper lunged toward Osborne, nearly dragging the filing-cabinet drawer off its runners. Rosco was forced to interfere, physically restraining Pepper while the chief warrant officer drew back and squared his shoulders. Every inch of his perfectly pressed uniform glittered disdain.

"Mr. Polycrates, sir, kindly remove this civilian from the installation immediately. I have an operation to run." Then Osborne barked an order to the chief petty officer. "Uncuff him and conduct him to the detective's vehicle." CWO Osborne turned on his heel and stalked into the corridor.

"I'm going to get your bars for this, Jack!" Pepper shouted after him. "You can count on that!"

"All right, let's take it easy." Rosco's hands still gripped Pepper's arms. "We're not accomplishing anything here." He waited another forty seconds until Tom showed signs of cooling down. "Let's walk out of here quietly . . . Then we'll go back to your house and regroup . . . All right?"

Pepper nodded slowly, but didn't speak.

"Good. I have my car outside. Okay, Mr. Pepper . . . ?"

Accompanied by the chief petty officer, the two men walked to the Jeep in silence. It was only as they drove through the gate that Pepper's surly humor revived. "What about my car?" he demanded.

"You brought it onto the base . . . They're holding the keys. It's their prerogative."

"Dammit." The word was bitten and irate. "Dammit."

"I'll send someone over to pick it up later, Mr. Pepper . . . Now, if you don't mind my asking . . . What did you intend to accomplish back there?"

Pepper let out a long, weary sigh. "I'm sick and tired of waiting, Rosco. I want to know where my wife is . . . Is that too much to ask? . . . I pay taxes. I pay those bozos' salaries, but they disconnected me every blasted time I called . . . I just wanted to look this Osborne character in the eye, and see if he was telling me the truth . . . I know when people are lying, Rosco, and when they're not."

"What would the Coast Guard have to gain by lying to you, Mr. Pepper? They want to find your wife as much as you do."

"What if they already picked her up and aren't telling anyone?"

"Why would they do that?"

"I don't know. Maybe she's badly injured. Maybe *they* injured her with their damn 'SAR Op.' Maybe they botched their rescue attempt, and they're covering their tracks . . . They should have found Genie and Jamaica by now. It's clear as a damned bell out there!" Pepper pointed back toward the Green Point base. "They're lying for some reason, Rosco. I could see it in Osborne's eyes. He wouldn't look at me . . . And where the hell is Evans hiding?"

"Mr. Pepper, the lieutenant is in charge of a huge operation."

"Osborne couldn't look me in the damned eye!"

Rosco continued in a calming tone. "I spoke with CWO Osborne before I picked you up. I talked to Lieutenant Evans earlier. These men are professionals, Mr. Pepper. Let's give them some leeway . . . Now, they both explained that a rubber dinghy, like the one on the *Orion,* will not sink. Even if it's been deflated, the rubber still floats and the outboard motor isn't heavy enough to take it down. Trust me, they're doing everything in their power to find it—and your wife."

"Sixty hours . . . She's been in that water sixty goddamn hours." Tom turned his anguished face toward Rosco as the Jeep passed the Yacht Club and headed out toward the point. "Do you think it's possible for anyone to stay alive for sixty hours in October in Buzzards Bay? Be honest, Rosco . . . I'm losing my mind with this thing."

"People have survived for months in an open boat, Mr. Pepper. There's also a possibility your wife and Miss Nevisson were picked up by someone sailing a boat without a radio."

"But what if they've been in the water all this time?"

"I couldn't speculate on that, Mr. Pepper."

"It's not knowing that's driving me crazy. I love my wife . . . I guess that goes without saying, doesn't it?"

Rosco didn't answer; instead, he exited the main road and entered the tree-shaded lane that led to Pepper's drive. Five hundred yards from the wrought-iron gates, he stopped. Still seated in the Jeep, the two men stared at the circus unfolding before them. Rosco spoke first.

"It's like the president's press corps up there, Mr. Pepper . . . Do you have a service entry?"

Pepper didn't take his eyes off the scene. "At the rear . . . But we'll have to drive through those bozos to get there."

"Slide down in the seat. They won't bother this car."

Rosco tapped the accelerator and headed straight for the

mass of reporters and TV crews encamped at the entrance to Pepper's property. There were three satellite vans and at least ten press cars; an enterprising Newcastle vendor had even set up a sandwich wagon in their midst.

As Rosco drove toward them, the bodies gradually parted and allowed him to pass. He recognized four or five reporters as local; the rest were strangers—down from Boston or up from New York. A few wore bright satin jackets embroidered with call letters starting with a *K*; Rosco assumed they'd traveled all the way from Los Angeles to get the latest scoop on Jamaica.

After he passed the gauntlet, he said, "We're through. What now?"

Tom remained crouched in the seat. "Another hundred yards or so, the drive veers off to the right. You'll see a dirt lane on your left. It looks like it belongs to the next property, but it's ours. There's a locked gate, but the key is with my car keys . . . I'll have to buzz the maid on the intercom."

Rosco followed Pepper's directions, but as he approached the gate, he noticed two cars parked beside it—and two men smoking cigarettes leaning against the driver-side doors. Nikon cameras dangled from straps around their necks.

"Well," Rosco said, "at least, we've improved the odds . . . Although, maybe I should be the one to call your maid."

Tom sat up in his seat and looked at the men. "Nah. She won't release the lock if she doesn't recognize the voice. Just pull up. We can handle these clowns."

Before Rosco could set the Jeep's parking brake, Pepper jumped from the car and began advancing on the reporters. The two men didn't miss a second of photographic opportunity. Equipped with motor drives, each camera squeezed off ten or fifteen shots of Tom's fury before he grabbed one Nikon, yanking it so ferociously from its owner's neck, the leather strap snapped like an ancient rubber band. Tom smashed the camera into the owner's windshield and turned on the second man.

"This is private property, you bloodsucker."

The reporter scuttled into the underbrush while Pepper returned his attention to the first man, who was now cowering against his damaged car. "I want to know who you work for!" Pepper grabbed him by his jacket lapels and hurled him into the side of Rosco's Jeep. "Who sent you here, you bloodsucker?"

Rosco stepped between the two. "Take it easy, Mr. Pepper," was all he could think to say.

But Pepper's wrath was up. He pushed the detective aside as if he hadn't heard him. "I asked you a question, creep! Who's your boss? Because, I'm going to sue him for every penny he's worth."

Fear seemed to make the man incapable of speaking.

"Open your mouth, you piece of scum, I want to know who your boss is. This is private property. If you want to leave in one piece, you'd better talk."

"*S-S-Shooting S-S-Stars*. But I'm a f-f-freelancer."

"And what about that other snake?"

"Come on, Mr. Pepper," Rosco urged. "These guys aren't worth the effort. Just let it be."

"I want some answers," Tom roared in response. "What rag does that other creep work for?"

The reporter took a step backward. "Please don't hit me."

"Who does he work for!"

"I don't know, man . . . He wouldn't tell me . . . Honest."

CHAPTER

10

B elle was gazing solemnly into a cookbook when the doorbell rang. "I'm coming!" she sang out, grabbing a tea towel as she ran through the stark and shadowy living room to fling open the door. The force of her gesture was so powerful the door's edge nearly hit her in the head. "Well? What happened at the Coast Guard?"

On the porch, bathed in the navy-blue darkness of an autumn night, Rosco grinned despite his raucous encounter with Pepper. "I could tell you out here, or . . . you could ask me in."

"Oh! In . . . Come on in." She led the way toward the kitchen while Rosco followed close behind.

"You might consider another lamp, Belle . . . I'm like a moth, attracted to illumination."

She turned back to survey the scene. "I don't know," she said slowly. "This home-decorating business has me awfully confused. The choices seem so . . . so permanent."

"I was only suggesting a lamp—"

"I know. But that's the problem ... In *theory*, a lamp should 'complement' a couch, which, in turn, 'reflects' a table which 'matches' a rug which 'echoes' the pictures on the wall ... See what I mean? One wrong step, and you've got a design disaster on your hands; the fashion police are called in, and you're forced to throw out everything and start from scratch with Lava lamps ... Besides, I've been considering candles as a less demanding alternative ..."

Rosco chuckled. "Candles don't give off a heap of light."

"But they're very romantic ... *A World Lit Only by Fire* ..." Her voice was dreamy. Then, in typical Belle fashion, the conversation spun around 180 degrees. "Well, what happened with Pepper and Green Point? I've been on pins and needles ever since our phone conversation. I gather there's no news on Genie and Jamaica?"

But Rosco wasn't ready to discuss that subject yet; instead, he said, "I take it you're quoting a line from a poem." He moved beside her, and slid his hands around her waist.

"It's a book title ... William Manchester ... A discourse on—"

Rosco's kiss stopped her words. When they finally backed away from each other, Belle fondly gazed into his eyes. "You're an anti-intellect, you know that? With a one-track mind."

"Sometimes I lose control ... So, it was a discourse on ... ?" A quiet weariness had crept into his voice, but Belle didn't yet hear it.

"I'm not going to tell you," she answered as she entered the kitchen. "There's wine in the fridge ... Achaia, like we had on our first date ... And *dolmades* ... I drove clear across town to get them ... The rest of the menu isn't quite so reliable ..." A self-deprecating grimace accompanied this statement. Then Belle returned to her original query. "So, tell me what the Coast Guard said."

Rosco didn't answer; instead, he studied a glass bowl in which a pound of raw, peeled shrimp was marinating in a thin, bluish liquid. Belle joined him, presenting the bottle of Achaia and a corkscrew. "Shrimp Pernod," she announced. "But I substituted Ouzo—in your honor."

"Ouzo ... there's an idea ..." he said, failing to conjure up a more positive response. "Ouzo, instead of Pernod ..."

"I figure they both have a licorice flavor ..."

"Hey, the world loves experimentation ... Blue shrimp."

"Why not? Anyway, there are spinach timbales if the shrimp dish fails ... I haven't made them before, but I figure you can't go wrong with spinach ... I hope ... Anyway, it's green—and a food group ... No, perhaps not ... Darn. How does that food-pyramid-chart thing work? ... Spinach must be on there somewhere—"

"Perhaps as a vegetable?"

"Very clever, Rosco. That part I know. But I think it also supplies calcium ..."

"Maybe we should leave this to the experts, Belle."

"I hope you're not insinuating that I can't cook anything except deviled eggs." She smiled as she spoke.

Rosco laughed. "Me? Never."

Belle raised amused eyebrows, then resumed her no-nonsense tone while arranging the *dolmades* on a stoneware plate. "So? What did the Coast Guard say?"

Again, Rosco hedged. "I thought you wanted to discuss your mysterious crossword puzzle ... or some discourse on fire ..."

"*A World Lit Only by Fire,*" Belle answered with a

happy grin as Rosco poured the wine and handed her a glass. "It's about the Middle Ages—"

"Well, here's to the modern world," he interrupted, "and a long vacation in Greece."

"And here's to someone who doesn't *willfully* change the subject—one-track mind or not." Belle laughed. "So? Tell me what that phone call entailed."

Rosco put his glass on the counter. "The Coast Guard had Pepper in the lockup . . . at least their version of one."

"What? You're kidding!"

"No . . . it wasn't a pretty scene. And things got worse when I drove him home . . ." Rosco described the situation at Green Point, then proceeded to the violent run-in with the reporters. "He really lost it, Belle . . . I couldn't control him; and I don't think he could control himself . . . He's going to wind up slapped with a lawsuit if he's not care-ful . . . There's nothing these slander sheets like better."

Belle listened to Rosco's words while intently studying his face. "You've had a tough day," she finally said, then changed tack with a worried: "Will the Coast Guard press charges, do you think?"

"I don't imagine so. They've got better things to worry about . . . Why do you ask?"

"Well, I had a lot of time to think this afternoon. And I remembered Sara and her brother, Senator Crane, and how grateful they are for your work on the Briephs case . . . I'm sure the Coast Guard is being as diligent as possible, but if it were necessary to apply a little pressure to get quicker results—or well . . . Hal Crane is a U.S. senator after all . . ."

Rosco considered the suggestion. "I don't know, Belle . . . Sara isn't keen on Pepper, and I'm not certain she'd want to get involved if she knew his potential for volatile behavior."

"He's just worried about his wife," Belle said. "Can you blame him?"

Rosco studied her compassionate face. "No, I can't."

While the rice steamed, Belle produced the crossword puzzle. "Shakespeare," she insisted, slapping it down on the countertop. "That's one of the through lines . . . another is a nautical theme. It's obvious the constructor is linking the actress, Jamaica, and a boat . . . Look at 14-Across. ORION. It can't get clearer than that."

Rosco leaned over her shoulder to study the cryptic while she continued her guided tour of clues and answers.

"Don't try anything funny, Rosco. This is serious . . . You'll note that many of the Bard's quotations are from *Much Ado About Nothing*."

Rosco stared at the graph paper. "Where does it say that?"

"It doesn't. I just happened to recognize the lines. I've always liked the play. I guess I relate to Beatrice. She's too brainy for her own good . . . an intellectual snob."

"You're hardly a snob, Belle."

"You didn't know me in my younger days." Then she shoved aside the crossword, yelping, "Oh jeez! The rice."

A solid mass of glutinous white stuck tenaciously to the pot. Belle looked sorrowfully at it. "I'll begin again," she said gamely. "What's an extra cup of rice? Anyway, to get back to the clues . . . Jamaica Nevisson did *Much Ado* a few years ago. I went up to Boston to see it. I was surprised how good she was in the role—and blond! Almost totally unrecognizable from her offstage appearance. Whoever constructed this puzzle has done his homework . . ."

Rosco retrieved the puzzle and ran his fingers over the letters. "What makes you think it's a man?"

"A hunch . . . A *strong* hunch. Look at the Down column . . . *Ship prefix; Naut. engine type; Mil. rank; Antiaircraft fire* . . . Definitely guy stuff."

Rosco looked hard at Belle. "I don't want you trying to
scare off any more prowlers," he said. "There's a serious
sicko out there." His expression was so grave, Belle's grew
pensive as well.

"Why do you say that?"

Rosco paused. "Your well-known involvement in the
Briephs' case, for starters. *'Cryptics Queen Collars Killer.'*
Remember that headline? One of many, I might add."

Belle remained silent for a long minute. "Are you suggesting this crossword is merely a copycat situation? That
it has nothing to do with the *Orion*?"

"Oh, it does, Belle. It definitely does. And that's exactly
what makes it frightening. Someone is playing a really
perverted game. I saw those reporters gathered at Pepper's
estate . . . They're giving constant updates, satellite feeds
across the nation . . . which only increases a weirdo's
desire to be involved in the action . . . Promise me you'll
listen to that little voice that warns you *not* to *personally*
chase away strangers?"

Belle frowned but didn't speak.

"Please, Belle. I want you to take this seriously. Whoever brought this puzzle to your house could well be a bor-
derline crazy. And crazies are fond of armaments."

Belle walked over to the shrimp dish, absentmindedly
dumping the Ouzo marinade down the sink. When she
realized what she'd done, she let out a yelp of dismay.
"Oh, drat! . . . Drat! I guess we'll have to sauté the shrimp
instead, what do you think?"

Rosco smiled gently. Dining on Belle's cuisine was
always unpredictable. "Sounds good to me."

"Garlic, do you think?" she asked.

Rosco's smile grew. "You can't go wrong with garlic."

While Rosco peeled and chopped garlic Belle tackled the necessary onion, celery, and parsley for the "original recipe." As she sliced and diced, she returned to her premise with a thoughtful: "I disagree with you, Rosco. I think this crossword contains a special message for me— something that will help unravel the mystery of the *Orion*'s fire . . . This is how the Briephs case was solved."

Rosco turned to face her. "And that's *exactly* why I'm convinced that the puzzle is the work of a deranged mind . . . Fame can be a dangerous thing Belle. A *very* dangerous thing."

CHAPTER

11

C onvincing Belle that there might be dangerous people traversing the globe, people who wouldn't think twice about harming another individual, was like trying to persuade a lemming not to jump off a cliff. Her approach to *any* situation was to leap in with both feet and forge ahead until she reached her goal. Rosco had never known anyone with such a jubilant and determined spirit. There was no doubt about it, she was an exceptional catch. One he hoped to never lose.

Driving his Jeep out of TX Bio-Lab's parking lot, Rosco smiled at the memory of his evening with Belle while the clean light of early morning washed the sea air and the ruddy bricks of the city's older buildings. The white trim etched around windows and doors looked as dazzlingly bright as a sandy beach at full noon. Rosco pulled into traffic, reminiscing about the previous summer: Belle in the ocean with her long tan legs splashing through the waves, then picnics on the sand, the hot and salty smell of beach blankets, the crumpled sandwich wrappers, potato-chip shards, and the drowsy sound of the breaking surf. The memories made him deeply regret that he wasn't on his way to her house, instead of visiting his former partner, Lieutenant Al Lever of the New-castle PD cops—even good guys like Al—just didn't measure up.

Rosco sighed once, then made a left onto Thomas Paine Boulevard, the wide thoroughfare that bisected the city, and turned his attention to Bio-Lab's preliminary report.

The blood samples lifted from the *Dixie-Jack* weren't what he'd expected; on the gauges, the blood had come from a marine source—obviously the tuna—but the samples he'd taken from the throttle arm were human—type A pos. Rosco figured Al should be informed. Maybe the blood had bearing on the *Orion* situation.

The station house on Winthrop Drive was unchanged from the days Rosco had worn a badge: institutional-green paint peeling from plastered walls, hallways that smelled of prepackaged doughnuts and stale coffee, and a cinder block-lined basement that served the multiple purpose of morgue, detention area, and forensics lab.

Rosco casually greeted several officers as he strolled past the duty desk and proceeded up three steps to a door marked HOMICIDE. He tapped once and walked in. He and Al had been rookie cops fifteen years before; they never stood on ceremony.

"Good to see you, Polly—Crates." A "Back Bay" twang

stretched out the syllables, a running joke Lever never seemed to tire of. When they'd started working together, Rosco had gotten the impression Al had never met anyone of Greek descent. "Still the 'barefoot boy,' eh, Polly—Crates? I guess it never gets cold enough for you to grab yourself a pair of socks."

Lever, a couple of years older than his former partner, already had a couch-potato build topped off by a "follicly challenged" hairline. He also had a constant smoker's cough, which now kicked in violently.

"Damn allergies," he said. "Summer, winter, they never leave me alone . . . It's murder, I'm tellin' ya . . . Now, what can I do you for? . . . Your phone call said it was important."

Lever broke into another small coughing fit. After it subsided, he lit a cigarette and tossed the match into an overflowing ashtray.

Rosco sat across from Lever's desk and waved a meaty cloud of smoke from his eyes. "Tom Pepper hired me to look into this *Orion* mess."

"Uh-oh, something tells me this is going to cost me a lot more than the ten minutes you asked for."

"Actually, I've done you a big favor, Al . . . Not to mention some of your homework." Rosco pulled a business-sized manila envelope from his jacket and tossed it onto Lever's desk. "Blood samples. One's fish, the other's human, type A pos. TX Bio-Lab got that much for me. I don't care about the fish, but I'd like to get a DNA run on the type A pos. I thought—"

"Nah, nah, nah, hold on there, Rosco. I'm not touching this with a ten-foot pole. Pepper's a good guy and all that, and I feel sorry as hell for him . . . but I got enough around

here to keep me busy for a year." A large, pudgy hand gestured toward a row of pending files stacked on a folding
metal table.

"I'm just asking you to run it down to your lab, Al. Have
Abe or someone draw me a printout. TX doesn't do DNA
work. They have to send it to Boston. Takes forever."

"Rosco . . ." Lever shook his head as if he were speaking to a child. "You know full well I can't run blood work
through my lab without opening a file on it."

"Right . . . Well, you're going to have to investigate this
thing sooner or later, so I figured—"

"That's where you're wrong, bucko. That boat burned at
sea, as far as I'm concerned. And I don't care where it was
towed—or by whom. It's federal jurisdiction. This entire
matter has nothing to do with my department. You want
DNA work? Go talk to the feds."

"Come on, Al, the FBI won't do this kind of thing for a
PI, and you know it. All I want to know is: Whose blood
did I lift? It may be nothing—a boating accident, no more.
But where's the harm in checking? At least get me a
male/female readout."

Lever sighed, smashed out his cigarette, leaned back in
his chair, and placed his hands behind his head. "You
never give up, do you, Polly—Crates? A shame you didn't
stay on the force. We need cops like you." Then, almost to
himself, he added, "Damn shame about the Peppers . . .
Tom's a solid citizen. He's been real good for this burg."
After that, Al resumed his gruff demeanor.

"Where'd this stuff come from, anyway? Not off the
Orion, because I looked her over . . . On my own time . . .
Hell, a celebrity goes to Davy Jones's locker . . . In Buz-
zards Bay . . ." He shrugged. "What can I say, it piques

your interest. I've even watched that 'soap' on occasion . . .
And, yeah, before you ask me . . . I also took a gander at
those photos in that tabloid . . . Some looker . . ."

Rosco chuckled. "A gander, Al?"

"Hey, come on, Polly—Crates, you know how it is . . .
The wife buys one of those rags at the supermarket . . . It's
lyin' there on the kitchen counter—"

"Uh-huh . . ."

But Al was not to be bested. "You gotta get yourself a
wife, buddy, if you don't believe me."

Rosco's thoughts inadvertently leaped to Belle. He
couldn't imagine her purchasing supermarket tabloids, but
then there were facets to her personality he hadn't yet discovered. "I had a wife, Al, if you remember."

"Two years don't count. It's like a trial run. A 'starter
marriage'—like the comics say." Lever lit up again and
immediately started hacking. "Besides," he wheezed, "that
was a long time ago."

When the coughing attack had subsided, Rosco said,
"I took the samples from the boat that hauled in the
Orion."

Lever sat up straighter in his chair. "So?"

"So, I thought you might be interested."

The answer was a grudging: "I'm all ears, Polly—
Crates. But make it snappy. This isn't a social gathering."

Rosco chortled again. Despite the curt response, he
knew he had a fish on the line. He began sharing what
he knew about the *Dixie-Jack* charter, Ed Colberg, and the
disappearance of Stingo and Quick. Rosco omitted Pepper's run-in with the Coast Guard—and Belle's bizarre
crossword puzzle. He sensed quotations from Shake-

speare might stretch the limits of Al's patience—or imagination. After Rosco had finished, Lever picked up the
manila envelope and tapped it thoughtfully in the palm of
his hand.

"So, what are you saying?" he asked.

"I'm saying that something's fishy, Al. And I'd like your
help. Just have your lab identify whether the blood's male
or female—how's that?"

"I can't buck the FBI. I have no jurisdiction here, Rosco.
Besides, even if I prioritize this, it would take Abe over a
week to get me any lab results. This holds no priority over
his backlog. You know that as well as anyone."

Rosco groaned and slid the envelope back into his
jacket.

"You're making too much out of this, Polly—Crates.
Colberg's not stupid enough to scuttle a boat and risk a
manslaughter charge while he's at it. Especially not with a
TV star on board. You've investigated him before. You
know that he's slicker than that."

"Uh-huh . . . Well, thanks, Al. I'll see ya around. Maybe
play some handball like old times . . ."

Rosco stood and walked to the door, but before he could
reach for the knob, Lever's phone rang.

"Yeah. Lever here."

Rosco watched him listening intently for a second or
two, then turned to the door.

"Hold on a minute, Polly—Crates." Lever had the
receiver cupped in his left hand. With his right hand, he
indicated for Rosco to wait, then hurriedly scribbled notes
on a pad of paper, said a terse "Got it," and hung up the
phone.

"What was that all about?" Rosco asked.

"Someone found the *Orion*'s tender washed up on Munnatawket Beach."

Rosco smiled, and tossed the manila envelope back onto Lever's desk. "Sounds like it's your jurisdiction, Al."

CHAPTER

12

"Munnatawket Beach, huh?" Rosco said as he slid into the passenger's side of Al Lever's unmarked car: *unmarked* being a stretch of anyone's imagination. A light brown, four-door Ford sedan with bench seats, huge black tires, and three extra radio antennas was the type of car that had never seemed especially unmarked to Rosco. "Who found the dinghy?" he asked Lever.

"Some guy walking his dog. Phoned in on his cell phone." Lever placed a red magnetized emergency flasher on the roof of the Ford and headed east on Thomas Paine Boulevard, passing through traffic signals as he picked up speed. "There's an officer out there now; I told him to keep this guy at the scene."

"Does the Coast Guard know yet?"

"No. I'll radio from Munnatawket Beach after I confirm the find. I'd hate to have them scale back the search if it's not the correct inflatable tender." Lever glanced over at Rosco and added, "That's a dinghy."

"Thanks, Al." Rosco gave the response a fair amount of sarcasm. "You're loaded with information."

"Well, I wasn't sure . . . I know how you are with boats and water."

Lever leveled off the Ford at fifty miles per hour as they passed the Patriot Yacht Club. Another seven or eight minutes and they were abreast of the lane that led to the Pepper estate.

Rosco shook his head. "This is going to be tough on Pepper," he said. "If the inflatable does belong to the *Orion,* the Coast Guard will scale back its SAR-Op . . . or cancel the search altogether . . . You know that, don't you?"

Lever thought for a moment. "We're looking at close to seventy-two hours in the water in October . . . A good swimmer, with good body fat, lasts four, six hours at the most. And I mean, real good body fat."

Rosco unconsciously glanced at Lever's paunch, and then back to his own lean waistline.

Lever laughed. "That's right, buddy-boy, I'd survive longer than you out in the deep blue sea. There are genuine advantages to *not* being such a dapper dan . . . Strict doughnut training is what I recommend for a build like mine."

They rounded a sharp curve in the road and immediately recognized the blue, red, and white strobe lights of a patrol car. It was parked beside a low stone wall that separated the pavement from the beach—a mile-long stretch of sand that had been named Munnatawket centuries ago by the Native Americans. A rough translation—"Beautiful Place." In the distance, Rosco could see small waves gently lapping at the shore. He found himself wishing Belle were with him, not Al, and that they were on their way to this secluded spot for an undisturbed afternoon picnic.

The two men stepped from the car and walked through a break in the wall designed for access by summer bathers. A sign stated that the beach was PRIVATE, NEWCASTLE RESIDENTS ONLY, and that anyone wishing to use it must wear or carry an APPROPRIATE TAG. Despite the intrusive modern directive, the place seemed timeless and serene. Rosco gazed at the scene while he trudged through the sand beside Al.

The depth of Munnatawket Beach varied with the seasons. During the summer, at low tide, it was close to fifty yards from the stone wall to the water's edge; in winter, the beach was often eroded to fifteen feet or less—then miraculously returned the following summer. It was one of those natural phenomena that never ceased to amaze Rosco.

On this day, there were nearly thirty feet of sand; and the *Orion*'s rubber dinghy rested at the midpoint between the stone wall and the water. A uniformed officer stood beside it talking with a man in his late thirties. He wore a black windbreaker and baggy crimson shorts with HARVARD embroidered on the right leg. A medium-sized brown-and-black dog of questionable parentage trotted around with a frayed tennis ball in her mouth. She had white paws and no tail. When she saw Rosco, she bounded toward him and dropped her ball at his feet; her eyes were winsome; she recognized him as an easy touch. Rosco played into her hands, picking up the ball and tossing it down the beach. By the time they'd reached the inflatable, she was back, again depositing the ball at his feet. He tossed it a second time. The dog's owner laughed and said, "There's a sucker born every minute.

She'll never leave you alone now; she's a definite ball-a-holic."

"That dog should be on a leash," Lever said, directing the complaint to the uniformed officer.

The officer, dog owner, and Rosco all looked at him as if he'd lost his mind. "It's October," they muttered in unison.

"City ordinance," Lever answered, although his tone was surprisingly mild.

He and Rosco began pacing the tender's perimeter, studying the dinghy without disturbing it. The word *Orion* had been stenciled on both sides of the black rubber bow, while a large gash had opened the port side, leaving the tender as deflated as a discarded inner tube. An eight-horsepower outboard engine was still bolted to the stern, the propeller arm partially covered in drifted sand like the limb of a French Legionnaire long dead in some Moroccan desert. Two feet of nylon towline remained attached to a hard plastic cleat at the bow.

Lever again focused on the uniformed officer, "So, what do we have here, Stuart? Talk to me."

"Well, Lieutenant, this is Mr. Mitchell." He pointed to the man in the Harvard shorts. "He found the inflatable about an hour ago. He knows more about it than I do."

Lever glanced at his watch, then to Mitchell. "About eleven-thirty? That's when you showed up?"

"Yep."

"You didn't touch it, did you? You didn't move it?"

"Nope. Just called 911." Mitchell instinctively pulled his cell phone out of his windbreaker.

"Stuart? You touch anything?"

"No, sir, I didn't move anything either."

"What about these footprints? Those belong to you, Mr. Mitchell?"

"I guess. Most of them, anyway. I walked around the

tender a little. I wasn't sure what it was at first. It looked like a beached sea turtle from a distance. There've been a few of them lately. The water's been really warm this year—"

"How often do you come out here?" Rosco interrupted.

"Just about every day."

"So this wasn't here yesterday?"

Mitchell thought for a moment. "Actually, I didn't come out yesterday. I had a lunch meeting. But it definitely wasn't here the day before. Tuesday, that is."

Rosco looked up and down the beach. There wasn't another soul in sight. "Aren't there usually more people out here?"

Mitchell also studied the scene. "Not this time of year. I can go for weeks without running into anyone . . . That's why I don't keep Sally on a leash. There's no one for her to bother."

"Do you live nearby?"

"No. That's my Saab over there." He pointed to a green car on the other side of the wall. "I live downtown. I just bring Sally out here at lunchtime to let her run off steam. She drives me crazy if I don't."

Lever sighed and said, "I'm going to radio the Coast Guard. I hate to say it, but there's no point in them searching for something they won't find . . . My guess is that the ladies just made the missing-and-presumed-dead list." He dropped his hands into his pockets and strolled slowly back to the Ford.

Rosco stepped away from the dinghy and looked toward Buzzards Bay, then studied the sand. "Does the tide usually come up this high?"

Mitchell picked up the tennis ball and tossed it for Sally. "Well, that's the strange thing. No, it doesn't . . . We had a full moon, though, so I suppose the tide could have been running unusually high . . . But I didn't see high-water marks in the sand near the inflatable . . . On the other hand, we've had a lot of rain . . . Maybe it erased the Tuesday night's waterline . . . Or, someone could have pulled the tender up here, and didn't bother to report it."

Mitchell again threw the ball for the persistent Sally, who went tearing after it for all she was worth. A spray of sand flew in her wake. "But, if that's the case," he continued, "whoever it was would have had to carry the tender, because there aren't any drag marks in the sand . . . Leaving you with a lot of possibilities, but no real answers, huh?"

Rosco smiled. "You should be a detective, Mr. Mitchell. Is there anything else that seems unusual to you?"

"I don't know. I wish I'd paid more attention to the footprints when I walked up. I can't tell if they're all mine or not." He crouched down and studied the long gash on the inflatable's port side. It appeared as if the rubber boat had been sliced open with some rough-edged power tool.

"What do you think did that?" Rosco asked. "Do you know anything about sailing?"

"Not much. I do a little surf fishing, deep-sea, once in a while . . . Maybe a swordfish could do something like that. But I don't think many come into the bay . . . Maybe a propeller, if the tender were submerged and was hit by a motorboat . . . There are sharks, of course." Mitchell shook his head. "I really feel sorry for those women. I didn't know them, but it's sad when something like this happens. I almost wish I hadn't found the thing."

"What's up?" Lever asked in a disinterested tone as he returned from the Ford.

"Not much," Rosco said. "We were just trying to figure

if the tide carried the tender this far—or if someone dragged it out of the water. What did the Coast Guard say?"

Lever lit a cigarette and tossed the match into the sand at Rosco's feet. "As far as they're concerned, the party's over. No one could make it this long in that water . . . They're diverting all efforts. They've got a Japanese tanker taking on water off the cape and they're scrambling to contain the oil spill and airlift the crew. It's a matter of priority at this point."

"Pepper's not going to like that . . . What about opening an investigation? Now that you've got the dinghy."

Lever gave Rosco a forced smile. "Thanks to you, my good friend, the Coast Guard has asked me—and my over-worked department—to conduct a preliminary into this one. My forensics people will check out the inflatable and the *Orion*. If they come up with anything *fishy*, the feds will make a decision on how to handle it . . . Thanks, Rosco, old buddy, I really needed this one."

Rosco held his hands in the air. "Hey, I'm here to help."

"Great . . . Happy to hear it. Why don't you start by 'helping' Stuart load that tender into the back of his squad car. Maybe he'll even give you a lift into town if you're real nice to him." Lever turned and walked toward his Ford. "I've got work to do," he muttered.

"Have the lab check out the *Dixie-Jack*, too," Rosco called after him, "and check out those blood samples."

The three men watched in silence as Lever drove off. "You guys need a hand with this thing?" Mitchell eventually asked.

Stuart shrugged. "I think we can handle it, Mr. Mitchell." He positioned himself over the outboard motor and added, "You'd think the weight of this engine would make it sink, wouldn't you?"

They looked at each other, then at the deflated tender, then back toward each other. Rosco was the first to speak. "I can double-check with Ed Colberg, but it's my understanding that the dinghy would remain seaborne—despite the loss of air. Rubber's pretty buoyant. Look at all those empty tires that wash up. They're full of water and they still float."

"That's it," Mitchell said as he snapped his fingers. "I knew there was something else I thought of while I waited for you . . . Look at this beach."

Rosco and Stuart stared at the length of empty sand.

"Yes?" Rosco asked.

"Waterlogged tires. That's just it! There aren't any. No driftwood. No dead turtles. That's what makes this such a great beach in the summer; no seaweed or debris . . . and that's also why no beachcombers are here off-season . . . There's something about the way the cove is situated in the current . . . It's really unusual for anything to wash up here."

After Rosco and Stuart had stowed the inflatable in the trunk of the patrol car, they returned to Newcastle at a leisurely pace. The officer dropped Rosco at his Jeep, then continued down the ramp leading to the morgue and forensics lab below police headquarters. Rosco slid behind the Jeep's wheel, started the engine, then entered his office number into his car phone and waited for it to pick up. He had three messages: the first from Tom Pepper, anxious for information; the second from a man claiming to work for A.M.I.; the third message was from Belle.

Rosco smiled at the sound of her voice, but the longer he listened to the message, the more his smile faded.

"Rosco, it's me . . . Where are you? I've been trying your car phone like crazy. Call me as soon as you get

this . . . No wait, don't call me. I'm starved. I'll be at
Lawson's Coffee Shop . . . It's quarter to one right now. I
don't have any food in the house . . . well, nothing *you'd*
call food . . . You're not going to believe this. Someone
sent me another crossword puzzle. I'll bring it to Lawson's. I won't order anything until you get there, so don't
take forever . . ."

Across

1. Turncoat
4. Thigh toppers
8. Decathlete Johnson
13. Freak ending?
14. Demi——, "St. Elmo's Fire" actress
15. Build
16. "Fee,——, foe"
17. Portuguese man——
18. Wanders
19. Shakespeare quote, part 1
22. Canvas coupler
23. Picnic pest
24. Bests
27. Coat type
29. Hunts for clues
31. Classic car
32. Gushes
34. Year in Trajan's reign
35. *Hamlet* houses?
36. Quote, part 2
39. "All my——remembered," *Hamlet*
40. Baron ender?
41. Beam & L.O.A., e.g.
42. Grade C, abbr.
43. A as in——
45. Nitrogen, comb. form
46. Morro——, 1934 shipwreck
48. 1984 and 2001, abbr.
50. "——and the Man"
53. Quote, part 3
56. Smithy
58. Vowel run
59. Garden tool
60. Chemist's gold
61. Mother-of-pearl
62. Terminate
63. "The 39——," Hitchcock film
64. First man
65. *The Catcher in the*——

Down

1. Improvisations
2. Not Occidental
3. Castaway's mirage
4. Nicholson title role
5. Hawkeyes
6. Down, but not out
7. Dry
8. Old TV?
9. "——by any other name"
10. "Show virtue her own——own image," *Hamlet*
11. Continental grp.
12. Hwys.
14. One of the Stooges
20. Knots?
21. Themes
25. "For——sake!"
26. Mayday!
28. Dread
30. ——of rage
32. Hindu destroyer
33. Thief
35. "Lifeboat" actor Walter
37. Biff's bro.
38. Psych. grp.
39. Defense grp.
43. Security devices
44. Beethoven symphony
47. Get ready to drive?
49. *The Perfect*——, Junger book
51. Listless
52. 56-Down employee often
54. ——Lake, Blue Nile source
55. Shade
56. Fjord flier
57. Hovel

PUZZLE 2

CHAPTER

13

Belle was already ensconced in the far-window booth at Lawson's Coffee Shop when Rosco opened the glass-paneled front door. His arrival was heralded by the noisy peal of a rusting tin bell attached to the upper hinges, an early-warning device left over from the 1950s when Lawson's had been built. True to form, none of the aging waitresses—also relics of the poodle-skirt era—turned a mascaraed eyelash, although one shouted out a raucous: "She's seated in the back, angel."

"Thanks, Martha." Rosco nodded at the speaker as he walked past the long, green Formica counter. Martha was as much an institution as the coffee shop. She never called customers by name, but that didn't mean she didn't know each and every one of them—and most likely their parents, too. Martha, with her defiantly flaxen beehive hairdo and rustling candy-pink uniform, was a font of information. She prided herself on keeping her eyes peeled.

"What happens next?" Belle asked while Rosco slid in beside her on the banquette. The motif, here, was also fifties flamingo pink, but the seats' aging vinyl covers were cracked and the tabletop chipped and scarred. Regulars like Rosco and Belle wouldn't have changed this homey ambience for all the tea in China, however. To them, Lawson's was as important a landmark as Newcastle's historic district or the resuscitated clipper-ship wharves. "Now that the inflatable's been found?" Belle continued, then added, "I take it the discovery ensures that Al Lever is officially involved?"

But Rosco didn't want to discuss the PD's role yet. He knew Lever's conclusion that the women were now "presumed dead" would be difficult for Belle to assimilate and accept. To buy time, Rosco asked to see the second crossword puzzle.

"I swear I'm not in any danger," she said, placing it between them on the table's scratchy surface. "This one was faxed—also anonymously—but I called the sender's number. It's that enormous new office-supply store, Papyrus, near the interstate . . . The woman who accepted the order is *supposed* to call me back when she returns from her lunch break . . . However, the exceedingly officious person who answered the phone said that *supplying* client information is a breach of privacy. In that case, I'll simply go out there and weasel pertinent details from them . . ." Belle was on a roll; Rosco could feel kinetic energy bounce from her body; her skin smelled like gardenias and warm wool. He was sorely tempted to wrap his arm around her shoulder.

Instead, he said, "I don't think that's wise, Belle."

Her monologue stopped mid-word; she stared in surprise. "What do you mean?"

"I don't think you should go out to Papyrus."

Belle continued staring.

"Look," Rosco continued, "if these puzzles are the work of a sicko—something I strongly suspect—then you'll be playing into his hands."

"It's a public place, Rosco . . . It's no different than walking into Lawson's—"

Rosco interrupted her. "In a case of arson, who do you think is usually the most noticeable person extinguishing the blaze? The perpetrator. The bigger the fire, the more obvious that person's heroics. And those antics aren't confined to arsonists . . . People of that type get their jollies from participating in the chaos they've created. It's a giant ego trip . . . I'll bet this kook is hanging around Papyrus right now waiting for you—which will only escalate an already problematic situation by encouraging his behavior."

Belle continued studying his face. Rosco could see her weighing, then gradually accepting his theory. "Okay, so scratch Papyrus, but I still believe someone is trying to tell me something—something about Genie and Jamaica . . . Look at the clues, Rosco . . . Look at these answers." Her fingers jabbed at the cryptic, making crosses where the Across and Down lines intersected.

"3-Down: THE LAPPING SHORE . . . See that running down the puzzle? And, PRACTICALLY DEAD at 6-Down? Isn't that scary? No matter what you say—and it's convincing, I have to admit—intuition tells me this isn't the work of a crazy . . . Someone is trying to tell us that these women are in terrible danger."

Martha sauntered over, armed with tall, laminated menus across which *Lawson's Coffee Shop* was printed in cherry red. "Want to take a peek? Or do you two want the usual?"

Rosco and Belle's heads swiveled toward her in unison. "The usual?"

"What you folks always order: grilled-cheese sandwiches, and a side of French toast with syrup, blueberry sauce, and whipped cream . . . coffee light for the lady, black for my man, here . . ." A smug smile wreathed Martha's primrose-painted lips.

"Always? We always order that? I didn't realize we'd become so predictable," Belle murmured.

"Everyone is, angel. Not to worry . . ." Heavy-duty support garments creaked beneath Martha's uniform while her left hand extricated a pencil from her lacquered hairdo. She poised the pencil above a pad marked *Guest Check* in faded lime-green lettering. ". . . So, what'll it be while you two palaver about that missing actress and Tom Pepper's hoity-toity wife?"

This time it was Rosco's turn to look stunned. But Martha didn't give him a chance to speak. "Why else would you lovebirds look so frazzled?" Then she marched off toward the kitchen, yelling: "Double cheddar melt and Froggers, extra crisp on the Froggers."

Shy grins crept over Rosco and Belle's faces. Involuntarily, they sat up straighter—and farther apart. Both toyed with their stainless-steel cutlery. Belle was the first to resume conversation, returning doggedly to her narrative as if Martha hadn't said a word.

"Of course, there's another nautical theme here, Rosco . . . 14-Across: *St. Elmo's Fire actress;* 41-Across: *Beam & L.O.A., e.g;* 46-Across: *Morro——, 1934 shipwreck;* 35-Down: *Lifeboat actor* . . . And here . . . look at this! 26-Down: *Mayday!* Could anything be more plain? Mayday! From the French *m'aider* . . . The international call of distress! And what's the answer? S.O.S.!"

Belle's tone had increased in speed and fervor; her

cheeks were flushed; turning to face Rosco, she almost glowed. "I know I'm right, Rosco. I just know it! . . . Wait, don't answer yet. There's more . . ."

Again, her fingers stabbed at the crossword puzzle. "See this? Starting at 19-Across? A series of three lines across that combine to form a quotation from *Macbeth*? Everyone in theater knows it's unlucky to say the play's name . . . It's referred to as *The Scottish Play* instead . . . So, that's a message in itself."

"It's no good, Belle," Rosco finally said.

"You've got to hear me out, Rosco. This wasn't constructed by some media-crazed weirdo. This is a warning. And it was sent to me, because I can discover the hidden meaning. 'FALSE FACE MUST HIDE,' she quoted, 'WHAT FALSE HEART DOTH KNOW.' " She clasped her hands in impatience; her fingers were taut. "I even looked it up. Me! . . . And this one from *Hamlet* at 10-Down; it's from the famous 'mirror to nature' speech: '. . . show virtue her own feature, scorn her own image'!"

"Belle. Please . . . listen to me . . ." Rosco slipped his hands around hers. "It's no good because Lever has decided to shift the investigation's focus. And with justifiable cause. I saw the dinghy. It has a mile-long gash . . . It's totally deflated. It could never have supported human life. If those women were on it, they weren't there for long . . ." Rosco took a beat while allowing Belle to process the information. " 'Missing—presumed dead' is how Lever's officially listing their disappearance . . . I'm sorry, Belle."

Belle stared at the crossword puzzle. Rosco could see tears forming in her eyes. "But . . ." she said, "but . . ."

"And, whether you like to hear it or not, this puzzle— and the other one—are the work of a nutcase. A smart one, I grant you, but a lunatic nevertheless . . . And I am genuinely concerned about your proximity to such a person. Especially someone so obviously clever."

Belle looked out the window. Across the street was the limestone, granite, and marble home of the *Newcastle Herald,* the *Evening Crier*'s rival newspaper. The building stood, noble and imposing, a paean to the turn-of-the-century publishing industry. The grassy area fronting the facade and the cars parked neatly at the curb were dwarfed by the *Herald*'s lofty demeanor.

"I want to publish this puzzle," Belle said while still gazing at the street. "In my column. I want to invite the constructor to come forward and claim authorship."

A clatter of dishes interrupted them. Soon the table was piled with cholesterol hell. Belle absentmindedly dabbed whipped cream on a slice of grilled-cheese sandwich, then ate it without seeming to notice.

"I really advise against that, Belle. You don't want to flush this loon out into the open. With Lever's official read, this thing will blow over, and Mr.—or Mrs.—Psycho will disappear. On the other hand, if you give this type of person additional attention, you risk further upsetting an imbalanced psyche. There's also a matter of 'transference'—turning you into this character's weird obsession."

Belle stabbed a piece of French toast dredged in blueberry sauce and maple syrup, then chewed with fierce concentration. "But if my theory is correct, Rosco, and the puzzles have genuine linkage to the case, then printing this crossword will send a message that we're ready to talk."

CHAPTER

14

T he offices of the *Evening Crier* were not so handsome or so stately as those of the *Herald,* but they were far more lively. Voices ricocheted along the corridors, bouncing though open doors that smelled of too many frenzied humans working at too frantic a pace. Although Belle could never think under such rattling conditions, she enjoyed her sojourns to her office—if only to watch in wonder as a tide of verbiage and ink flowed down stairwells, up halls, around watercoolers and computer terminals to create a daily newspaper filled with fact and whimsy. Belle was part of the whimsy.

So was Bartholomew Kerr, whose *Biz-y Buzz,* with its whiff of British elitism, had become the newest staple of Newcastle society. Kerr was so fond of affixing pseudo-royal titles and pet names to those fortunate enough to appear in his columns that a stranger to the city might have imagined that the entire global monarchy had encamped on the Massachusetts shore.

"Naturally, he's doing everything in his power to *connive* a means of acquiring those precious photographs," Kerr was now complaining to Belle, "but I intend to foil those efforts at every turning." The gossip columnist trained his enormous glasses upward onto Belle's face as if the lenses were telescopic in intensity. "And that's all I have to say on a *very* sordid subject."

Standing in the *Crier*'s second-floor corridor, a wide red-and-black linoleum avenue intersected by doors with frosted-glass panels, two elevators, a janitorial supply room, and numerous pendant fluorescent-light fixtures, Belle realized Kerr's statement was misleading in the extreme. Obviously, he had a good deal more on his mind. And, knowing Bartholomew, he didn't intend to remain silent for long.

"Simply because the man boasts of a national readership— although of dubious powers of discernment, I might add— doesn't mean I should acquiesce like some junior scrivener . . . like some hopeless neophyte . . ."

Belle hadn't the slightest idea what had so enraged Bartholomew, but she was enjoying the display. She breathed in the invigorating pressroom scent of waxed linoleum, spilled coffee, and endless reams of inky paper as she listened to Kerr pour forth his disgust. His accent, she decided, must have been created somewhere in the middle of the North Atlantic; it wasn't English; it definitely wasn't American or Canadian. She wondered if acquiring a new voice and persona could occur mid-flight, like a spy changing clothes and hairstyle in a plane's rest room.

". . . So tawdry, really . . . attempting to *cajole* another member of the fourth estate into *relinquishing* sources and photographic information . . . Almost demanding the negatives? Well, *negatives*, my dear girl, is exactly what he received from me, in the form of: 'No, no, no!' Now, if

he'd requested that I *consult* with him on the subject . . .
suggested I maintain my own *byline* . . . What do you
think Annabella?"

"Belle," she corrected automatically while Bartholomew
Kerr just as quickly said, "You know, my dear, it simply
makes no sense whatsoever for you to abbreviate your
handsome moniker . . . It makes you sound like someone
Ethel Merman would have played—to the hilt, I might
add . . . Belle Starr, the outlaw bandit queen . . . Besides,
Annabella Graham has such a mellifluous—and dare I say
germane—association with your craft: 'Anna-Gram' is
how it would be pronounced in the dear old motherland. Of
course, you can appreciate the connection—"

Belle winced. "Please . . . Bartholomew . . . I was tortured with that nickname when I was a kid—"

"No matter, then . . . *Tant pis* . . . *tant pis* . . . Well, I'm
off to do more electronic battle with the odious toad who
torments me . . . I assume his next suggestion is that we
meet in some darkened hotel bar to hand off these print
negatives—as if exchanging government secrets . . . I did
that once, in Istanbul, you know, but the quarry was
the offspring of a prince—and that young gentleman's
bride . . . Ah, well, giddier times . . . giddier times . . ."

Belle had begun to edge her way down the corridor.
Bartholomew might be amusing, but she reminded herself
that she was on a mission.

". . . If I wind up missing like La Nevisson, my dear, tell
the constabulary that I'm *hors de combat*."

Belle's ears pricked up. "What's this about Jamaica
Nevisson?"

Bartholomew smiled with the smugness of a man who
knows himself superior to all mortals around him. "That's
precisely what you and I have been discussing . . . This
perfectly *wretched* reporter from *The Globe* who's been

telephoning and e-mailing me unmercifully, harassing me at *all* hours simply to obtain photographs of our vanished actress—a series I shot at the Patriot Yacht Club dinner dance . . . the last known likenesses of her, as it turns out. There are also several of you, Belle, in the not-too-distant background . . . I must say, you and your swain looked simply *splendid* that evening—"

"Is this the same man who snapped those bizarre pictures of Jamaica on Catalina Island?"

"I wouldn't have the foggiest, my dear."

But Belle recognized the falsity of this statement. Kerr knew very well who the man was. What she didn't understand was why the columnist would lie.

"Flack is simply another sordid huckster, Annabella . . . a benighted devil attracted to tragedy . . . the desire of the moth for the flame—"

" 'The desire of the moth for the star,' " Belle murmured unintentionally while Kerr pivoted his oversized spectacles in her direction. "It's a line from a poem by Percy Bysshe Shelley," she added. "The conclusion is: 'The devotion to something afar / From the field of our sorrow.' " Belle's bright eyes flashed with a sudden revelation. "What did you say this man's name was again, Bartholomew?"

"Who? Reggie Flack?"

"Flack . . . yes, that's it . . ." Her brain raced through a myriad of possible connections to the name or word. Then she remembered the mysterious crossword puzzle she'd received on Wednesday. The word FLACK was one of the answers; the clue had been *Antiaircraft fire, var.* She remembered it because the constructor could have used another definition—and omitted the ubiquitous *var.* Flack was the colloquial term for a press agent.

"I see you're noodling over serious thoughts, Belle—" Kerr began in a prodding tone, but she cut him off.

"And this Reggie Flack wants the photos you shot at the Yacht Club?"

"Dear me! Have I been talking solely to these dreary walls?"

"Why does he want them?" Belle demanded. "What's in the pictures?"

Kerr's answer was a flippant: "You, for one thing."

But Belle ignored the remark. "What does Flack intend to do with photographs of a social gathering in Newcastle?"

"I imagine the man is obsessed with La Nevisson. Whatever else could it be, my dear? Assuming you are not his obsession . . ."

"His name appeared—" Belle stopped herself—although not in time. Kerr's sharp ears never missed a single innuendo or inadvertently dropped secret.

"Yes?" he said.

Belle considered her options. She could either confide in Bartholomew or lie; if there were less extreme choices, they wouldn't have entered her decisive mind. Belle's thoughts flew forward, gauging possible outcomes. If she maintained secrecy, discovering new information on Flack would be extraordinarily difficult. But, if she confessed all to Bartholomew, what would be the result? On a sudden whim, she decided to share her suspicions about Jamaica's and Genie's disappearance.

"I received a peculiar crossword puzzle on Wednesday," she said. "The word FLACK was in it . . . So was JAMAICA . . . and GENIE . . . and ORION. There were also numerous nautical themes. And, quotations from *Much Ado About Nothing*—a play Jamaica did in Boston. Very well, too."

"Oh, my dear," was all Bartholomew could think to say.

"Rosco felt it was the work of a sick prankster, and I

was inclined to agree—until today. Today I received a second cryptic. Not only does the nautical theme continue, but the Shakespeare quotes do as well . . . Now, I seem to recall that this *Globe* photographer liked to reference the Bard."

"Oh, my dear!" Kerr repeated in a burbling gush. "I believe you're quite right . . . This is all terribly exciting. What do you—"

But Belle's brain had spun forward. "I intend to publish this newest crossword, Bartholomew," she said, "in hopes of flushing the constructor out into the open—sending a message that his voice has been heard . . . But now I'm wondering if you could do me an enormous favor."

"Oh, yes!" Kerr's thick lenses glinted.

"Could you report this conversation? . . . Drop it into your *Biz-y Buzz* column as if it were a piece of Newcastle gossip."

The black-rimmed glasses bounced up and down. "I can picture the lead," he nearly sang. "And maybe a pull quote—to catch the readers' attention . . . Of course I can, my dear! Bartholomew Kerr to the rescue. But . . ." The glasses drooped; the head sagged.

"But?" Belle asked.

"But the earliest I can get it printed is tomorrow's edition. This afternoon's is already trundling its way to the news vendors."

"Friday is fine, Bartholomew." Belle beamed down at the tiny man. "And let me know, won't you, what other information you hear from Reggie Flack?"

"The very moment, Belle. The very instant . . . Reggie has met his match."

The woman's hand shook as she punched in the telephone number. Semidarkness obscured her features and the room around her. All that was visible was the outline of an unmade bed, a low chest of drawers, and a lamp with a dented shade. The lamp had not been lit.

A seemingly interminable amount of time passed before the call was answered, and another several silent seconds elapsed before the woman decided to proceed.

"Is it all right to talk?" she asked. Her voice was low, a monotone created by purposely compressing the larynx. The accent was equally difficult to ascertain; there was an undertone of a Tennessee drawl overlaid with the crisply bitten consonants of Maine.

The male speaker at the other end produced a disturbed, nervous laugh. "Hey! How are ya?" Then the register dropped to a whisper, and the collegial tone became bitten and hard. "You're not supposed to call me here . . . It could be traced in a second. That was the deal—"

"That *was* the deal." Her voice caught with a sound like unexpressed tears. "But what am I supposed to do? You left me high and dry here—"

"Look,"—the voice was barely audible—"I don't know who's nearby . . . I can't talk."

"Then find a time when we can—"

"That's impossible! You know the rules. No contact until this is over."

"They found the dinghy."

"They were *supposed* to find it, remember?"

In the small bedroom, the woman's free hand clenched spasmodically against her thigh. She started to speak, but only produced a strangled groan that finally gave way to a gasp of desperation. "Something's gone wrong," she said in an accent clearly approaching her own. "Hasn't it?"

"I can't tell yet . . ." Then the man's voice changed timbre again, becoming loud, robust, and businesslike; he was obviously talking to someone else. "Okay," he called out.

"I'll be there in a minute . . . Tell them to hold their horses . . . Okay . . . Okay . . . I get the picture!"

Another moan broke from the woman's throat; this one was more like a snarl. "I can't stand this!"

"Well, try!" was the biting response.

"We should have had a contingency plan . . . I shouldn't have listened to you!" she spat back.

"Hey, babe, whose idea was this?" was his equally vicious reply.

Her voice descended to a weeping whimper. "I'm going crazy here."

"I've got to go," he said.

"When will you—"

"I don't know. Don't call me again. I'll find a way to contact you . . . And listen, next time work on your voice—"

"I'm going crazy here," she sobbed again in response. But he'd hung up before she'd completed the sentence.

CHAPTER

15

E ven though the autumn days were growing shorter, Rosco believed dawn was now purposely arriving earlier each morning. Sunlight radiated through his bedroom blinds long before the clock radio produced its annoying and persistent buzz. Friday was no different; at six forty-five A.M., when the alarm finally sounded, Rosco was already awake, sitting up, staring at the blinds and wondering what kind of sick mind would create the puzzles Belle had received.

He reached over and tapped the clock's Off button, causing the radio to switch to the *Imus in the Morning* program. The I-Man and his merry band of jesters were laughing so raucously at some lascivious witticism that Rosco could barely make out a word of conversation. On this particular day, Rosco found the gang a little too happy for his liking. He dispensed with Don, Charles, Fred, Bernard, and Company and walked grimly into the bathroom to shave and shower. He wasn't looking forward to his meeting with Tom Pepper. After perusing the inflatable tender the previous day, Rosco felt that he, and the world, had let Tom Pepper down.

At seven-thirty A.M., Anson opened the front door of the Pepper estate. "Ahh . . . Mr. Polycrates . . . It's good to see you again. I trust you had no trouble forcing your way through our media encampment?"

"I think they recognize me as a nonplayer."

Anson smiled in a formal fashion that made him look both uncomfortable and deceitful. Again, Rosco was struck by the way the man's appearance belied his position. Whatever Anson had been before his arrival in the Pepper household, it hadn't been a butler. "A nonplayer," he echoed. "Yes, sir . . ." Then he added a hasty: "Please come in. Mr. Pepper is expecting you."

"Okay, okay," Tom barked from somewhere in the invisible interior. "Take the man's jacket, Anson . . . Rosco, I want to see you in my office . . ." His voice disappeared, leaving Anson holding the offending jacket while Rosco found his way to the command center on his own.

The moment the detective entered the room, Tom's forceful speech resumed: "I appreciate the hell out of you coming so early, Rosco. I've got a heavy workload today. Sit down."

Rosco remained standing. "I'm all right."

"Suit yourself. So . . . what have you got for me?"

"Well, nothing more than what you've heard from the Coast Guard . . . They've suspended their search. There's an oil tanker—"

"I know all about the Japanese sailors. Cigar?" Tom opened a humidor and offered one to Rosco.

"No thanks."

"The only way to start a day." He lit up, inhaled, and

leaned back in his chair. "You know, Rosco, I can't help but laugh at the irony of this situation. My old man was stationed at Pearl Harbor in December of forty-one. He was lucky to come away with his skin . . . Now our guys are ditching my wife in order to save a bunch of sailors from Yokohama." Pepper pronounced the word "yoo-koo-haa-maa" with a long sarcastic emphasis on the final diphthong.

Rosco felt his temperature rising; he was well acquainted with prejudice, but he held his temper in check. "The Coast Guard has been examining all facets of the situation, Mr. Pepper. I realize it's not a pleasant thought, but in reality no one could survive for ninety-six hours in Buzzards Bay. From a tactical standpoint—"

"Yeah, yeah, I know . . . My Genie's gone. No doubt about it." Tom took a long hard pull from his cigar. "End of chapter. End of story . . ." Pepper inhaled again. "My frankness probably astonishes you, doesn't it? Look, I've had a night to sleep on this thing—or not sleep, as the case may be. I know a great deal about these past ninety-six hours. I've been personally involved with each one of those nasty buggers . . .

"But I'm a businessman, Rosco. The clock is either my biggest enemy, or my savior. This week it beat me—but good . . . However, I've had time to think things through . . . Think about what Genie would have wanted . . . What she would have *insisted* on. You didn't know my wife, but she was one hell of a lady . . . a racing skipper . . . You know that? . . . A real gutsy gal and all-around class act . . . Jamaica, too—" Pepper's voice broke. After a long, and icily quiet moment, he regained his eerie composure.

"I'm not a whiner, Rosco. I'm a self-made man, and I've never asked anyone for sympathy or help . . . and I'm not one of those damn depression addicts—popping pills and feeling sorry for myself . . . Genie's dead. Nothing I can do will bring her back—"

Rosco started to interrupt with words of consolation, but Pepper overrode him:

"However, I can make whoever was responsible pay. *Big time.*" His left fist slammed the desktop and remained clenched there while his right hand continued to grip the cigar. Rosco was surprised the hand-rolled cylinder didn't snap in two. "So I'm asking myself . . . what's the next step? Where do we go from here? What would *Genie* have asked me to do?"

Rosco recognized these as questions he wasn't expected, or encouraged, to answer. He gave his shoulders a slight shrug while watching Tom suddenly stab the tip of his cigar into an etched crystal ashtray on the center of his desk. Although Pepper appeared cognizant, even resigned, to the loss of his wife, Rosco found his behavior alarming—the antithesis of the man ranting about the ineptness of the Coast Guard and the intrusiveness of the media two days earlier. Rosco began to wonder how long this pseudo calm would last; in his experience, grief always took its toll. Sooner or later Tom's tough facade would crumble. What would replace it, the detective didn't know.

Pepper continued. "So what we do is this: We take that SOB Ed Colberg to the cleaners. I don't care what it costs or how much time it takes; he's going to pay and pay big. I want him out of business. I want his inventory seized, and I want him in jail. And then I want the damn media crawling down his throat. I want him to burn . . . What have the police found?"

"Why don't we discuss this later, Mr. Pepper? After you've had time to adjust—"

"Hell, no! We want this creep, we've got to strike while the iron is hot!"

"Well . . ." Rosco reluctantly began. "There's a forensics team scheduled to go over the *Orion* this afternoon. They'll also examine the fishing boat that towed her in . . . The department is pressed for personnel right now, so the detective working on the case is from homicide. You couldn't ask for a better man—"

"I want you to stay on top of them."

"I plan to be at Mystic Isle Yachts when they examine the boats." Rosco caught himself about to add "sir" to his answer.

Pepper dragged on his cigar again. His chest swelled; he seemed to be holding everything inside: smoke, sorrow, rage, guilt, grief. "Good," he finally said. His jaw looked tight enough to crack.

"They have the inflatable tender in the police lab for tests as well."

"What?"

"The dinghy."

"I know what a damn inflatable tender is, Polycrates! Why didn't you give me that information the moment you walked through my door, dammit?"

Rosco was about to reply, but Pepper cut him off. Again, his demeanor had suddenly altered. The voice was now quiet to the point of exhaustion. "Why the hell are they wasting their time with that piece of junk? Genie's gone . . . Studying her final last seconds on earth won't bring her back . . ."

Rosco allowed a moment of silence to elapse before he answered. "Well, Mr. Pepper, for one thing, they'd like to determine what caused the gash in its side. It might give them an idea of how far your wife might have traveled from the wreck."

"And what's that going to prove? Listen, I don't need to know all the gory details of how Genie died . . . I don't want those media bloodsuckers speculating on half-truths. The whole situation's ghoulish enough as it is." Again, the determined stance showed serious signs of breaking. Rosco watched sorrow and frustrated rage etch themselves across Pepper's face. "I'm not a religious man, Polycrates . . . never had much time for it . . . And now? Well, I don't know . . . But the dead should be allowed to rest in peace. I don't want to imagine my wife's last breaths . . . terrified, alone on a huge, hostile ocean . . . sharks, whatever . . ." Pepper shut his eyes tight. When he opened them again, his expression had resumed its determined serenity. "Who's this homicide detective? How well do you know him?"

"His name is Lever. We were partners when I was with the department."

"Good. Then we can use this clown."

Rosco squinted and said, "Clown's not a word I would use for Lever."

"Whatever . . . See if you can get him to concentrate on the *Orion* and the fishing boat . . . That's how we get Colberg—and that's the key to this situation . . . not wasting precious time on some dinky rubber boat . . . Genie died . . . my Genie died because of a maritime fire. We find the cause and affix blame."

Rosco recognized the anguish Tom was experiencing. "I see your point," he replied gently. "But if Colberg was negligent in providing proper safety equipment for the *Orion,* i.e., the tender, it could be an important factor in establishing blame—"

"Who's paying you, Polycrates! I'm telling you I don't want to know about the inflatable!" Pepper's voice had risen ominously. "We go after the yacht—and that's all . . .

If I have to see pictures of that damn rubber raft spread all over the tabloids, I think I'll lose my mind . . . Now, do I have to call Lever myself?"

"I'll talk to him."

"Good. Make sure you do." Pepper sagged in his chair.

Rosco cleared his throat. "I don't suppose you know your wife's blood type?"

Tom turned in his chair to face a desktop computer. "I have it here somewhere. What do you need it for?" He made an entry on the keyboard.

"There was some blood on the *Dixie-Jack* . . . A positive."

Tom studied the computer screen. "Nope . . . Genie was O negative."

"Well, that's—"

"Excuse me, sir," Anson said as he tapped lightly on the mahogany door. Rosco had not closed it when he'd entered.

Pepper answered with an aggravated: "What is it?"

Anson stepped toward Tom's desk. In his left hand he held a business-sized envelope. "This just arrived for you, sir. I was told it was most urgent."

"Now what?" Tom groaned, then stared hard at the handwritten address. A spasm of pain shot across his face. This time he couldn't conceal it. He pulled a long letter opener from the middle desk drawer and quickly slit the envelope open. His hand was clenched, his face gray. He stared at the butler. "You're not needed here."

After Anson left, Tom looked at Rosco. "Nosiest man in the whole damn world," he said bitterly. "I hired a butler, what I got was a snoop. I wouldn't be surprised if he tries to sell his story to those harpies outside . . ." Pepper slid a piece of paper from the envelope, unfolded it, studied it for fifteen seconds, then tossed it onto his desk toward Rosco.

It was a hand-drawn crossword puzzle, worked out on single-sided quarter-inch graph paper. Tom gritted his teeth. "There are too many sick people out there, Polycrates."

"I'll be right back." Rosco sprinted from the den, then returned three minutes later.

"What was that all about?" Tom asked.

"I wanted to speak to whoever delivered it."

"Well . . . ?"

"He was gone. I couldn't catch sight of him. Anson said he'd never seen him before. A kid in a Red Sox hat driving a beat-up Honda. A Grateful Dead fan, judging by the amount of stickers." Rosco picked up the puzzle and shook his head slowly.

"What is it?"

"Belle has already received two anonymous puzzles like this."

Tom jabbed his cigar into the ashtray and lurched forward in his chair. His voice had become exhausted and gravelly. "Dammit, man! Why haven't I been told about this?"

"Our assumption was that they'd come from a sicko . . . Someone to be wary of, yes, but better off ignored . . . What made *you* say that about sick people?"

"Look at it, it's addressed to Genie."

Rosco glanced at the envelope.

"And the graph paper has today's date on it. Four days after her disappearance."

Rosco watched Tom for a second or two. His hands were trembling, and his controlled demeanor definitely beginning to fail. "Do you ever do these puzzles?" Rosco asked.

"No." A hard laugh accompanied the word. "But Genie did . . . She was a member of a crossword club or something. I don't pay any attention to this stuff, but clearly,

whoever sent this must have the information . . . a mailing
list . . . I don't know. The person who did this is after
something, Rosco. I sense it . . . I don't like this. I don't
like it one bit."

"What could they want?"

"Money? Notoriety? . . . A sadistic thrill? . . . Hell, I don't
know what these Looney Tunes want!" Pepper jumped to
his feet and pointed at Rosco. "That's what I'm hiring you
for, dammit! To get me some answers!"

Again, Rosco could feel his own irritation escalating,
but the sensation was mitigated by Pepper's pain. Rosco
picked up the puzzle and placed it in the envelope. "Do
you mind if I take this? Belle can fill it in . . . Then I'll
compare it with the other two and return it."

After what seemed like a long silence Tom mumbled,
"Don't show it to the police."

"Pardon me?"

He raised his voice. "I said, don't take that thing to the
police. At this point it's privileged information shared
between you and your client. If this ends up being some
sort of bizarre extortion plot, I'll handle it . . . I just don't
want . . . I don't want . . ." Pepper's voice broke, and he
sank back into his chair.

"Sure, Mr. Pepper . . . If that's the way you want it . . .
In fact, until we get this puzzle solved, we have nothing
that would interest the police. But I feel it's my duty to
inform you that if this turns out to be an extortion attempt,
the police and FBI have far greater resources at their dis-
posal. They have—"

Tom lifted his hand and stopped Rosco in midsentence.
"This is my show, Polycrates, and I'm running it. After
that stupid puzzle's solved, we'll discuss the police. But I
don't . . . I don't want . . . Why would someone do a horrible thing like this? Two women are dead . . ." Pepper's

head fell back into his leather chair. His eyes stared glassily into the ceiling. "I've got work to do," he muttered, "a busy day . . . Get that snoop of a butler to show you out."

Three minutes later Rosco was in his Jeep and heading toward Newcastle proper. He punched star-1 into his car phone. Belle answered on the first ring.

Across

1. Counterfeited
6. Boleyn and others
11. Age
14. Fighting——of Notre Dame
15. Sub finder
16. Get a flat?
17. Nautical information, Shak.
20. ——shu, Chinese script
21. Convex moldings
22. "——on Me," Freeman film
23. "If you wrong us, shall——?" Shak.
27. Femmes——, Jamaica Nevisson & others
30. À la Keats
31. Bakery worker
32. N.Y. Shakespeare Festival wish
33. Prop for 6-Down
36. ". . . ——the search," Shak.
41. Ant. opp.
42. Bay
43. ——voce!
44. Loafer
45. Least hard
48. "Let no such——," Shak.
52. Mine, Fr.
53. Greek portico
54. Little sizes, abbr.
57. "If I——upon the hip . . ." Shak.
62. "I Go to——," Peter Allen song
63. Receiver
64. Eat away
65. Switch settings
66. Printer need
67. You're in a——situation

Down

1. Rat
2. Site
3. New Zealander
4. Turn in the road
5. Maître——
6. Houston nine
7. Ryan specialty
8. Wind dir.
9. Corn unit
10. ——Lanka
11. "Act of Vengeance" actress Burstyn
12. Mark down
13. Repent
18. "And then there were——"
19. "Mute Witness" actor Guinness
23. Trepidating
24. "——Cop," Weller film
25. Rework
26. A——from the Bridge, Miller play
27. Starts partner
28. Sore
29. Young adult
32. "——False Move," Paxton film
33. French cheese
34. 4-whlrs.
35. "All——glisters is not GOLD"
37. Pain
38. "The love of money is the—— of all evil"
39. "Be it——so humble"
40. "Ars Amatoria" poet
44. Little guy loaner, abbr.
45. "Neptune's Daughter" actress Williams
46. Yours, Fr.
47. Salts
48. Large, comb. form
49. At full speed
50. Insider trades?

PUZZLE 3

51. Theatergoer?
54. Con
55. Fifteenth-century date
56. Exposed
58. Alarm Co.

59. Also
60. TV news org.
61. Spanish GOLD

CHAPTER

16

B elle polished off her last deviled egg simultaneously with inking in the crossword puzzle's final clue. "Well," she said. "Well . . . well . . . well . . ."

She licked her fingers as if a delightful residue of beaten hard-boiled egg yolk and mayo remained there, sighed contentedly, then glanced up at Rosco, who had been hovering near her shoulder—when he wasn't pacing the floor of her office or pretending to read one of her foreign-language dictionaries. "It's almost painfully obvious, isn't it?" she asked, but was rewarded with a perplexed grin.

"Well, it's a crossword, if that's what you mean," he answered slowly.

"No, I mean the clues! The references . . . these quotations . . ." The hand holding the pen flew around in the air, describing loops and dips of frustration at Rosco's seeming obtuseness.

He shook his head; the grin spread. "I think we have to change your diet, Belle."

"Are you crazy?" she demanded. "I couldn't possibly give up deviled eggs. I'm *addicted* to them!"

"Maybe it's too much brain food." Rosco laughed. "Let's start from the beginning. What's so obvious?"

"*The Merchant of Venice* . . . The references are as plain as the nose on your face."

Rosco thought for a moment. "Okay," he said. "I'm with you . . . Shylock, right? . . . And . . . and Portia . . . And she said something about mercy—"

"And what was Shylock's profession?" Belle's tone was solemn and patient.

"A loan shark?"

"Well, 'usurer' . . . but it's the same diff—"

"Look, Belle, I know you love these games, and I appreciate your enthusiasm . . . Really I do. But some nut planted this on Tom Pepper . . . And if it has no bearing on the case, then I should let him know. The man's in a lot of pain. In fact, I'm worried about his mental health."

Belle's large eyes seemed to grow in size and luminosity. "But that's just it, Rosco! This crossword puzzle has everything to do with Pepper . . . He's an investment banker, right? A *merchant* prince? A man who gambles on potentially problematic ventures? . . . That's exactly what Shylock did! Whoever constructed this puzzle is comparing the two men—and it's not a kind comparison . . . The person who delivered this cryptic to Tom is sending a message saying, 'You've got money'; 'I have something you want.' "

"Where? Where does it say that?" Rosco scanned the clues and answers.

"Well, it's an *inference*," Belle admitted, then added a reluctant: "I'm pretty familiar with the play . . ."

Rosco raised his eyebrows, chuckled, strolled to a window, and turned back to level a scrutinizing gaze at Belle.

"Actually, I know most of Shylock's lines," she said softly.

"Curiosity?" he prodded. "Parental encouragement? No, wait . . . You had a cruel high school teacher who forced you to memorize entire passages of text before you were allowed out on the basketball court. Or no, better yet, you dated the sixteen-year-old sap who considered himself the reincarnation of Laurence Olivier."

Belle stared at her desk. "I did Shylock," she murmured.

" 'Did'? What do you mean 'did'?"

"I acted the part . . . in school . . . tenth grade, in fact . . ."

"You were an actress? Well, live and learn . . ." Rosco started to laugh again, then realized his reaction might be misconstrued. "What I mean is: That's a man's role. Besides, I thought you were into poetry—"

"The boy acting the part got sick." Belle's eyes remained fixed on her cluttered desk.

"There weren't any other guy kids to take his place?"

"I was the only person who knew the part." The reply was barely audible.

This time Rosco allowed himself a hearty chuckle. "Aha! Just as I thought! That little ferretlike brain of yours memorized the entire play—just for fun!"

Belle glanced up; her cheeks were endearingly pink and shiny. "I was the prompter, Rosco, I had to learn the lines."

He laughed harder. "And how did you fare as the old Venetian merchant?"

Belle grinned. "Terribly . . . I decided to act old by wobbling around and limping a lot . . . but I can still recite most of the speeches . . . Want to hear?"

"I hope you don't practice in the shower."

"Hmm . . . there's an idea I hadn't considered . . ." Then

she grew serious again. "I *know* this crossword refers to Pepper, Rosco, and I know it's intended as some type of threat. My hunch is that Genie and Jamaica may not only be alive, but are being held for ransom . . . On the other hand—and this is a far crueler scenario—the puzzle could be a form of extortion preying upon the fears of an already terrified husband."

"Say again?"

Belle's lips pursed into lines of both sorrow and anger. "What if the constructor has *no* connection with Genie and Jamaica, and is only *pretending* in order to make Tom believe this is a kidnapping scenario?"

"The envelope was addressed to Genie . . ."

"But *after* her disappearance. If it had been addressed to Tom, it might not have received such a quick response."

"Good point . . . So, what you're saying is: The women are dead—accidentally drowned, as originally reported— and this kook is pretending he has them?"

Belle nodded unhappily. "Look at this," she continued. "35-Down and 61-Down . . . Both clues have the word *gold* spelled out—but in capital letters—just like the acronym for Tom's Global Overseas Lender Development Fund . . . And here: 27-Across: *Femmes———,Jamaica Nevisson & others*. The answer, of course, is the French FATALES, but in English that's translated as plain old fatal . . . 23-Across: REVENGE is in the answer . . . 11-Down: the clue is *Act of Vengeance actress* . . . Whoever created this puzzle is an angry person."

Rosco considered Belle's words. "Not a pretty picture— either way," he said after a long moment.

"Let's hope the women are still alive and being held hostage."

"As remote as that sounds, in my way of thinking, that's a distinct possibility . . . Especially since we don't have any bodies yet." Rosco picked up the crossword and gazed at it. "I have to return this to Tom, Belle. He's—"

"I'll photocopy it before you go." Belle jumped to her feet and reached for the puzzle.

"Ahh . . ." Rosco hedged, "that's privileged information . . . You're the only person I'm permitted to show it to. Technically, that makes you a subcontractor of the Polycrates Agency."

"I like the sound of that. Subcontractor . . . I hope it pays well." Belle smiled, then returned to her serious tone. "I think you should soft-pedal this idea with Tom, though, if you can . . . Maybe he won't notice the revenge motif—or the several banking references. Because if I'm wrong . . . Well, it would be terrible to get his hopes up about Genie." Belle thought for a second. "Pepper won't reconsider calling in the police department, will he? They could be a help . . . maybe set up surveillance around his house . . ."

"No," said Rosco. "He was adamant on that point. I think that receiving this crossword rattled him more than he knows. I guess he expected—maybe *hoped* is a better word—that the clues or answers would reveal some form of demand. Tom certainly must have recognized the word *gold* in the clues . . . But he's a hard guy to figure out . . . I don't know, maybe he's already jumped to the kidnapping conclusion."

Belle stared through the windows. From the flattened shadows in her yard, she guessed it was about noon. Friday's *Evening Crier* would be hitting the stands in a few hours. "I think we'll learn more after the *Crier* publishes that other anonymous puzzle I received—and also after Bartholomew's column appears . . . If there's a kidnapper or blackmailer out there, we'll be playing his game . . . That should bring him out of the woodwork."

"Hey," Rosco said in a low and gentle voice.

Belle turned back to face him. "Hey, what?" she said.

"I can see the wheels spinning. I only agreed to your publishing-the-puzzle scheme if you promised to stay in the shadows, remember? I want you to be careful . . ."

"Safety's my middle name . . . Anyway, in a pinch I can always spout old Shylock . . . 'Hates any man the thing he would not kill?'—*par exemple* . . . That should set any malefactor dozing . . ."

While Rosco returned to Pepper's house, Belle drove to Sara's home, White Caps. Their conversation on Monday had begun with Tom Pepper; and Belle had a hunch that a lady as ensconced in Newcastle's hierarchy as Sara Crane Briephs would know *everything* about the man and his business dealings. Belle even suspected Sara might be able to describe the G.O.L.D. Fund's intricate structure.

Naturally, it was Emma who escorted Belle from the entry foyer through the long somber hall to Sara's pleasant parlor. The grand old lady was finishing a tray lunch: tuna fish salad on crustless white bread—a quintessentially WASPy meal. A McIntosh apple and two gingersnaps completed the picture. Old-line New Englanders didn't maintain their longevity by being lavish.

"A sandwich, Belle?" Sara asked while Belle took the same seat she'd occupied the previous Monday.

"I already ate, thanks . . . I think."

Sara's imperious blue eyes swept Belle's face. "That is not an encouraging answer, young lady. The brain and the body need sufficient fuel in order to function properly. Without decent food, one cannot think."

Belle suddenly remembered her luncheon menu. "I had deviled eggs," she said. "Several . . . or maybe four or five . . ."

Sara's face grew wistful. "My favorite treat," she murmured. "You know, in my day, one could not attend a party—any type of party—without deviled eggs being among the canapés. Unfortunately, at my age, that amount of cholesterol is not . . . ah, well . . . plummier times . . ." Stoicism straightened the old woman's shoulders and spine. "Now, Belle, what can I do for you? When you phoned to suggest this visit, discussing hard-cooked eggs was obviously not part of the plan."

Belle hesitated for only a second. *Subcontractor of the Polycrates Agency*, she heard her brain repeating. The term, she felt, gave her a certain flexibility—and power. She pulled her photocopy of the newest crossword from her purse.

"This is the third anonymous puzzle I've completed in as many days, Sara. The first two came to me at my home, this third was delivered to Tom Pepper." Then she added a knowing: "It's highly confidential—as I'm sure you realize. I could get into a good deal of trouble for divulging information, but I'm convinced it pertains to the fire aboard the *Orion,* and the disappearance of Genie Pepper and Jamaica Nevisson."

Belle passed the crossword to Sara, who perused it with her customary alacrity.

"I'd say that's an understatement, Belle. If my son had seen this, he'd concur wholeheartedly." She studied the word game further. "*Gold* referred to twice," she said. "*Insider trades* at 50-Down . . . *The love of money* at 38-Down . . . Very intriguing . . . very intriguing, indeed . . . How can I help you with this investigation? I take it this *is* an investigation?"

Belle explained Rosco's connection to Pepper, and her own subsequent involvement, while Sara nodded astutely. "And you suspect that I may have the skinny on Pepper and any potential enemies he might have?" she said.

When Belle smiled at this antique colloquialism, her hostess responded with a tart, "I am not so antediluvian as you think, young lady. Contrary to public opinion, I didn't speak in iambic pentameter as a girl . . . Now, to return to Mr. Edison 'Tom' Pepper . . . I'm afraid that I'm in the minority in my dislike for him. Newcastle seems to have deified the man."

"The other day you mentioned that you didn't trust him, Sara, why is that?"

Sara pondered the question. "He makes money too quickly," she finally said, then, responding to Belle's quizzical expression, added: "My father was a wealthy man—a very wealthy man—but he didn't believe in so-called speculation, nor in this execrable 'leverage' business, 'stock options,' 'hedge funds,' 'skyrocketing technology stocks,' et cetera: all the tactics these new portfolio managers quote—and espouse. Fortunes, in my father's day, were made on tangible assets: railroads, shipping lines, oil fields, silver mines, commodities of trade . . . Pepper makes money from money; I'm afraid it seems like so much thin air to me."

"But he's greatly increased the endowment funds of many Newcastle institutions, hasn't he?" Belle asked. "That new children's wing at the hospital . . . isn't it being constructed as a result of Pepper's expertise in managing the hospital's charitable gifts?"

Sara smiled a lovely, rueful smile: age acknowledging youth. "As I said, Belle, I'm in the minority . . . I've been told that Pepper promised to double his investors' portfolios in the space of six months."

Belle's eyes widened. "That's an *enormous* profit," she said. "No wonder he's treated like royalty."

"Indeed. Indeed . . . A prince among men . . ." Then Sara's glance returned to the crossword. "These long quotations are interesting," she said. "17-Across . . . fifteen letters . . . the answer's a variation of Shakespeare's famous line 'What news on the Rialto?' Are you familiar with the play *The Merchant of Venice*?"

Fortunately, Sara's gaze was intent on the cryptic in her lap; she didn't see how deeply Belle blushed. "Yes, I am . . ." was the reluctant answer.

"And so you're aware of the financial deal Shylock strikes . . . a hefty loan predicated upon the safe arrival of several heavily laden trading ships?"

Belle looked up and caught Sara's keen stare. "All of which sink before reaching port and discharging their lucrative cargo," the young woman answered.

"And what happens to Shylock's daughter—his dearest female companion—as this disaster unfolds?"

"She disappears," Belle said. "And her name begins with a *J* . . ."

CHAPTER

17

After he left Belle's house, it had taken Rosco only twenty minutes to retrace his path to the Pepper home. He'd been informed by Anson that Tom was deeply involved with pressing matters surrounding the G.O.L.D. Fund and had given strict orders not to be disturbed— "under *any* circumstances," according to the butler. The injunction brought Rosco a certain sense of relief; after his discussion with Belle, he had no desire to be called on the carpet about possible hidden meanings in the perplexing crossword.

With Anson hovering at his elbow, Rosco wrote the following on the back of the envelope containing the completed puzzle: *Mr. Pepper—look this puzzle over and let me know your thoughts. I suspect it's the work of a disturbed mind, but if you feel there may be more to it, give me a call.*

He handed the envelope to Anson and left. Pepper

would make his own inferences on the crossword's clues and answers—or he would not.

Lieutenant Al Lever and his forensics expert, Abe Jones, weren't due to start work at Mystic Isle Yachts until four P.M. As a result, Rosco gauged that he had plenty of time to drive out to Warren and investigate the elusive truckers, Moe Quick and Bob Stingo. Establishing their where-abouts would hopefully fill in a large piece of the puzzle.

Warren's run-down neighborhoods were as unwelcom-ing as they'd been on Tuesday, and the Stingo house appeared consistently dark and unoccupied. Rosco banged on the front and rear doors, but the house's interior remained silent. The home also emitted a morguelike chill, the feel of a building that's been without heat or human habitation for several days. He stood pressed to the kitchen door for a couple of long minutes, but detected no odor of cooking gas, food preparation, or dishes either washed or piled in the sink. The house smelled only of standing water, cold concrete, and aged vinyl siding.

He returned to his Jeep. The neighboring homes seemed equally devoid of life, although Rosco was certain he was being watched—if only by a nosy populace. He considered approaching one or two of those dwellings, then realized his current attire had "official snoop" written all over it. If he hadn't been singled out as an undercover cop, he proba-bly looked like something worse: a repo man or enforcer from a rental agency. None of these folks would open their door to such a heinous character, so Rosco turned his Jeep toward Duxbury Court and the Quicks' mobile home.

Doris Quick seemed truly frightened to see him. Her ruddy complexion blanched; and she slammed the door in his face without speaking. But before Rosco had time to call out or knock again, he heard her voice whisper through the door. "Okay, okay, I'll open it." The inflection made it impossible to determine whether the response was intended for Rosco or someone within the trailer. She reopened the door, but only enough to show her eyes, nose, and mouth. "Sorry," she said in a halting tone. "I . . . I thought you were someone else." She attempted a smile but failed.

Rosco assumed his most wholesome demeanor. "Better safe than sorry, I always say."

Doris studied him, trying to determine his motive. "I suppose you want my husband."

"Right . . . Just for a minute or two, Mrs. Quick. Is he home?"

"Nope, he ain't."

"I thought I heard another voice . . ."

"You didn't." Her jaw muscles tightened. Rosco could see she wanted to slam the door shut again. "And I told you, I don't like being called Missus . . . makes me feel older than I should."

"All right, then . . . Doris . . . I'm assuming your husband has finally checked in with you—that you have spoken to him since I was here on Tuesday?"

She took her time before responding. "I can't say I recall when I last talked to him."

Rosco scratched the back of his head and sighed as if in total sympathy with women married to fickle men. At the same time he was convinced she wasn't alone. Rosco raised his voice. "Would you like to know where I'm headed right now, Doris?"

"Can't say that I care."

"I'm off to Ed Colberg's marina. Do you have any idea who I'll be seeing there?"

Doris didn't answer.

"The police department, Mrs. Quick. They're investigating the possibility that the *Orion*'s fire might not have been accidental."

"I don't know nothin' about that boat! I told you already!"

"I'm sure you don't . . . But as your husband was one of the men who found the *Orion*, Newcastle PD will want to speak with him. Now, you're certain you can't contact him? No phone number? No emergency address? No motel he might stop in?"

"He could be anywhere."

"The police will check your telephone records if they have a probable cause, Mrs. Quick. They'll check the records of *everyone* involved in this thing. They'll know exactly who you've called—and when."

Doris thought for a moment. Her studiedly bland expression had become a frown of concentration. "Just a minute. I left something . . . cooking on the stove."

Doris slammed the door and returned two minutes later. Before she could open her mouth, Rosco stepped up close to the entry. "Do you mind if I come in and get a drink of water?" He coughed. "I seem to have something stuck in my throat."

"You have to go. I can't talk anymore."

Rosco placed his hand on the door to prevent her closing it. "It'll only take a second." He rubbed his throat and coughed again. "I don't know what it is . . . Must have been a piece of dust or something."

"You have to leave."

"Are you alone, Doris?"

"Please go." She leaned her entire weight against the door. Although Rosco realized he could easily push past her, he opted not to. He had no legal right to make a forced entry. Instead, he stepped away, and heard Doris Quick slide the door's drop bolt in place. Then he left the small concrete stoop and walked to the back of the mobile home. All the drapes had been closed, making it impossible to observe the interior.

Rosco returned to the street, slid into his Jeep, and checked his watch. He didn't have time to wait and see who—besides Doris—exited the trailer; Lever was due at Mystic Isle Yachts at four, so Rosco eased the Jeep out of Duxbury Court, merged onto the interstate, and pulled into the marina parking lot at precisely three fifty-two.

The *Orion* and *Dixie-Jack* were berthed in the same locations Rosco had previously visited. The only difference was that both were now cordoned off with yellow crime-scene tape ordering POLICE LINE—DO NOT CROSS in bold black letters. Ripped yellow tail ends fluttered in the ocean breeze like kite tails, but those playful gestures only made the crime tape's presence more incongruous in an otherwise wholesome picture. Inboards, outboards, and sailboats, not under official scrutiny, bobbed gently along the piers. For yachting buffs, the view would have been tempting. Unfortunately, Rosco wasn't one of them. Even the rhythmic slap of halyard rope against yardarm made him feel vaguely queasy.

There was no sign of Lever or his "unmarked" car, so Rosco entered the marina office, where he found Colberg working on the *Crier*'s crossword puzzle. The boatyard owner seemed to be filling in answers with surprising ease.

He barely glanced at Rosco; his nod was even less perceptible. "Polycrates," he groaned in a tone that most people reserved for the discovery of poison ivy or a parking ticket.

"Lever still planning to stop by?" Rosco asked.

"Far as I know." Colberg glanced up briefly, then resumed his efforts. It was obvious to Rosco their conversation wasn't going to have an easy flow.

He gestured toward the puzzle. "Looks like you're pretty good at those things Eduardo."

Colberg answered with a grunt, then added a dismissive: "If you've been doing them as long as I have, it's second nature. Like filling out a tax form."

"Right . . . Well, some folks have a little trouble in that area, too."

Ed tapped the newspaper with the eraser end of his pencil. "Seems this Graham babe's on a Shakespeare jag today. *Macbeth . . . Hamlet . . .*"

"You know a lot of Shakespeare, then?"

Colberg finally looked up. Cynical pride creased his face. "Hell, I was English lit. in college. VP of the theater club, too. Big yuck, huh? Me . . . You try earning a living with a damn degree like that. Course, that was before I took to the beaches." He paused. "Sales are where the action is my friend. Find something someone wants, dangle it in front of their nose, and sell it to 'em. Of course, in the yacht business it pays to know who has the bucks and who doesn't."

"Like Tom Pepper?"

"Not a buyer . . . a looker. Don't let him fool ya."

"I always thought the sign of a good salesman was being able to sell someone something they *didn't* want." Rosco said this with a smile, but his eyes remained watchful and hard.

"I got work to do, Polycrates. If you want the good lieutenant, why don't you wait out on the dock?"

Rosco responded with a cheery, "6-Down: fifteen letters—PRACTICALLY DEAD . . . Good luck with the 'work,'" then stepped outside just in time to see Lever's brown Ford angle into the parking lot. The lieutenant lumbered out from behind the wheel and walked to the car's trunk, where his forensics expert, Abe Jones, joined him.

Jones looked like a young Harry Belafonte—a fact not lost on a stunningly large and ever-revolving list of lady friends. Sometimes Jones's cronies at NPD even referred to him by this pseudonym, although a hearty dose of envy accompanied the jest—especially among those men who were married. Jones accepted their gibes as compliments, which only intensified the macho banter.

He and Lever each hefted a large black case from the Ford and headed toward the *Orion*. Rosco met them halfway.

"Why does it never surprise me to find you lurking in the underbrush, Polly—Crates?" Lever said as he extended a beefy paw to Rosco.

After they exchanged a handshake, Rosco said, "I like to keep on top of things, Al. It's amazing how uncommunicative guys like Colberg become once the cops show up." Rosco looked at Jones and added, "How's it going, Abe?" The detective was one of the few who had never called Jones "Belafonte."

"I'm not complaining, Rosco."

Lever muttered a resigned: "Someone who looks like he just stepped out of *GQ* better not complain."

"Exercise, Al, that's all it takes." Jones grinned.

"You've never exercised a day in your life, my friend."

"Well, there's many different forms of exercise, Al. I work out nearly every evening. Hey, if you don't believe me, I'll give you a list of corroborating witnesses. Maybe their phone numbers, if you play your cards right."

"Ho, ho, ho."

They reached the *Orion* and immediately switched into serious business mode. Jones placed his case on the dock and sat next to it, letting his feet dangle over the boat's charred gunwale. He remained silent for nearly two minutes while he studied the wreck. Finally he said, "What a mess. So . . . what do we need to know, Al?"

Lever pulled a pack of cigarettes from his shirt pocket and waved it over the *Orion* as he searched for a match with his other hand. "Let's start with what started the fire and what put it out . . . How and when the women exited . . . Did they make it to the inflatable? Or were they forced to jump overboard?"

Jones laughed, shook his head, and said, "Hey, that's simple enough." He slid down onto the boat.

Lever found his matches and turned to Rosco while he lit up. "Not much to do but watch."

Rosco shrugged. ". . . You never know."

"By the way, I called L.A. It turns out Jamaica Nevisson's blood type was A positive."

"One call? That easy?"

"Never let it be said that Al Lever is a man without friends."

"A pos. . . . Same as I pulled off the fishing boat."

"Right. But we don't know if that was boy or girl blood, do we? Mrs. Pepper was O neg."

"Yep," Rosco said. "I got that from Mr. Pepper." He decided to move the dialogue forward at a brisker pace. "I took a gander at the *Dixie-Jack* before you got here, Al. It's been scrubbed down . . . looks like a brand-new boat. You're going to be hard-pressed to find anything worthwhile on her."

Jones's voice interrupted them. "Well, this is interesting," he called from the *Orion*'s hulk. "What'd you say put this fire out?"

Rosco looked in his direction. "One of the guys who

towed her in said a squall blew in. He figured the rain doused it."

"That's not what I'd call a real accurate statement."

"What makes you say that, Abe?" Lever asked.

"Well the rain might have *started* to do the job . . . slow it down, anyway. It's hard to tell because it rained the other night, but there's still CO_2 residue all over this thing."

"Meaning . . . ?"

"Meaning somebody hosed her down with a fire extinguisher. But good."

"So, the women did it—and then jumped ship?" Lever asked. He made no attempt to hide his confusion.

"No way. If they'd done it, we'd detect footprints; rain or no rain. Two women extinguish the blaze, meanwhile passing through heavy CO_2 residue and ashes to reach the boat's inflatable . . . There's no sign of that type of activity . . . Besides, the towline is scorched, but also nicely sliced at the end—meaning the inflatable was cut loose while the boat was still burning . . . From the angle and buildup of CO_2, it appears that the blaze was extinguished from above . . . My guess is that a larger vessel pulled alongside and dowsed the fire—"

"Let me get this straight," Lever demanded. "We're talking about another boat coming to the rescue?"

"Something like that," Jones answered. "Someone had to be *above* this fire to extinguish it. The rain helped, sure, but two women in an inflatable sitting alongside in the ocean wouldn't have had sufficient maneuverability—or height—to fight this kind of fire . . .

"Besides"—he hoisted two blackened cylindrical objects—"here are the *Orion*'s fire extinguishers. The dials have melted, but judging by the weight, they're still holding full charges . . . Safety codes require boats up to

forty feet to carry two type B-1 extinguishers—which
we have here . . . I'm willing to bet this is the only fire-
prevention equipment the boat possessed . . . And no one
used them. The pins are bent around so tightly it would
take someone with a pair of pliers to get them out. A stupid
way to keep them . . . useless in an emergency . . ."

"I'll be back," Rosco said. He jogged down the pier,
crossed to the adjoining dock, and jumped onto the *Dixie-
Jack*. Colberg had left the hatch unlocked in anticipation of
Lever's arrival. Rosco poked around for two or three minutes before returning to the marina office. Colberg was still
hunched over the crossword; there were only a few blank
spaces left.

"When's the *Dixie-Jack* going out again?" Rosco asked.
Ed didn't glance up.

"Not until the cops are finished with her, why?"

"You might want to check her fire extinguishers."

"What's the problem?"

"All four are empty."

CHAPTER

18

After Rosco reported the problem of the *Dixie-Jack*'s depleted fire extinguishers to Ed Colberg, he strolled down the dock and shared the information with Al Lever.

"So it looks like your bartender 'friend' lied to you, doesn't it, Rosco?" was Lever's smug response.

Rosco shrugged. "He's no friend of mine, Al."

"Well, at least it would indicate he probably didn't start the fire," Jones said.

Rosco looked down at the *Orion,* where Abe was still making his inspection. "You're suggesting this was intentional?"

"I don't know . . . It's hard to tell at this point. I'll have to get these samples back to the lab. But *initially,* I'd say the boat was torched. First off: we've got a diesel engine here—or what's left of it. Igniting diesel fuel requires a lot of effort; it doesn't usually happen accidentally. The fuel won't explode like gasoline. It takes more than a wire short or spark to get it going . . .

"Another thing: most of these newer boats are constructed with flame-resistant materials. You have to work to activate a solid blaze. Obviously it can be done. Douse a surface with a combustible . . . something like that. Look what happened here—" Jones waved a hand above the *Orion*'s remains.

Lever interrupted. "So, what's your call, Abe?"

"Well . . . it seems like we've got the remains of a couple of oil lamps in what's left of the cabin. Definitely a no-no on any type of boat. Why anyone would have them is beyond me, but I'm guessing the lamp oil probably instigated the fire . . . Now, you can suggest that the things rolled off the table when the *Orion* slapped into a wave, but my mind doesn't work that way. It's fishy; it stinks; it doesn't belong in the picture . . . Besides, it's my understanding that these women were too experienced to carry that type of lamp in the first place—"

"But it's possible . . ." Lever said, thinking out loud.

"Sure . . . But to tell the truth, my lab work will only confirm that the lamps were *involved* in the blaze—if that's the case—it won't tell you who or what—"

Again, Lever interrupted. "Anything's possible until we prove otherwise . . . What else, Abe?" Al lit another cigarette, took a long drag, and coughed loudly.

Jones hesitated until Lever's coughing jag slowed, then resumed his analysis. "Well, let's continue with the *premise* of arson . . . Now, whoever started this fire was smart, but not quite smart enough. *If* the intention was to send this baby to the bottom real quick, then whoever torched it seriously miscalculated the propane tank—"

"What do you mean?" Rosco asked.

"Well, most people would expect propane to build a fire's intensity, but depending on the position of the tank, it can have an opposite effect, like it probably did here . . . See, when the propane tank gets hot enough, it blows like a giant firecracker. That's because of the natural expansion of the gas. It doesn't matter whether the stuff is flammable or not; the same thing could happen to a scuba tank . . ." Abe looked from Lever to Rosco for signs of comprehension. Both men nodded.

"Now, on the *Orion,* the explosion sent the entire deck skyward—the deck and most of the cockpit—opening up the boat's interior, as you see here . . . Actually, I'm surprised the Coast Guard didn't find pieces of composite Fiberglass floating around out there . . . Anyway, as the propane burns off, it quickly dissipates in the atmosphere. So, the explosion and concussion it causes can effectively blow *out* a preexisting fire . . . I'm betting dollars to doughnuts that's what happened here . . . The propane explosion may not have suppressed the fire *entirely*, but it sufficiently reduced it—allowing our three fishermen to finish the job with handheld extinguishers."

"But who started it?" Again, Lever was thinking out loud.

"What about this guy Colberg?" Jones said, pointing to the office. "I mean, come on, fellas, we all know he scuttled those boats three years ago for the insurance money. No one's ever proved it, is all . . ."

Rosco shook his head. "I'm no Colberg fan, but I doubt he'd risk killing two people in the process. Insurance fraud's one thing, murder's something else."

Lever coughed again as he took another drag on his cigarette. "Anything's possible."

"You're sounding like a broken record, Al." Rosco said this in a friendly tone, then grew serious. "If Abe is correct and the fire was intentional, then the boat wasn't the target. The women were. I'd say we're talking homicide."

Lever stiffened at the suggestion. "I'd like to see some bodies before I open up a murder case."

"They'll wash up," Jones said. "They always do. Might take a couple of weeks, but you'll find them . . . unless the sharks got them . . . Then you just find a few pieces . . . But they'll show up. Trust me."

"The sharks in this case might be three fishermen."

"Whoa . . . Whoa . . . hold on there, Rosco," Lever said, "That's making a huge leap. Where did that come from?"

"Like you said, Al, anything's possible. Without any bodies, how can you rule out the potential of a kidnapping? I pulled Jamaica's blood off of the *Dixie-Jack*."

"You pulled A positive, Rosco. We don't have confirmation on whose blood that is and you know it."

"All I'm suggesting, Al is that *anything's* possible . . . The women could be alive, for all we know—and in the custody of kidnappers. Maybe not our fishermen, maybe another boat got to the *Orion* first . . . Or picked the women up in the dinghy . . . Or . . . yeah, they could be dead."

Jones cleared his throat and said, "Don't look now but here comes trouble."

Rosco and Lever turned to follow Jones's stare. Marching down the dock toward them was a bulldog-shaped man in his early sixties. He was almost bald, but what remained of his snow-white hair was buzzed as short as a Marine drill sergeant's. Clint Mize, senior insurance adjuster for Shore Line Mutual, had fond memories of his years in "The Corps." He nodded briskly to the men as he approached.

"Lever . . . Jones . . ." Mize shook Rosco's hand and cracked what he considered to be a joke: "You back with the NPD, Polycrates?" Then he cocked his head toward the *Orion*. Again, the gesture resonated with Marine-Corps precision. "What's the official status here?"

"That's just what we were discussing." Rosco gave Mize a quizzical look. "I thought Colberg said the *Orion* was insured by A.M.I.? What's Shore Line's interest in this?"

"Well, let's say my boss doesn't like writing checks for five million dollars without having me poke around."

"Whoa, whoa, whoa . . . come again?" Lever blurted out.

"Genevieve Pepper. Shore Line carried a life-insurance policy on her. Five million smacks."

Lever lit another cigarette and spoke through the smoke. "Kinda shoots a hole through your 'kidnapping' theory, there, Polly—Crates."

Rosco was as shocked as Lever and Jones; he was left stammering slightly. "What? I mean . . . who's the beneficiary? I'm working for her husband, Clint. He didn't mention anything about a policy."

"Maybe he didn't know . . . Our records show that she paid the premiums, not him."

"And Pepper picks up five mil?" Lever said, shaking his head. "That's the kind of wife I need."

Mize held up his hands and said, "Not so fast, Al . . . Pepper isn't the beneficiary."

"Who is?"

"A guy by the name of William Vauriens. Genie's half brother. He lives up in Boston. Rumor has it that Old Man Pepper sends him sizable bucks every month just so he keeps his distance. I guess there's no love lost in that family." Mize chuckled slightly as if pleased at his witticism.

"You're saying Pepper knew nothing about this life-insurance policy?" Rosco asked.

"I can't say one way or another . . . I tried to get him on the line, but he's not taking my calls. Hell, he's your client . . . Why don't you ask him?"

Rosco's thought process had finally assimilated Clint Mize's news. "What else do you know about Vauriens?"

"Not much . . . Can't seem to hold a regular job for any length of time. Has an on-again-off-again relationship with a woman in Back Bay. She's been picked up twice for kiting checks. Never served any time—"

"Have you spoken to Vauriens?" Rosco said while he jotted down the name.

"Not in person. I drove up to Boston . . . poked around a little . . . talked to his lady friend. She says she hasn't seen 'Billy' in well over a week. Same with his boss. Vauriens was working construction—part of a pickup crew . . . Hey, but for five mil, the guy'll turn up sooner or later. They always do." Mize said this almost regretfully.

"I don't suppose you'd like to share the lady's name and number?" Rosco said as he offered Mize his pad and pen. "I might take a run up to Boston tomorrow morning myself."

"Hey, it's no skin off my teeth. The sooner I catch up

with 'Billy' Vauriens the better." As he scribbled into Rosco's pad, Mize cocked an eye in Abe Jones's direction. "What's your guesstimate on this fire, Abe?"

"Torch job, Clint. Torch job, all the way."

CHAPTER

19

BARTHOLOMEW KERR'S "BIZ-Y BUZZ": CRYPTIC NEWS FROM QUEEN B

The hive was positively humming when our para-
digm of puzzlers shared a none-too-cross word yesterday. Seems Queen B received an encoded letter
game apparently referring to the disappearance of
the Lady **Nevisson**. Don't tell the drones, but Begum
Belle is a busy biscuit—and I don't mean **Graham**
flour, sweeties . . .

"I t's me." The male voice on the phone slurred the words
drunkenly, but they didn't lose their tension or their
fear.

"Where are you?" the woman demanded.

"Where I'm supposed to be," he answered. She could

hear a dangerous measure of defeat enter his tone. She was tempted to carry the phone to the window, yank wide the curtains, throw open the sash, and bring a breath of welcome fresh air into the claustrophobic room, but she remained where she was: frozen in inactivity beside the rumpled double bed.

"You saw the newspaper?" she asked. "The gossip column?"

The response was a bitter: "Oh, I've seen more than that . . . There's a crossword puzzle in the same edition . . . a snotty-nosed, incriminating word game only an idiot could ignore . . . This Graham chick's a wild card I never bargained for."

"What are we going to do?"

Again, his reply was bitter. "It's your call, babe . . . I've been dancing on live coals over here . . . I'm about played out." He laughed; the sound was hollow and mean.

"You creep," she hissed, then thought, but didn't say: *You can't fall apart on me now!* The pause while her brain examined and reexamined the facts was deadening; at the far end of the receiver, the hiatus seemed endless. "How much does this Graham broad know?" she finally asked.

"No telling, toots . . ."

Rage exploded from her. "Don't you care about this situation at all?"

His response was equally infuriated. "You know damn well I do!"

"Well, don't give up on me, then!" Again, the woman thought for several long moments. "We've got to scare off little Miss Annabella Graham. Make her retract whatever comments she supplied . . . make her *vanish*. She's a loose cannon."

"And how do you propose doing that?"

"Leave it to me," she answered. "*Cherchez la femme . . .* , that's French, in case you didn't know."

"Hey, you're a surprise a minute."

Belle's phone rang at the grotesque hour of three A.M. She fumbled for it in her sleep, first upbraiding herself for oversleeping—she imagined it was daytime, then glanced with half-closed eyes at the alarm clock's illuminated face. Her next sensation was worry—something terrible must have happened to Rosco! Her third was irritation—this was clearly a misdialed number. When she answered the phone, it was with a cross "yes?"

"Belle Graham?"

"Speaking."

"I didn't wake you, did I?"

Belle almost said no—such is the conditioning of the human spirit; no one is supposed to be too sleepy or unconscious to make a full and intelligent response. Instead, she answered a disbelieving, "It's three in the morning!"

"I did wake you, then . . ."

Belle sat up straighter in bed, punching her pillow into a cushion behind her back. She realized she had no idea who her caller was, nor could she identify whether the person were male or female. The accent was equally impossible to place. It could have been South African; it could have been northern English; it could have been German or Dutch with a British education. Or it could have been plain, old American pretending it was something more exotic. "Who is this?"

"Let's just say someone concerned with your well-being."

"Then perhaps you should have let me sleep."

The person laughed, a malevolent sound that caused

Belle to reach for the lamp on the nightstand. But when the room was bathed in light, she felt no more secure.

"Good try, Belle, but not, I'm afraid, appropriate under the circumstances. Strong-willed women like you can be your own worst enemies. Do you understand my meaning?"

"Who is this?" Belle repeated.

"That's for me to know and you to find out." Again, the malign laugh. "Now, let's have a little chat about the Pepper case."

Belle was tempted to lie, and protest ignorance, but suddenly realized a phone call like this was precisely what she'd hoped to instigate. Her tone changed; she became conciliatory and chatty. "Are you calling about the anonymous crossword puzzle I published?" she asked.

"That—and the gossip column."

"Are you the constructor?"

"What?"

"Are you the—" A warning whistle rang in Belle's brain. The caller didn't know the term for a crossword creator was "constructor." "Who is this?" she demanded for the third time.

"Let's say that I am not your friend . . . Let's say, *we* are not your friends."

In the golden lamplight, Belle's gray eyes grew huge and agate-colored. She didn't speak.

"And let's further add that we want you to walk away from this Pepper business . . . that we strongly *advise* you to forget every detail . . . make like it didn't happen. Get it, Belle?"

Belle nodded to her empty bedroom.

"Because otherwise you might vanish like those two dumb broads. Understand?"

"Where are they?" Belle asked. "Do you know? . . . You do, don't you?"

"Cut the chat, sweetie. Those babes are no concern of yours."

Belle realized that the caller's vocal quality had taken on an obviously masculine tone. "I could help you, sir . . . if you'd let me . . . take a message to Mr. Pepper perhaps—"

The laugh at the other end of the receiver was piercing. "Bodyguard city!" the voice scoffed. "And then, you and who else would be in on this gig? . . . No, I'm telling you to butt out, honey. And I mean now!"

Belle was silent, playing for time. "You won't harm them, will you? . . . Genie and Jamaica, I mean?" she finally asked.

"That depends on you, little lady. You walk away, those dames may see the light of day . . . You keep sticking your nose in this mess, you're gonna find yourself stuck in one big tragedy!" Then the phone went dead; the caller had gone.

"Tragedy," Belle repeated. "Tragedy." Comedy . . . tragedy . . . Shakespeare . . . Was it possible the caller was connected to the puzzles, after all? But if not, who was he? And why did he call? She fell asleep pondering the questions.

The bedside lamp burned through the rest of her fitful night. When she awoke, she stared up into its hot, incriminating bulb. "Oh, darn," she muttered, reaching automatically to turn off the switch, then suddenly recalling why she'd lit it. She swung her feet from the bed in a trice, threw on her robe, and dashed down the stairs. She had an overwhelming urge for the soothing comfort of a deviled egg—or maybe two.

Hideously, the refrigerator was empty. Belle stared woefully at the stark shelves, then straightened her shoulders and decided to walk to the mom-and-pop store at the bottom of the lane. Mayo, capers, and eggs were only a couple of minutes away. Relief was at hand.

She walked resolutely to the front door, opening it to assess her wardrobe choices on this autumnal Saturday morning. But her gaze was arrested by an envelope tucked halfway beneath the mat. She opened it with trembling hands. Inside was another crossword puzzle.

Across
1. Sonny &———
5. Criminal to the end?
10. Asian Reds, abbr.
13. Rescue
14. Furious
15. Buckeye state
17. When?
19. Skirt type
20. Revenge, with up
21. Danger
22. Bribed
25. Blithers
26. Tavern quaff
27. "Eating———," Bartel film
29. Fixer-upper
32. What?
36. Coming———wing and a prayer
37. Turncoat
38. Sign up, var.
39. Why?
41. Earthquake
42. Wide open
43. Western hemisphere grp.
44. Liar
47. Stealing
52. Loafer
53. "The———in Winter," O'Toole film
54. Genuine
55. Where?
61. British peer
62. Single
63. Beehive State
64. Meadow
65. 60s things
66. Asian weight

Down
1. 40-Down foe
2. Black———, bad guy
3. The devil made her do it!
4. 1-Down general
5. A cat has nine
6. Dunne of "The Awful Truth"
7. Actress admirer
8. JFK stat.
9. Rock band
10. How?
11. Nautical map
12. Woodland elf
16. Bribes
18. ———Perón
21. Trims
22. Astronaut John
23. Till over
24. "Beautiful———"
25. ———Pot
26. Tosca's final breath?
28. Beginning of rations?
30. Who?
31. ———game; extortion scheme
32. Ensnare
33. Genie & Jamaica's craft
34. Hose type
35. Shade trees
40. Union battlers, abbr.
44. Fate of 33-Down
45. Perfect
46. Trumpet
48. Bygone
49. Pigeons, e.g.
50. *To Kill a Mockingbird* character
51. Supply
55. Voice-over
56. Naut. heading
57. Red Baron's milieu
58. Give———chance
59. No to Burns
60. Orr org.

PUZZLE 4

CHAPTER

20

Finished with the newest cryptic, Belle sat hunched at her desk as if expecting it to speak. In a blue terry robe that had seen happier days, her body shivered with cold, but she didn't seem to notice. One slipper had fallen off, leaving her toes exposed and icy; again, she appeared unaware of physical discomfort. Her total concentration was dedicated to the crossword puzzle and the message it relayed. With clues indicating *Who?*, *What?*, *Where?*, *When?*, *Why?*, and *How?*, the constructor's intent had become plain as day.

COME ALONE. Belle stared at the answer to 10-Down, then moved to 32-Across: TELL NO ONE. She remembered the threatening phone call she'd received just four short hours earlier. Someone obviously hadn't wanted her involved in the Pepper case, but she now held in her hand proof that another person definitely needed her help. There was her name spelled out at 30-Down; the location was found at 55-Across: DEW DROP INN, a derelict resort spread across one hundred wild and scenic acres on the promontory known as Allyn's Point an hour south of Newcastle.

Or, could it be, she wondered, that the puzzle was a means of luring her into danger? Invented by the very same person who had just phoned her the night before? The old inn's grounds would be particularly empty of hikers or picnickers at this time of year. She'd make an easy target. Belle almost wished she owned a weapon, but then reminded herself that she didn't know the first thing about guns. If she faced some hideous adversary, she'd probably discover she'd left the pistol's safety on—and then her defenses would be reduced to throwing a two-pound piece of metal. She couldn't throw any better than she could shoot.

Belle scanned the clues and answers again. *When?* was at 17-Across. The answer: AT ELEVEN AM. 33-Down spelled out ORION; 44-Down: FIRE; PERIL was the answer to 21-Across; SAVE at 13-Across. *Genie* and *Jamaica* were among the clues. *Ensnare; Liar; Criminal; Revenge*. Her attention returned to 32-Across: TELL NO ONE. The intent was plain; Rosco was not to be included in the excursion.

Belle stood and realized her slipper was missing and her foot asleep. She sagged toward the floor, grabbed her wayward scuff, then limped across the office while her toes revived. All the while her brain kept jumping to possible scenarios, solutions, and a raft of unanswered questions. One fact remained abundantly clear, however; she had been designated as liaison. If Genie and Jamaica were indeed alive, and if they were to be rescued, Belle would have to follow the crossword's instructions implicitly.

She hurried out of her office, taking the stairs' bare treads two at a time. She then rushed into her bedroom, threw on a pair of jeans, an Irish fisherman's sweater she'd owned since her senior year in college, and white canvas Keds that had turned a permanent gray beige. In case she encountered a birder or late-season beachcomber, the costume was appropriately outdoorsy and nondescript.

Belle drove her car down the remaining loop of Captain's Walk, turned right on Thirteenth Street, then left on Congress heading for the interstate south, the bridge crossing the river, and the long stretch of sparsely inhabited blacktop that led to Allyn's Point. It was, she suddenly realized, a beautiful fall day.

The Dew Drop Inn had been built in the early twenties. Despite its pixielike name, it was a mammoth place and wholly incongruous with its primitive surroundings. For one thing, it was stuccoed with as much panache and abandon as a villa on the Riviera; for another thing, it was pink. Overwhelmingly so. The cupolaed, porticoed, mansarded, gabled, and multiwindowed fantasy-by-the-sea looked as if it had been carved out of spun cotton candy, and seventy-plus years of salt spray, snow, ice, summer sun, hurricanes, and winter windstorms had not diminished one note of this eccentric tonal palette.

Belle stepped from her car and approached the place. The wide porch was more desolate than she'd remembered it; it was also showing serious signs of neglect. Every ten years or so, some developer would purchase the building with the intention of restoring and refurbishing it to "its original glory"; sometimes these incarnations lasted a couple of years; mostly they did not, and the Dew Drop Inn would then slide back into its woeful state. The property was an acknowledged white elephant, a valuable tract of land with an unusable building no one had the courage—

or the zoning approval—to raze. Local realtors had now dubbed it "The *Pink* Elephant."

Beyond the inn proper, the salt waves of Buzzards Bay surged around the rocky promontory, spilling into numerous small inlets the sea had rubbed from the stone. Where an incoming wave met one receding, the friction produced huge plumes of spray that erupted in the air, dousing the craggy boulders until they were as black and slick as oil.

To the left of the promontory, a pebble-strewn beach stretched toward what had once been the inn's cabanas and oceanside restaurant—also vivid pink. To the right was a wide green cliff grown wild and woolly with tangled brush, bittersweet, and desiccated honeysuckle vines. Belle gazed at the scene. She was totally alone.

She circumnavigated the main building, looking at it, and then away. She wasn't certain what she'd expected, but decided the spot was a rendezvous. COME ALONE; the implication was that someone else would arrive.

Finished with one pass of the inn, Belle began a second loop. She slowed her pace, walking methodically as if her body language could transmit an appropriate solitude to a distant observer. She had the definite sensation of being watched.

With her second tour of the building finished, she began a third, this time walking in the opposite direction, as if the choice might send another signal. No one appeared; the only sound was that of the surf crashing against the promontory, and of seagulls wheeling boisterously in the sky. Belle noticed that the sun was almost directly overhead. Eleven A.M. had come and gone.

Perhaps she'd been mistaken about human contact, she decided; maybe a message had been attached to the building. She approached the porch; leaves and brush flung there by countless storms lay in deep eddies beside the doors and under the windows. More than a few floorboards had rotted away. She carefully kicked aside the refuse to continue her inspection. What a sad place, she thought; the utter abandonment of the building made her suddenly want to cry.

It was the slamming of a car door that made Belle snap to attention. She spun toward the sound. A woman dressed in jogging tights, a gray sweatshirt, white socks bunched at her ankles, and black running shoes was walking to the rear of an obscenely large sport utility vehicle. Her hair was blond—or wanted to be blond; long, dark roots spiked through an unruly mop that was tied in an elasticized terry band as if she'd just finished an arduous aerobics class. She glanced apprehensively at the figure on the porch through the lenses of large dark glasses.

Belle nodded encouragement and gestured toward the inn's facade as if she were no more than a curious hiker. But the woman only scowled, opened the rear gate of her car, and allowed a shaggy black dog to amble down. "Come on, boy," she ordered. The dog paid little heed; instead, his fur bristled and he loped toward Belle. "Come on, boy!" The woman shouted again. This time the tone was more urgent, even angry. "Come on! Come here, dammit!"

Belle detected fear in the voice. Apprehensively, she backed into a protective corner, but the dog suddenly stopped, arrested by some compelling scent in the unkempt lawn. When it finally looked up, it turned its head from Belle toward its frustrated owner, then slowly sauntered back to her side. Belle peered at the cracked and grimy window behind her head. In the dim reflection, she saw the muzzy outline of the rebellious dog and its owner running toward the beach.

When they were out of sight, she continued her inspection of the inn's porch. No sign of human intrusion was evident, although several windowpanes were missing—victims of wind-borne debris. Belle peered inside at the chilly, vacant reception rooms. Again, a sense of ineffable sorrow swept over her.

She shook off the feeling and retrieved the folded crossword from her purse, searching for clues she might have missed or misconstrued. 7-Down: *Actress admirer*; 16-Down: *Bribes*. The answer to 39-Across—*Why?*—was: AN ENDGAME. What did it mean? Surely whoever had called her to this spot possessed some answers.

The door closest to the promontory was slightly ajar. Belle pushed, but couldn't move it. She leaned her weight against it; the door reluctantly gave way, and she forced her way inside. Several chairs and tables littered the interior, which was overhung with a pall of dust and gritty sand. Cobwebs obscured many of the windows; nesting material from birds or rodents lay festering on the grimy sills.

Belle studied the floor; there didn't seem to be any trace of previous footsteps. Briefly, she wondered if the space was safe to walk across, then began gingerly edging her way across the room. She'd been summoned to the inn, there had to be a message somewhere.

In a blind corridor between rooms, she heard the thud of feet on the porch. Her heart pounded within her chest; she felt her mouth go dry. She waited, only able to half see the area she was approaching; the one she'd left behind was now invisible—as was the building's exterior. The footsteps continued, navigating the porch's rotten flooring and piles of castaway branches and leaves. It became obvious that her unseen visitor was seeking an entrance.

Slowly, she turned and began retracing her steps. Fear

caused her ears to ring; she was aware of staring without seeing. She clutched the crossword in her hand as if its presence could ensure her safe passage. Bizarrely, she felt as though she were entering some grade-school test for which she'd memorized all the answers. DEW DROP INN, she wanted to say, AT ELEVEN AM.

Suddenly a gust of wind billowed through the dust-filled air; Belle realized that the door she'd entered had been pushed wide open and closed.

She froze. She simply could not force herself to move. Then she heard a dog barking; it was very near. No human voice responded, and the animal continued yapping. Belle drew a breath and walked toward the entry.

"Hey . . ." It was the woman in the jogging clothes. She shifted forward on her toes as if Belle's appearance had badly frightened her. Then she stared disbelieving at the puzzle in Belle's hand.

Belle found her own glance descending to the crossword. She realized how stupid she looked—trespassing in a derelict building with a sheet of graph paper clenched in her fist.

"You'd better be careful that your dog doesn't fall into one of those holes on the porch," she said, attempting a nonchalant smile.

"I tied him up," the woman said. She didn't move, and didn't smile. In fact, her body language seemed downright challenging.

"Are you . . . are you one of the owners of the building?" Belle asked.

The dog started another spate of barking, and Belle remembered her mission. COME ALONE, the crossword had warned, but here she was talking to some disagreeable female while her equally contentious pet announced to the world that the Dew Drop Inn was less than deserted. Belle walked past the woman and yanked open the door. Annoyance at herself and this unwanted visitor made her shoulders rigid.

"What are you doing in here?" the woman demanded.

"Looking around," Belle answered without turning to face her. "That's not a crime, is it? Besides, unless you're an owner, you have no more right to be here than I do." She looked at her watch. It was one o'clock. The person or persons attempting to contact her had obviously decided against it.

"Those word games are a big waste of time," the woman announced to Belle's retreating back.

"To each his own." The answer was frosty; Belle added an equally irritable, "Your dog doesn't seem too happy."

"My dog's fine."

Belle didn't answer. If the woman wanted to pick a fight, she'd have to look elsewhere.

"Don't you worry about my dog!" she called out. "Animals have as much right to run around free as humans do. It's people like you who make their lives miserable, not the folks who own them!"

Amid this tirade, Belle marched to her car, slid into the driver's seat, and locked the doors. A subcontractor for the Polycrates Agency, she told herself. What a joke! If Genie and Jamaica *are* alive, I've probably done them more harm than good.

CHAPTER

21

R osco hit the roof—as Belle had anticipated he would. "What do you mean you went out to Allyn's Point? Alone?" his voice demanded through the telephone line. Fear for her safety magnified the outrage in his tone.

"If someone actually kidnapped those two women, Belle, that person is playing for keeps. And *if*—as you suggested in another scenario—this is an extortion scheme targeting Pepper and his millions, and the women are already dead . . . Then you're still dealing with a hardened criminal . . . and a sadistic one, to boot . . ." He waited a second or two, then added, "Belle, are you listening to me . . . ?"

"I am, yes." She stared out her office window. She knew he was right, but that didn't make the dressing-down any easier to take. In fact, her own criticism of herself made his more difficult to accept. Besides, she hadn't even told him about the threatening phone call. Not that she was about to share *that* piece of information posthaste.

"You should have called me, Belle," Rosco concluded. His anger had given way to old-fashioned worry.

"The puzzle read, 'Tell no one.' "

Rosco sighed. "Belle, you're a word person—some might say an egghead . . . but you're not a cop."

In spite of herself, Belle bristled. "What's that supposed to mean?"

"It means that you should have basic training in law enforcement before dealing with criminals."

"Tom Pepper told you he didn't want the police brought in on this—and you listened to him."

"That's because I used to be a cop. I know what I'm doing."

"As opposed to me? The *egghead*?" Belle's question was delivered in the flat, challenging tone of a statement.

Rosco paused. Belle could hear him breathing slowly and deliberately. "Look, you're a very smart person, that's all I meant," he said. "I can't quote Shakespeare. You can. French and Latin phrases don't roll off my tongue. You can jump hoops between languages. On the other hand, I've been through the police academy, and I've been out on the streets . . . I've learned to anticipate problem situations." The particular stress he put on "problem" painted a vivid picture of just what those times entailed. "I also know when to carry a gun, and how to use it if I have to."

Belle didn't speak immediately. Instead, she continued gazing through the window. Midafternoon was giving way to dusk. The sky was still blue, but the color looked heavier and darker, as if the panes of intervening glass had been tinted an amber brown. "Rosco, I may not have sufficient experience with criminal investigations, but everything in that crossword indicated that I'd been designated as a liaison. If I hadn't gone alone—"

"Why you, Belle?" Although Rosco's tone was gentle, Belle found herself growing irritable again.

"Why not me? You're working for Pepper. Most folks consider us to be . . . to be . . ." Annoyance at the situation wouldn't permit her to say the word "couple"; instead she opted for a noncommittal "involved."

"Only people we know."

"What's that supposed to mean?"

"That you're presupposing this kidnapper—or extortionist—is a local who's attuned to the personal relationships of every citizen of Newcastle."

Belle could see Rosco's point, but her stubborn streak refused to concede the argument. "Then why were those first two crosswords sent to me, the third to Tom, and the fourth delivered to me again?"

Rosco's response was a weary: "Those are questions we don't have answers for yet."

"But I do! The first puzzle comes to me; I answer the clues, but fail to respond—or so the constructor assumes . . . Ditto with the second crossword . . . although, meanwhile I decide to publish it—and talk to Bartholomew Kerr . . . The puzzle's printed version and his gossip column don't appear until yesterday—Friday . . . But in the meantime the constructor becomes frustrated at my seeming inattention and targets Pepper, knowing he'll pass the puzzle along to me—"

"You're making a big assumption—"

"No, I'm not, Rosco! This is common sense. I know I'm right!"

"No, Belle, you don't *know* it. You *believe* it . . . That's a whole different thing . . . I don't mean to lecture you, but it's important not to jump to conclusions here—"

"You play hunches all the time. You told me so yourself . . . Besides, Sara 'wholeheartedly' concurred that the crossword Pepper received had direct bearing on the case. 'Wholeheartedly' was her term, not mine."

"Tell me you didn't show that puzzle to Sara."

Belle remained silent, so Rosco pushed harder. "You showed that puzzle to Sara?" He could feel himself steaming up again. "When Pepper practically *ordered* me not to inform the police!"

Belle's tone—and verbiage—turned immediately defensive and grand. "As a subcontractor of the Polycrates Agency, I felt it within my jurisdiction, yes . . . Anyway, Sara—"

"Where did you get that high-flown term 'subcontractor'?"

"From you!"

Rosco's frustration echoed through the telephone wire. "And so this employee of mine takes it upon herself to investigate a situation without informing her boss—"

"Well, you're not my boss, for one thing. Let's not get carried away—"

"Aha!" Rosco almost shouted. "Now we're getting somewhere . . . So this *non*employee decides to investigate a case in which she has no jurisdiction . . . not to mention authority—"

But Belle was not to be bested. "Rosco! Two women's lives are at stake!"

"We don't actually know that, Belle—"

"Yes, we do!"

"Belle—"

"Okay, okay . . . my *assumption* is that this is a kidnapping . . . But isn't that the only way for us to proceed? By hoping that these crosswords lead us to Genie and Jamaica?"

Rosco didn't answer, and both, in their separate rooms, backed off. Belle glared through the windows. Evening was now marching forward; soon the panes of glass would turn black and cold. She flicked on her desk lamp, but the circle of light did nothing to dispel the sense of hastening gloom.

"Listen," she said, "this latest cryptic arrived first thing this morning—today, Saturday . . . After the threatening phone call last night, it made perfect sense that I—"

"What phone call?" Rosco's tone was again on edge.

Belle groaned. She couldn't think of an answer that would assuage his fears. "I didn't mean to tell you," she said quietly.

"Well, that's just swell," was his exasperated response. "That's just terrific! You put yourself at severe risk, and you don't have the courtesy to tell me?"

"It had nothing to do with courtesy, Rosco. I knew you'd try to dissuade me from going."

"You're right! That's exactly what I would have done— dissuade. And with good reason."

"But I'm trying to tell you I *had* to go out to Allyn's Point alone!"

"Speaking of *points,* that's mine . . . Someone wanted you there alone—and that person is most probably a character you shouldn't meet face-to-face."

"But he—" Belle began, but Rosco overrode her.

"Belle," he said, "If you love someone, don't you want to protect them? Whatever it takes?"

Belle was silent for a long time. How could you stand on principle when someone said they loved you? "Yes," she finally answered. "Yes, you do."

"You worry about me, right?"

"Yes," she answered.

"Well . . . ?" he asked.

In response, she frowned at her desk, and at a well-thumbed Oxford edition of Shakespeare's complete works lying open on its surface.

"What's good for the goose . . ." Rosco said gently.

"Is good for the gander," was her mumbled response. Then she added a quick: " 'Young blood must have its. course, lad, / And every dog his day.' It's from *Water Babies* . . . Charles Kingsley . . . The poem has a goose in it. That's why it came to mind, I guess . . . although there was this dog out at Allyn's Point . . ."

"We need to talk about that, Belle," Rosco answered softly. "Listen, what do you say I take you out to dinner? We can hash over the entire situation then . . . parameters, safety, appropriate information-exchange policy, *subcontractors*, the works . . ."

"Promise you'll never call me an egghead again."

"Only if you positively swear you'll start considering the consequences of your actions."

"I'm not sure I know how," was Belle's quiet response.

"That's why I worry about you." Rosco chuckled a little. The stalemate was broken. "Is half an hour okay? And maybe the Athena? Besides, I've got my own news to share. One item being that Genie Pepper's half brother— and no friend of Tom's—is the beneficiary of her *generous* life-insurance policy. The second being that he up and quit his job. No one in Boston has seen hide nor hair of him since last Saturday."

"Yikes!" was all Belle could think to say.

CHAPTER

22

The Athena Restaurant on Front Street in the resuscitated City Pier area had been the scene of Rosco and Belle's first dinner together. With its cozy, romantic ambience, checkered tablecloths, and evocative, wall-sized murals of Greece, the eatery had remained a favorite; Belle and Rosco felt almost as if they'd been transported to some exotic vacation spot when dining there. Tonight, however, business intruded. Or, perhaps, discussing the Pepper case was easier than addressing the push-pull of their own emotions. Both of them had been deeply affected by their argument that afternoon; love, they knew, could make people unreasonable, sometimes possessive, often anxious. It could also bring joy beyond measure.

"So . . . let's see . . . You were telling me that Billy Vauriens can't be found . . ." Nervous energy and a sudden shyness caused Belle's pale blond hair to bounce as she spoke. She smiled, but the expression was almost too bright. "Doesn't his girlfriend find that odd?"

Rosco tried to match her impersonal mood. "Not from what she said . . . I gather they have a pretty loose arrangement."

"I'd hate that," Belle blurted out, then stammered an embarrassed, "For me, I mean . . . Or, rather . . ."

"I wouldn't like it either," Rosco said. "For myself, that is . . ."

"To each his own," Belle answered.

"Absolutely," was Rosco's swift reply.

In the awkward silence that ensued, he divvied up the remaining *dolmades;* and the waiter removed the plate from the red-and-white-checked tablecloth, then poured white wine into their glasses. Rosco waited until he and Belle were again alone before speaking.

"You and Vauriens' lady friend don't have much in common . . ." he began, then attempted a less intimate tone as he watched her attack her last stuffed grape leaf. "Unless you've been kiting checks, that is." Finally, he added a quiet: "I'm glad you didn't starve out there on Allyn's Point . . . Or harm yourself in any other way . . ."

"I was fine, Rosco. Really I was," Belle murmured, before returning to the safer subject of Billy Vauriens. "I still don't understand his situation with his boss."

Rosco toyed with his glass. Belle could see he had something on his mind that didn't include Genie Pepper's half brother. When he answered, however, it was Vauriens' situation he addressed. "I gather Billy's part of a pickup crew for construction work. Nonunion, usually working off the books . . . sometimes only marginally skilled . . . They're not the most dependable folks to hire."

Belle followed his lead with an equally pragmatic: "So, why didn't this boss question Vauriens about his decision to quit?"

"The guy's got a site under construction. Probably running

behind schedule would be my guess . . . He barely had time to talk to me. Anyway, he's used to these part-timers coming and going. He's got better things to do than keep track of them."

"Hmm . . ." Belle nodded. "Hmm."

Flat soup dishes containing *avgolemono* were placed in front of them. "Lemon soup." She sighed. "You know how much I love this stuff."

Rosco smiled as he watched her. "It's not that hard to cook."

"For someone named Polycrates, maybe!" Belle returned his warm glance, but her pronouncement suddenly brought a welter of disturbing thoughts—accompanied by the single damning and unshakable word Jamaica had leveled at her during the Patriot Yacht Club dinner dance; "transitional" clanged in Belle's ears.

"So . . ." she continued after several moments, "after you went gallivanting all over Boston looking for Vauriens, then what?"

"Then I drove back to Newcastle, called Pepper, and told him I'd been hunting for Billy . . . It's a good thing we were talking on the phone, because I'm not sure I would have been able to handle that much hollering in person . . . Pepper clearly despises his brother-in-law."

"Half," Belle corrected reflexively.

"Right . . . Genie's *half* brother."

"And Tom didn't know anything about the five-million-dollar policy?"

"Not a peep."

"And this forensics expert, Jones—what's his first name again?"

"Abe."

"That's right," Belle said. Rosco could see her searching for a mental association to remember the name.

"It's not what you think," he offered. "Abraham Lincoln and emancipation . . . Abe stands for Absalom or Absolon—something like that."

Belle looked thunderstruck. "Absalom Jones? As in one of the founders of the African Methodist Episcopal Church?"

"I wouldn't have pegged Abe as a religious guy—"

"I'm talking about his namesake, Rosco! A late-eighteenth-century former slave . . . an extraordinary leader and orator."

Rosco stared, nonplussed. "Does your brain have room for any additional information? Or do you have to throw away outmoded data every so often?"

"Rosco, he was famous!" Then she saw how crestfallen he looked, and softened her response. "I've used the name in my more challenging cryptics—cross-referencing King David's traitorous son, Absalom . . . It's fairly arcane stuff . . . Actually, I'm not certain how I originally came across the information . . ." The rush of verbiage began to slow. "So, this *Abe* Jones of yours said he suspected that the *Orion* fire was a case of arson?"

"King David's evil son," Rosco mused in response. "What do you know about that."

Belle grinned. "Polycrates was a Greek tyrant, if you don't mind me reminding you."

"Sixth century B.C.," was Rosco's rapid retort. "The family's become much less autocratic since then."

"That remains to be seen." Belle chuckled.

"Anyway, the guy was big on piracy—meaning he must have liked boats."

Belle laughed again. "So, you're saying Abe Jones believes the *Orion* fire was arson?"

" 'Torched' was the word he used, Belle. I've known

Abe for quite a while, and it's uncanny how right on most of his initial insights are. If he feels it was arson—"

"And you don't think you should share that piece of news with Pepper?"

Rosco hesitated. "Not yet . . . Ultimately there's still nothing confirmed . . . and I don't want Tom going ballistic over a situation that could be misinterpreted . . . Until we have concrete evidence, we have to consider the possibility that the fire may have been accidental—no matter how slim the possibility. It's never a good idea to pass half-truths onto a client. I get paid to deliver facts."

"But what if the *Orion were* set on fire?" Belle asked.

"Well, then I'd say the situation doesn't look promising for Mr. William Vauriens."

Belle's eyes wandered to the murals in the restaurant's candlelit alcoves. The scenes they replicated made her yearn to be in Greece. On one wall stood an island village full of ancient, whitewashed houses. On another were olive trees on a sea-breeze-swept hillside. One painting was a bird's-eye view of a tawny valley dotted with toppled marble columns.

"Five million dollars could buy a lot, couldn't it?" she murmured almost unconsciously.

Rosco followed her glance. His response was equally thoughtful. "It sure could."

Instinctively, their hands met on the tabletop. "I'd like to take you there, sometime," Rosco said quietly.

Belle didn't speak; instead, her entire being seemed transported by the suggestion while the term "transitional" suddenly and miraculously vanished, leaving her mind as full of tranquillity and hope as the images on the restaurant walls. "I'd like that," she said at last.

Rosco squeezed her fingers again. They were both smiling in earnest, although not yet at each other.

"So . . ." Belle finally asked, "so . . . what else did you learn about Vauriens?"

"Vauriens," Rosco answered, and sat up straighter. "Right . . . Well, apparently, Genie kept trying to get him to clean up his act. He's not unattractive, from what I heard—'killer looks' according to the girlfriend—"

"The one with the 'loose' relationship."

Rosco raised his eyebrows, but sidestepped the interruption and its implication. "Anyway, Genie decided Billy should study acting . . . Something to 'keep him off the streets.' "

Belle completely failed to see where this revelation was heading. "So?"

"So, she got him an apprenticeship at a theater in Connecticut . . . the Avon Shakespeare Festival . . ."

"Oh my . . ." Belle said.

"He left Connecticut at the end of the summer. It seems the part of Balthazar in *The Merchant of Venice* didn't offer him enough of a stretch."

"Oh my . . ."

"Now do you see why I worry about you?"

Belle's eyes met Rosco's. "Where do we go from here?" she finally asked. Both realized the question had nothing to do with Billy Vauriens.

CHAPTER

23

Sunday morning in Newcastle's dockside was no different than any other honky-tonk neighborhood nursing a hangover. The peal of eleven A.M. church bells could be heard in the distance, but no one on the waterfront strip was making a mad dash to slide into a favorite pew for a much-needed lesson in Judeo-Christian ethics. The final remnant of Saturday night's revelers had stumbled from the grimy pavement toward darker hiding places when the sun made its dawn appearance; in their wake lay the detritus of determined partying: discarded liquor bottles, empty cigarette packages, gnawed-on pizza crusts, and mangled fish-and-chips wrappers. Sticky ketchup smeared the wrappers; the substance had begun to resemble drying blood.

Rosco studied the scene as he drove toward the Red Admiral. The asphalt pavement fronting the tavern was nearly vacant; one lonely and rusting VW bus and two Harley-Davidson motorcycles were its only inhabitants.

Judging by the amount of trash accumulated nearby, the owners had been absent for some time. As he eased his Jeep to a stop, he heard the distinct sound of an aluminum beer can crunch beneath his tires.

"Better than glass." Rosco sighed, stepping from the Jeep to survey the waterfront and commercial docks facing Water Street's east side. Dark clouds ranged slowly across the bright October sky while a thin morning sun appeared above the harbor at irregular intervals, creating blinding reflections from any metal object it touched.

The west side of the street, however, emitted the dingy aura of a ghost town. Crushed plastic cups, pint-sized paper bags, and balled-up candy wrappers blew by like tumbleweed. Iron gates, heavy with layers of peeling paint, covered every window and door. The same held true for the Red Admiral. The shutters on its two ground-floor windows had been closed and padlocked; crisscrossed steel bars blocked the front entrance.

Rosco glanced up toward a second-floor window. It had been left open, and a faded green-and-white-striped curtain flapped in the breeze. From his previous visit, he knew that Vic Fogram lived above the bar. He wasn't the type to leave a window unlocked accidentally. Rosco decided the Admiral's owner was home.

He walked to the side alley, where he found a flight of rickety wooden steps leading to a second-story doorway. He realized there was no point in surprising Fogram—it was the type of thing that got people shot in this neighborhood; instead, Rosco trod heavily up the stairs, hoping the noise would announce his arrival.

As if on cue, Vic was waiting at the landing. Clad in a grungy brown, hooded terry-cloth robe, he looked like a deranged Franciscan monk. "Well, if it isn't our friend from Baltimore," he said with an ill-disguised sneer. "Back from Maine so soon? Let me guess; you couldn't find a motel and you need a place to crash."

Rosco reached for a business card. "I wasn't completely up front with you the other night. My name's Rosco Polycrates. I'm a private investigator."

Vic glanced at the card. "And a local PI, at that." He scratched the back of his head through the brown fabric. "I gotta hand it to you, pal, you're good. Everyone in the joint bought the Baltimore line." Vic pulled a pack of Marlboros from his robe, lit one, and tossed the match into the alley. His wary demeanor returned. "What do you want?"

"I'm looking into the *Orion* fire."

Vic gave a hint of a smile and shook his head. "I would have bet a hundred bucks you were gonna tell me Charlie Yarnell's wife hired you to find out who he's shackin' up with. Guess it's Charlie's lucky day and not mine."

"Can I come in?" Rosco asked. "Fifteen minutes is all I need."

Vic considered the request. He didn't speak, just inhaled long and deep. "I don't have anything to say about the *Orion*—other than to tell you to hit the road." Then he lazily flicked his half-smoked cigarette toward the ground and began to step inside.

"That's advice you might want to reconsider, Fogram," Rosco said.

"I didn't kill those babes."

"Who said they were dead?"

"You ever try swimming for ninety-some hours in Buzzards Bay in October?" The retort didn't mask Vic's sudden nervousness.

Rosco recognized how easily the tavern's owner had been rattled and decided to press his advantage. "There's another possibility, Fogram . . . Police scenario number two: the cops start looking for someone who might have staged the fire and kidnapped the women. In that case, your door is the first the feds knock on. I'm sure you can follow the logic there . . . Trust me, you're up to your keister in this . . ."

"I don't like being pushed"—Fogram glanced anxiously at Rosco's card—"Polycrates."

"Then I suggest you figure a way to keep yourself out of a federal lockup. Because those boys are notorious for their pushiness."

Vic reached for another cigarette, but found the package empty. He crushed the wrapper and flung it down into the alley, then gritted his teeth and appeared to make a decision. "I've got a lady visitor. I'll tell her I got company." He slammed into his apartment, banging the door shut behind him.

Rosco waited on the wooden landing with his arms folded across his chest, then watched in envy as a pair of seagulls glided by, riding the light wind. It seemed a preferable way to spend the morning. Three minutes into Rosco's bird-watching reverie, Vic yanked open the door. "Okay," he growled. "I'll give you fifteen—but that's all."

Rosco found the apartment's interior a surprisingly pleasant, open space. Kitchen appliances lined one wall; everything seemed fairly new and orderly. There was an oak dining-room table in the center of the room. A couch flanked by two armchairs faced a wall containing a TV, VCR, and CD player, with a wooden lobster pot serving as a somewhat arty coffee table. At the rear portion of the room, a beaded curtain separated the sleeping area. Rosco had little trouble discerning a large brass bed and the outline of a figure covered from head to toe with a patchwork quilt. Obviously Fogram's "lady visitor."

"Sit." Vic pointed to the couch. "I'm gonna have a beer . . . Hair of the dog."

Rosco chose the couch and waited for Vic to return with his Budweiser. As he flipped the top, he sank into one of the chairs. "What do you want to know, Polycrates?"

Rosco cocked his head toward the sleeping area. "You don't mind being overheard, I take it?"

"Listen, pal, I've got nothing to hide. From you or anybody else. I haven't done a damn thing . . . Who're you working for, anyway?"

"That's confidential."

"Right . . . So, you want me to talk to you, but you won't tell me jack about yourself. Well, not everyone's an idiot in this town. I got a C-note says you're working for Tom Pepper. Who else cares about those broads? No one I know. I'll tell you this: If you're looking for crooks, you'd better start sniffin' around your own backyard."

"Meaning?"

"Meaning Pepper."

"You mentioned something about that the other night . . . Something like: if you'd known the *Orion* had been leased by Pepper's wife, you would have just let it burn . . . What did you mean by that?"

"Exactly what I said. I got no use for these creepola money traders and numbers swappers. Let me tell you something: no one makes money without someone else losing it. A guy walks into my place downstairs and orders a Bud? What happens? I'm two dollars richer and he's two dollars poorer. That's how the world goes 'round."

Rosco smiled slightly. "Do you hate all rich people, or is Pepper someone special?"

"Let's stick to the *Orion*. I don't need a headshrinker."

"All right. So, what happened last Sunday?"

Vic retrieved a fresh pack of Marlboros from a teak box on the coffee table, slipped off the cellophane, and lit up. As he spoke, smoke escaped from his mouth and nose.

"Me and Bob and Moe were off Monomoy Island on the south end of the Cape, just north of Nantucket. We'd told Colberg we'd have the *Dixie-Jack* back before eight A.M. Monday, so we were heading in. Pulled some nice tuna . . . Anyway, we shot straight across Nantucket Sound, past the Vineyard, Woods Hole, and hit Buzzards Bay around midnight. We'd been throwin' down beers the whole way . . . so I can't vouch for the accuracy of the time, or the exact location of the *Orion* when we came on it, but obviously we picked her up somewhere between the Hole and Newcastle. Dropped a towline on her and towed her in . . . End of story."

"I see . . . So, you're saying the fire was already out when you found her?"

Vic's left foot started tapping on the wooden floor as if an imaginary tune were playing in his head. "Yeah . . . It was rainin' . . . a surprise squall had come up."

Now Rosco scratched the back of *his* head. "I'm having a little trouble with this one, Vic . . . We've got a squall, so we've got heavy cloud cover, right? It's also midnight— pitch-black under those conditions. And you find this boat? In the middle of nowhere? That's a big bay out there. How could you see a burned-out shell bobbing around? Sounds to me like the thing would be damn near invisible—" Rosco held up his hand as Fogram started to interrupt. "Before you answer, let me tell you that I know you guys blasted through all four fire extinguishers on the *Dixie-Jack,* and that CO_2 residue was found all over the *Orion.*"

Fogram jumped to his feet and stabbed his lit cigarette in the air. "I told you I don't like to be pushed, fella. Maybe you better just get the hell outta here."

Rosco remained seated, but raised his voice to meet Vic's. "Pushed . . . ? You're going to jail, Vic. You got a picture of what that looks like? Right now you're accessory to insurance fraud. And that's on the bright side, *fella*. Who knows what else you're in for—once all the pieces fall into place . . . Personally, I don't think you'd be stupid enough to kidnap these women, but I've been wrong in the past. You'd better start coughing up some information, because from where I sit, you and your pals look guilty as hell."

Vic slouched back down in his chair and rubbed at his forehead.

"Look," Rosco continued in a pseudo-friendly tone, "I've got no bone to pick with you, Fogram, I really don't, but you know how cops work; they get Bob in one room, Moe in the other . . . Before you know it, they're saying Vic planned the whole thing."

Vic jabbed his cigarette into a black Bakelite ashtray adorned with the Harley-Davidson logo. "I'm tellin' you, we didn't do nothin' wrong."

"But you did put out the fire? Am I right?"

After a long beat, Fogram spoke. "Yeah . . . we doused it . . . That's how we found her—by the flames. There was an explosion. Lit up the sky. We figured it was the propane tank."

"What about the women?"

"We didn't know nothin' about them. There was nobody on that boat. I swear it on my mother's grave."

"Why didn't you call the Coast Guard? Report the position? You know as well as I do, that's procedure."

Vic looked off to the sleeping area as if the answer might lie in his bed. He let out a tired sigh and lowered his voice to a harsh whisper. "Look, we were all looped to the gills by that time. The last people in the world we wanted to see was the damn Guard. I pulled the *Dixie-Jack* up to the *Orion,* and Moe and Bob started hosing her down with the extinguishers, making a party of it . . . I mean, they started really goofing around. Spraying each other while they were at it. Laughing their fool heads off. Anyway . . ." Vic looked at the bed a second time. "Anyway, I wanted to get out of there, leave the boat, but Moe saw the word 'Orion' painted on the stern and said he recognized it as one of Colberg's charters." Fogram lit up again, then said, "I need another beer."

As he walked to the refrigerator, Rosco noticed how unsteady his gait had become.

"What we figured," Vic continued when he returned, "was that Colberg had towed the *Orion* out and torched it himself. You know, for the insurance—like you said. He's done it in the past, trust me on that. Everyone knows it . . . Anyway, we didn't think anyone was on that boat—honest. Look, I did my time in the Navy. I'd still be out there looking for those broads if I didn't think this was another Colberg torch job . . . That tough talk about Pepper's wife . . . That was just yak, that's all."

"So, why did you tow the *Orion* back?" Rosco asked, uncertain how much of the tale to believe. Or whether to believe it at all.

"Moe wanted to play a big joke on Colberg. Set him up. Let him come to work on Monday and find the tub sitting there like a ghost come back to haunt him. Moe thought it would be a real hoot . . . So we sat around on the *Dixie-Jack* waiting for the sun to come up so we could see the expression on Ed's scrawny face."

"But you didn't get what you bargained for?"

Fogram shook his head and swigged at his beer bottle; Rosco had the distinct impression the man was hiding something. He shifted tack, assuming a sympathetic and credulous pose.

"And you didn't see any sign of the dinghy out there?"

"Didn't see it, didn't hear the outboard . . . I told you,

Polycrates, I was in the Navy. I swear I would have picked up those babes and brought them in. No matter who they were. I wouldn't leave nobody out there. I got a decent, legit business in this town. I'm not a crook."

Rosco studied Vic closely as he asked his next question. "What would you say if I told you that the police found samples of Jamaica Nevisson's blood on the *Dixie-Jack*."

The response was a measured: "I'd say you're a liar, pal."

"It was all over the gauges."

"The gauges? Hell, man that was plain old fish blood. We filleted them. Tuna meat's red and bloody. Ask anyone."

"Sorry, Vic. The police lab says there's some of both. Tuna and human . . . A positive. Same as Jamaica Nevisson."

Fogram stood and walked between Rosco and the sleeping area. "You're talkin' outta your hat. I got nothin' more to say."

Rosco also rose. "This isn't going to blow over, Fogram. It's going to get worse. Call me. You've got my card."

"That ain't likely to happen."

"You never know . . ." Rosco sniffed the air and gave Vic a broad smile. "Nice perfume . . . Say hello to Doris for me when she wakes up."

Fogram swung his left fist while Doris Quick bolted upright in the bed and yelled something indecipherable. Rosco ducked the first blow, but Vic countered with a hard right, slamming his beer bottle into the corner of the detective's left eye and instantly opening a half-inch gash below his eyebrow.

"Get the hell outta here before I kill you!" Fogram raised the bottle over his shoulder and heaved it toward the door frame behind Rosco's head. Beer suds and shards of amber glass rained down upon him as Vic continued to advance. "I'm gonna kill you, I swear . . ."

Rosco found the doorknob and jumped for the wooden landing. Fogram was right behind him. For a moment the two men stood, suspended in time one story above the grimy pavement. They stared hard at each other. "Get lost, Polycrates. And don't show up here again. This is harassment. That's what it is. I'll get a lawyer."

"That may not be such a bad idea . . . Thanks for the fifteen minutes," Rosco answered. "And the memento . . . I won't forget it too soon."

Rosco walked down the stairs, reentered the garbage-strewn alley, and dabbed at the cut with his handkerchief while he slipped behind the wheel of his Jeep. Then he twisted the rearview mirror to study the wound. The bleeding was slowing; it wouldn't require stitches. But his cheek and brow were already showing signs of swelling.

"Great," he muttered, "just, great. 'Another Black-eye Sunday Morning.' Sounds like a C and W tune . . ." He lifted his jacket to his nose. "I smell like a booze hound . . . And Bud, too . . . At least, it could have been an import . . ."

He balled up the handkerchief, applying it like a compress while he activated his phone and checked for messages. There was one from Belle, requesting that he "beam in" for some "vital information."

"Guess who just called?" she demanded the second she answered the phone.

Rosco didn't have time to answer; Belle's voice hurried forward before he could open his mouth. "Bartholomew Kerr." Her tone indicated that this was the important news she'd wanted to share.

Rosco massaged his swelling eye. "Little early for gossip, isn't it?" he asked, then decided: Ice. I've got to get some ice. It seemed ironic that the Red Admiral with its steady supply lay in plain view. He considered telling Belle what had just transpired, but opted against it. "What did *Biz-y Buzz* want?" he said instead.

"He just heard a peculiar story. It seems your pal Al Lever made an arrest late last night."

Rosco sighed. His eye and cheek were beginning to throb. "Anybody I know?"

"Did you ever hear of a guy named Reggie Flack?"

CHAPTER

24

After speaking with Belle, Rosco had U-turned on Water Street and headed the Jeep east on Fifth in the direction of Newcastle police headquarters. The eight-block ride had given him time to make two more phone calls: the first to Al Lever to ensure that he hadn't yet left the NPD building, the second to Tom Pepper.

"Mr. Pepper, the police picked up Reggie Flack last night—"

"Tell me something I don't know, Polycrates. Where the hell do you think they picked him up, Disneyland? He was in my kitchen."

"What . . . ?"

"He didn't start out there." Pepper said this with a low chuckle. "Anson and I caught the slimeball crawling through the rhododendrons at two A.M. last night. After I made the creep eat his camera, we hog-tied him and called the cops. Flack's going to rot in jail for twenty years if I have anything to say about it."

"I'm headed to the NPD now. I'll see what information I can get out of him."

"Well, good luck. He wouldn't say peep to me. Threatened to sue me for knocking out a few of his teeth, though. Hell, he's lucky I didn't finish him off. If I had a gun, I would have. And I would have been within my rights."

Rosco refrained from groaning and saying, That's debatable. Instead he only asked, "You're pressing charges, then?"

"Absolutely!"

The viciousness of Pepper's tone set Rosco's teeth on edge. "I'll keep you posted," he said in an attempt to defuse the situation.

"You do that! That's what I'm paying you for." The line went dead before Rosco even had time to consider an answer.

Arriving at the south side of the NPD building, he slipped his Jeep into a parking space marked OFFICIAL USE ONLY, then walked up the main stairs and tapped on the glass paneled door marked HOMICIDE.

"Yeah?" Lever grumbled from the other side.

Rosco stepped through the door. "You don't have any ice in here, do you, Al?"

"What happened? Don't tell me Pepper belted you, too?" Lever reached into his lower desk drawer and tossed Rosco a chemically charged cold compress.

"Thanks . . . Someone clipped me with a beer bottle. I'll get over it . . . You're working Sundays now?" Rosco twisted the plastic package to start the cooling reaction, then placed it over his left eye.

"Thanks to you, Polly—Crates. I had a ten o'clock

tee time. Kissed that baby good-bye a couple of hours ago."

"Hey, Al"—Rosco shrugged—"none of this is my doing. It all would have ended up in your lap anyway."

"Hmmph." Lever lit a cigarette and began coughing.

"What's with Flack?"

Lever inhaled again. "He's not a talker . . . insists he's waiting for *The Globe*'s attorney to get down from Boston. Bail's been set at a quarter mil."

Rosco whistled softly and said, "Wow. That much? How come?"

"Pepper's got friends in *very* high places. Judge Lawrence considers Flack a flight risk. Thinks he'll skip back to L.A. . . . Well, now he has a little incentive to return for a hearing if he does."

"What're you charging him with?"

"Trespassing, invasion of privacy, and criminal mischief."

". . . And two hundred and fifty thousand dollars bail?" Rosco laughed. "That has to be some sort of record, even if he is from Los Angeles . . . Mind if I talk to him?"

"He's down in the hole. Be my guest." Lever coughed again. "Damn these allergies. You'd think they'd let up by October, wouldn't you?"

"A 'killing frost,' that's what you need to get rid of pollen, Al."

"Since when did you take up gardening, Polly—Crates?" The question wasn't unkind.

"Maybe it's not allergies, Al, have you considered that?"

"Don't say it, Rosco. You . . . the wife, hell, even my doctor's turning against me since he quit smoking. Now get out of here; I got work to do." As Rosco headed for the door, Lever added, "Enjoy your conversation with our quarter-of-a-million-dollar man. Ask him if he likes being a local celebrity."

"The hole," as Al liked to call it, was composed of six large holding cells in the basement of the building. The compound sat at the end of a corridor bordered on the right by the Newcastle morgue and on the left by Abe Jones's forensics lab. The walls were institutional green, and the lab and morgue doors were reinforced stainless steel with small shatterproof windows. When Rosco reached "the hole," the heavily barred door was opened by a uniformed officer.

"Hey, Rosco," he said, "what happened to your eye?"

"Walked into a door . . . How've you been, Terry?"

"No complaints."

"I'm here to see Flack."

"Lever okay it?"

"Yep. Call him up if you want."

Terry grimaced. "He missed his Sunday-morning golf game—"

"So I heard."

"Flack's in number two," was Terry's wry response.

A double set of three cells lined a center aisle; each holding area was separated only by iron bars, privacy not being a luxury afforded to inmates of "the hole." Number two was the center facility on the left. One and three were empty; four, five, and six, to Rosco's right, held one man apiece—obviously gents who'd done too much Saturday-night partying. All three were asleep on metal cots suspended from the cinder block walls. The place smelled like an airless locker room after a wrestling match—and that was a genteel description.

Rosco dragged a folding chair to the door of cell two, dropped into it, and propped his feet up on the bars.

Flack made no indication of acknowledging his visitor; instead, he hunched over on his bunk, his feet planted on the concrete floor and his forearms resting loosely on his knees. One hand nursed a purple jaw. Although not a large or powerful man, he gave the impression of muscle and rage. When he finally lifted his head, Rosco recognized him as one of the two photographers Tom Pepper had pursued the afternoon of the incident at the Coast Guard station.

Under a "Geraldo"-type mustache, Flack's mouth was a pulpy red, and he had a long blue-black bruise on his right cheek. He hadn't shaved for three or four days, and his body gave off the rank odor of nerves and cunning. Lever's assessment was correct; the man would be a tough nut to crack; he'd been around.

Rosco continued to stare; he kept his arms folded across his chest.

After several minutes Flack decided to speak; his missing teeth produced a pained and irritable lisp. "What is this? The old 'good cop, bad cop' routine? You guys watch a lot of TV in this burg, do you?" He stressed "TV" as if any yokels not residing in L.A. existed solely through stories fed them by the entertainment industry.

"I'm no cop," Rosco said. "I work for the man whose house you broke into."

"I didn't break into anyone's house, dude."

Rosco smiled evenly. "The police cuffed you in his kitchen, from what I hear."

"Pepper and some two-bit Brit thug dragged me there . . . 'Blimey, matey, look what we have 'ere . . . a bloomin' 'orse thief—' "

"That's your story, Flack; I've got two policemen upstairs who maintain they found you in Pepper's kitchen . . . But, hey, the facts will come out in court, right? No point in our wasting time determining whose human rights might have been violated."

Flack looked up; he seemed to take Rosco's measure. "What's this about? I don't have to talk to you."

"That's your decision—Mr. Flack. But let me present my employer's view on this matter. If he drops charges, you're out of here in an hour. If he presses them . . . you're going to jail. Probably only for a year, but you will do time, and it'll be hard time. This is Massachusetts, not California. I'm sure you're smart enough to realize that Mr. Pepper is a powerful man in this 'burg' . . ."

Flack's head drooped again; he stared at the stained floor. After a beat he muttered, "Where's *The Hollywood Globe* attorney? I don't have to speak without legal counsel present."

"Good for you, Flack. So, you know your way around a station house, and *Miranda* v. *Arizona*? It doesn't surprise me. However, I don't operate under police guidelines. I'm just a messenger—here at Mr. Pepper's behest. The questions I'm asking are his. And he'd like them answered in a timely manner. In an hour or two he may not feel so lenient. Your bail's been set for a quarter of a million dollars—kinda high for a crime of this type, wouldn't you say?"

Flack ran his fingers through his limp and greasy hair, then wiped his palms on his trousers. "What does he want to know?"

"First off: your obsession with Jamaica Nevisson."

Flack's wiry chest produced a snort of contempt. "Those pictures have paid my rent as long as I can remember, dude. Let me tell you something, PR's a two-way street. Jamaica Nevisson needed me as much as I needed her. I wouldn't expect some bozo hick to understand the PR biz, but it was Jamaica's people—her agent, manager, press wrangler, et cetera—who put me onto her in the beginning. Her career would have gone nowhere without coverage in *The Globe*—or lack thereof." The statement was followed by a smug laugh.

"Since you raise the issue of privacy, do you mind describing how you got those nudies of her on Catalina Island?"

Flack chortled again, shaking his head in amazement as if he were dealing with a five-year-old. "Her 'mysterious male companion' set up the photo op. See, he's a newbie trying to jump-start his career. Just like everybody else on the Coast . . . So he supplies all the details of the trip, and I follow them out to the island . . . Buff young guy posing on muscle beach . . . Now he's hot, and Jamaica's not. *C'est la guerre,* dude, as the Frenchies say."

"And you followed them out to Catalina on a boat?"

"No, dude, I swam . . . I've always had this thing for sharks." Flack stared at the ceiling; sarcasm curled his thickened lips. "Welcome to Hicksville, Reggie," he muttered, then reclined on the bunk as if finished with the interview.

Rosco ignored the performance. "I assume this frenzy over Jamaica's disappearance has also benefited your career, Mr. Flack . . . Do you mind telling me when you arrived in Newcastle?"

The photographer lifted his head and squinted at Rosco. For the first time he seemed worried about his answer. "Last week, why?"

"I can always check with the airlines, but I was hoping you'd cooperate and supply something more specific— such as what day and hour? Was it before or after the *Orion* blaze?"

Again Flack turned evasive. "Come on, dude, what difference does that make?"

"As I said, it's easy enough to check with the airlines . . ." Rosco stood as if to leave. "Mr. Pepper doesn't like leaving loose ends—especially when it involves finding his wife—"

"Hold on." Flack swung off the cot and hurried across to the cell's bars. "I arrived last Saturday night—nine, ten o'clock . . . As soon as I heard Jamaica had lit out of L.A., I booked a flight."

"Who told you she'd 'lit out'?"

"Sources, dude, sources . . ." Flack started to sneer, then reconsidered the remark. His tone and body language grew wary. "Okay . . . the same guy she sailed to Catalina with. It's worth his while to keep her name in the papers."

"So you were here Sunday . . . You could have followed the *Orion* into Buzzards Bay."

"Hey, hey . . . back up there . . . What are you saying? That I torched the boat?"

"Who said it was torched?"

Flack forced an unsteady laugh. "Torched . . . accident . . . who cares? Listen, if I'd been there when those babes bit it, I would have gotten photographs of the whole damn shooting match."

"Who's to say you don't have them already?" Rosco stood for a moment, regarding Flack while the photographer mimicked unconcern. "Do you know what W. R.

Hearst wired to his illustrator Frederic Remington after sending him to Cuba in 1898?"

Flack shrugged. "That's what you cowboys talk about around here? Ancient history? Sorry, dude, that was a little before my time."

" 'You furnish the pictures; I'll furnish the war.' Some folks will stoop pretty low to sell a few newspapers . . . Or jump-start a career."

The photographer opened his mouth to speak, but Rosco cut him off. "Don't waste brain cells on a response, 'dude.' Like you said, before your time . . . And possibly beyond your acumen."

Then he turned and walked to the corridor. In the greenish glare from a line of fluorescent overheads, he saw Abe Jones leaving the forensics lab, a dark brown file folder in his left hand. Rosco trotted to catch up. "It looks like NPD has everyone working today."

Abe let out an elongated groan. "Overworked, is more like it . . . What happened to your eye?"

"Cut myself shaving . . . Did you get the DNA tests on the blood samples I turned in?"

"They won't be ready till Tuesday." Jones tapped the file folder. "I'm finished with the rest of it though—taking the results to Al now."

"Any surprises?"

Jones thought for a minute. "The fire was started by the two oil lamps—as I'd figured during my initial examination. Fingerprints were scarce. The few I lifted belonged to the women or to Colberg, but I also found a couple that didn't match. They've been sent to the FBI for analysis . . . I'll stay with my original theory that the propane tank blew and knocked out most of the existing fire. But someone definitely appeared at the scene later and finished the job with CO_2 extinguishers."

"Fogram, the guy who leased the *Dixie-Jack,* admitted he and his buddies doused it," Rosco said, then added a slow, "So, that's it, huh?"

"Not completely, no. The most intriguing data isn't from the *Orion* or the *Dixie-Jack.* It's from the inflatable."

"Oh?"

"First: the remaining portion of the *Orion*'s towline had been singed, but cut clean—not untied. The rope ending that was still attached to the inflatable isn't singed, although the sever marks cleanly match those on board. I'd say the women escaped in the dinghy rather than jumping overboard. The fact that it was cut points to a hasty escape, probably panic; even experienced sailors can run afoul of a well-tied knot—especially in the dark with an escalating blaze. Next: Colberg maintains the outboard was gassed up when the yacht departed. When we retrieved the inflatable, the tank was almost empty, indicating that it had been run for almost two hours."

Rosco mulled over the information. "The women could have reached any shoreline in the bay in two hours: Woods Hole, West Falmouth, even back to West Island . . ."

"In all probability, yes. But here's the real kicker, Rosco . . . The inflatable had no salt water in it."

"What're you getting at?"

"I'm not talking about deposits in and around the seats; of course there were traces of salt there . . . I'm talking about the bladder itself. If the dinghy had been punctured in Buzzards Bay and rendered unseaworthy, salt water would have seeped into the air pocket—and I would have found it."

Again, Rosco paused to assimilate the information. "So what's your theory?"

"I've got a few, but they all point to the same conclusion."

"What's that?"

"Dollars to doughnuts . . . those women are still alive."

CHAPTER

25

The sun was beginning to slink behind the scrub and dunes backing Munnatawket Beach when Belle and Rosco arrived. Their shadows etched the sand in front of them as they walked to the spot where the *Orion*'s tender had been found. Belle pulled up her jacket collar, then jabbed her hands in her pockets. In half an hour the beach would no longer be bathed in the soft gold glow of a waning October afternoon; it would be as cold, gray, and uninviting as congealing gravy.

Belle shivered in anticipation, then resumed her part of the conversation. "... I disagree with that concept, Rosco," she said as her Keds scuffed determined footprints in her wake. "From everything you've told me, it sounds as if Flack's guilty as sin. I'd bet everything I have that he knows where the women are—and how they vanished."

"But where's his motive?" Rosco asked her. He started circling the area where the inflatable had been beached.

"For kidnapping? Money, of course ... and maybe

some weird form of power, role reversal . . . something like that. Jamaica's been his prey for quite a while. I imagine he identifies strongly with her. Maybe he's gone off the deep end . . . You met him. Do you think he represents a picture of stability?"

Rosco studied the spot where the inflatable had been found. "Not really, but that's assuming this *is* a kidnapping, Belle."

"But aren't we going under the premise that the women have been nabbed? You told me that was Abe Jones's theory . . . You said he's convinced they're still alive."

"I'm not certain I agree with him, Belle. There are major pieces missing from the puzzle." Rosco knelt on one knee and stared at the now undisturbed sand. A wisp of seaweed, stuck in the heavier substance, had created a semaphore arc like something desperately signaling for release.

"Such as?" she asked.

"Such as no ransom note, for one . . . So far, four puzzles have arrived, right? Going under the assumption that they're connected to the women's disappearance, why hasn't there been a demand for money?"

"We haven't received it yet?" This was a question.

"And why not? It's nearly a week now."

Belle thought for a long minute. When she spoke again, the words spewed out rapid-fire: "It's a form of sadistic game—which supports my theory that Flack is involved . . . He won't contact Pepper with demands until he's put a worried husband through hell. That crossword Pepper received was the work of an enraged and vindictive person—"

"Okay," Rosco said. "I'm following you, but why is Genie in the mix if Flack is obsessed with Jamaica?"

"She just happened to be on the boat with her pal. A pawn like the young hunk in L.A. . . . Flack admitted he was using that guy, didn't he? The 'newbie' actor . . . Isn't that what he said?"

Rosco didn't answer; instead, he continued staring at the windswept sand.

"Besides, this cretin of a photographer is obviously comfortable on the water," Belle insisted. "He followed Jamaica to Catalina Island. That's a long way from the mainland. Think about it; whoever picked them up had to use a boat, right?"

"Fogram knows his way around boats, don't forget . . . Colberg, too. And then, there's Doris . . ."

"Right . . ." Belle answered slowly, "Vic and Doris . . ." She bent over to follow Rosco's sight line. "What are you looking for?"

"Inspiration?"

"Very clever." Belle chuckled briefly, then grew serious again. "Doris and her peculiarly absent husband."

"And the other trucker . . . Mr. and Mrs. Stingo—completely unaccounted for. Don't forget them."

Belle sighed. "What a mess," she finally said.

Rosco stood and Belle straightened up, touching hands instinctively and then just as unconsciously drawing away, as if personal emotions had no part in their conversation.

"The dinghy's outboard was gassed up when the *Orion* sailed . . ." Rosco began, while Belle finished the thought.

"But the engine was near empty when the tender was found—"

"Meaning it had been in use for two hours or so."

Belle screwed her eyes up and stared hard at the broad stretch of sand. "If it was discovered this high above the high-water mark, then someone must have placed it here," she said. "And whoever set the stage had to realize—amend that—had to *ensure* that the boat be found . . . It was part of the plan . . ."

She began to pace toward the ocean; Rosco followed close behind. "The fact that it was free of salt residue increases the probability that the criminal intended the discovery to indicate a kidnapping rather than an accident at sea: a gash *clearly* created on dry land. Whoever our criminal is would have been certain forensics tests would be run."

"Not necessarily. Amateurs don't think that far ahead. Plus—"

"Wait!" She suddenly turned in her tracks, and in doing so nearly collided with Rosco. "That's it!" she almost shouted. "Staged! The entire thing's been staged! Flack and Jamaica's boy-toy betrayer—the wannnabe actor! Those two guys have orchestrated the entire scenario! Just like they did at Catalina!"

Rosco looked at the ocean and then at Belle. "All right," he said slowly. "I'll play along . . . Flack gets tired of earning peanuts from celebrity shots . . . He decides to go for the big bucks . . . But that's assuming he could command a sizable ransom for Jamaica."

Again, Belle pondered the situation. "Flack must have had prior knowledge that Genie would be involved. He must have counted on Tom paying whatever he asked."

"Except that no demands have been made, cash or otherwise."

Belle pursed her lips; her eyes squinted in concentration. "Okay, okay, okay! I've got a better idea. Maybe Jamaica instigated the entire deal. Maybe she's the one calling the shots. A delayed ransom note would suit her sense of the dramatic—"

Rosco began to interrupt, but Belle overrode him. "Flack alluded to Jamaica's previous participation, right? He said PR's a two-way street—or words to that effect . . . Well, maybe Jamaica was worried about her career and trying to revitalize it . . . Maybe she contacted Flack . . . hired him to take those lurid pictures—"

"I love the way your brain works, Belle," Rosco interjected. "But I'm afraid you're way off the mark. Flack told me—"

"No, wait . . . let me finish. Flack might be lying through his teeth, you know—"

"What's left of them."

"Rosco, I'm not joking! Hear me out."

Rosco put up his hands in mock surrender. "I'm silent. I'm silent."

"Okay," she grumbled. "But I'd like you to take my suggestions seriously."

"I am."

Belle shot him a glance, then continued. Her words and tone were thoughtful. "So, here's my notion: Jamaica masterminds *The Globe* photo spread. Her 'mysterious male companion' is part of the deal—or not. That's an unimportant detail because who knows where, or *who* he is . . . When said cruel pix are published, the actress appears outraged. Whines to her best buddy, Genie, and furiously decamps the L.A. scene—only to tragically disappear at sea during a yachting 'accident' aboard said best friend's chartered boat."

"You've lost me again, Belle . . . What's the purpose of this hoax?"

In the waning light, Belle's gray eyes burned like smoldering coal. "How much publicity has Jamaica gotten out of this situation already?" The speech flew ahead without waiting for a response. "A lot! And what happens when the media learns the dinghy didn't sustain damage in the ocean? Where will speculation lead, then?" Again, Belle didn't pause for an answer. "Everyone will *assume* it's a kidnapping, Rosco! Beloved actress hideously abducted . . .

Fans of *Crescent Heights* and Jamaica's character will start tearing the tabloids off the shelves. When she reappears, shaken but unscathed, she'll be reinstalled as a star in the Hollywood pantheon."

"Okay . . ." Rosco said. "Supposing you're right . . . Just supposing . . . What's Genie's role?"

"She's giving her friend every bit of help she can. Think about it—a solid citizen is abducted as well. It's perfect. Who would suspect a hoax?"

Rosco was silent, mulling over the suggestions. "I don't know, Belle. This is pretty outlandish—"

"No, it's not. It's dramatic. It's Hollywood! And that's what we're looking at. A drama created by an actress. Two, if you want to be specific about it—"

"Where does Tom fit in? According to this . . . this theory of yours?"

Belle gestured toward the darkening waves as if their depths held answers. "Well . . ." she began, "obviously, Tom has to be aware of each detail in the plot . . . More than 'aware'; he's got to be a player, too . . . After all, he 'found' Flack in his home, had him thrown in the can—and insisted bail be posted at a quarter of a million dollars . . . Besides, Pepper has all sorts of alibis that point to noninvolvement. First, he's away hunting in Maine, then he hauls you in on the 'case'; next, he pretends to go ballistic with the Coast Guard, then feigns an attack on an unfortunate photographer—who turns out to be none other than Mr. Reggie Flack . . ."

Rosco didn't speak.

"Tell me you don't agree."

"I don't. For one thing, I don't believe Tom could possibly have faked the rage I witnessed. He was truly irrational; I told you I was genuinely concerned about his mental health—"

"But the setup is perfect, Rosco!" Belle insisted. "It's flawless!"

In the dimming light, Rosco took a long breath and shook his head. "Was," he finally said.

"What do you mean 'was'?"

"It can't be flawless if someone uncovers the *supposed* crime. And that's what it is; a crime. No one could pull a stunt like this without getting prosecuted."

"That's assuming they get caught." Belle sighed impatiently. "You don't believe me, do you?"

Rosco paused, then gently took her hand. This time the gesture was in earnest. "I think your idea's too complex, Belle. It involves too many players to be successfully staged."

"What about the CIA's tactics? What about the FBI stings?"

"Where did that come from?" he said with a smile, finding her looking overly alluring in the setting sun.

"Anything's possible. We haven't even considered the guys from D.C."

Rosco drew her close. "It's getting cold. What do you say we go home—"

"The crossword puzzles," she interrupted with a quick shake of her head. "I just remembered clues and answers that seemed insignificant earlier . . ." Her brow creased in concentration.

"You don't give up, do you?"

"Never!" she answered. "So you'd better get used to it." Then her words raced ahead. "FLACK appeared in the first puzzle I received. MOE was in the second puzzle—the answer to *One of the Stooges*—"

"Belle . . ." Rosco began.

"I know what you're going to say." She waved a hand in excited impatience. "But maybe *Stooges* doesn't refer to television clowns; perhaps it indicates another group—one more closely allied to finding the *Orion*. A 'stooge' can be a puppet, a straight man—or a stool pigeon. Think about the implications, Rosco. Vic Fogram admitted dousing the *Orion* fire, right? And he said his buddies were acting crazy. The puzzles must have been created by someone who witnessed their behavior."

Rosco tried to interrupt, but Belle would not allow it. "Then there's *The Globe*, Reggie Flack's newspaper—that was Shakespeare's theater."

"Flack doesn't publish the paper, Belle; he's not responsible for—"

"But everything fits, Rosco! It's all part of a bigger puzzle! Remember the quotations from *The Merchant of Venice*, the references to *Hamlet, Much Ado About Nothing*—those clues *had* to be Flack's creation, Rosco. Apt quotes from the Bard are his stock in trade, remember? Flack's the one who's been sending the crosswords. He's the one who staged Jamaica's kidnapping."

Rosco shook his head. "With her permission, I think you mentioned—"

"With her *collusion*!" Belle corrected vehemently. "And Genie's *and* Tom's! They're up to their eyeballs in this!"

Rosco leaned close, gently brushing a strand of blond hair away from her face. "I love your enthusiasm, Belle . . . along with everything else. Really, I do. But as a former cop, I've got to tell you—"

Belle studied him, her expression dangerously solemn. "You know, your eye looks worse than it did an hour ago."

"Listen . . . It was a good theory."

"It *is* a good theory," she insisted. "And don't try to change the subject. Your eye really looks awful. We should put more ice on it."

"I probably shouldn't have mentioned Doris's name, but

I was trying to get a rise out of Fogram," Rosco said with a rueful shrug.

"You certainly succeeded in getting a rise out of your eyebrow."

"You'd be surprised how much information can flow with a good burst of anger . . ."

She turned away from him and the water's edge and began to survey the now dusky beach.

"Belle, I'm serious; it's a good theory. We just need to bounce it around a little more."

After several thoughtful minutes she spoke. "You said it took two of you to stash the inflatable tender in the patrol car, right?"

"Correct."

Belle continued to stare toward the dunes. "If the dinghy had been driven to Munnatawket Beach and immobilized here, a good-sized vehicle would have had to transport it; and one person couldn't have wrestled the tender to the spot where you found it without creating a visible trail . . . And *if* it had been cut elsewhere and *then* driven here, two people would still have been involved."

"What are you getting at?"

"Flack must have an assistant who's still at large."

"Belle . . ." Rosco began. He walked to her and put his arm around her shoulder.

"Admit defeat, Rosco. I'm right and you're wrong."

"No surrender." He laughed briefly. "How about you're wrong and *I'm* right?"

Belle ignored the comment. "And I know just who the guilty party is, too."

"I'll just bet you do."

"Don't be so high-and-mighty, Mr. Ex-Cop."

Rosco sighed. "Okay, I'll bite. Who is our mysterious missing link?"

"Billy Vauriens!"

Rosco closed his eyes. "Don't make me laugh, Belle, please; it makes my eye sorer than it already is."

"Why not Vauriens?" she demanded.

"Well, for starters, why don't you tell me why his name sprang into your head?"

"Genie wanted her brother to go into acting, right?"

"Mmm-hmm . . ."

"But he couldn't tolerate bit parts in classical theater. It was below his talent. Isn't that the gist of what you relayed to me?"

"Something like that . . ."

"Then he disappears . . . his girlfriend's disgruntled; his work history is spotty—to say the least . . . Why couldn't he have been Jamaica's 'mysterious male companion,' the guy Flack *claims* set up the Catalina visit. Vauriens jets out to L.A. from Boston—maybe more than a few times. Maybe he's even serious about breaking into the movie biz—"

"Belle, give it up."

"Think about it, Rosco! You don't know what Vauriens looks like. Who's to say he wasn't that blurry male on the beach in Catalina?"

"Don't you think Tom would have told me that Vauriens—"

"Why would he, Rosco?" Belle interrupted. "If he's in on the whole thing? I know what you're going to say, but you've got to admit there's a good possibility of Vauriens and the 'mysterious escort' being one and the same man."

Rosco was silent for several seconds. "I don't know, Belle. This is a huge leap—"

"Not if you subscribe to my previous theory."

"Which I don't."

Belle threw up her hands. "You are really stubborn,

Rosco. I hope you know that . . . Besides, you told me you always played hunches. Well, this is my hunch. And it's a strong one. I believe Flack is the point man for an operation that Jamaica's clandestinely controlling—and that he has a very willing young assistant."

Again, Rosco didn't speak. "Let's hope a few of these ideas are correct," he said at last. "And if Tom isn't in on it, let's also hope he gets a ransom note soon. Because if you're wrong, the fact is that those women are still missing . . . And if they've been kidnapped by someone whose motive is money and revenge, they're still in a great deal of danger."

"I know," Belle said quietly. "I know."

In the early-evening gloom, the two walked to the Jeep. The sun had set, and the last residue of pink and orange long since gone from the sky. Rosco put the car in gear, and they began retracing their route to Newcastle.

Near the hairpin curve leading to the secluded point of land upon which the Pepper house stood, the rapid blue, red, and white flash of emergency strobe lights slashed across the darkened pavement. As the Jeep rounded the bend, Rosco and Belle spotted an ambulance and two police cars—one of which was Lever's unmarked Ford. An ancient orange VW Bug clung to the road's shoulder, its driver an equally antique lady who looked white and glassy with horror. Al Lever leaned down talking to her while two medics and another police officer attended to a body lying prone and lifeless in the road.

Without a word, Rosco and Belle jumped from the Jeep. Lever glanced up. "Bad news sure has a way of trailing me today, Polly—Crates. Tell me you two are out on a date, and this isn't business."

"Anything I can do, Al?"

"Yeah, tell me to go home." He turned back to the VW's

driver, then suddenly jerked his head in Rosco's direction. "Lady witnessed a hit-and-run . . . says she saw the whole thing . . . 'Some kind of truck' was 'driving recklessly, almost out of control.' The guy you see over there must have been walking along the opposite shoulder. Dead on contact, according to the EMS . . ."

Lever straightened and approached Rosco and Belle; his lips were tight. "ID states he was William Vauriens— Genie Pepper's half brother."

CHAPTER

26

"Who is this?" Rosco grumbled into the receiver of his bedside telephone. "What time is it?" He said this half to himself and half as an annoyed accusation to the early-morning caller whose raspy voice he hadn't recognized. Rosco fumbled with his clock radio, turning the dial toward the window in an attempt to attract predawn illumination.

"I couldn't sleep," the person said as if the answer would suffice as apology for calling at such a heinous hour.

"What time is it?" Rosco repeated.

"I don't know . . . five . . . five-thirty . . . Maybe earlier." The words slurred over themselves, fading in and out. "Hell, you used to be a cop. You must have worked night shift. Able-bodied seamen can tell the time by the stars."

"Who is this?" Rosco demanded again, then suddenly remembered Belle's menacing phone call. "Unless you identify yourself, I'm hanging up."

"Fogram . . ." Rosco finally heard. "Vic Fogram . . . the Red Admiral . . ."

Rosco fumbled with the alarm clock. "You don't sound like the Vic I met," he said.

"Fogram . . . Vic Fogram." Again, the words had a muzzy sound. "You came up to my place yesterday . . ."

Rosco finally succeeded in illuminating the clock's face. It was five-ten A.M. "The Red Admiral . . ." he heard repeated. "I had me too many shots and beers last night. Too many smokes. I can't sleep . . ." The conversation had spun full circle; Rosco decided to shake it loose. He pulled himself upright in the bed. "How's Doris?" he asked.

The response was a ferocious expletive.

Rosco smiled to himself, then remembered the welt above his eye. "Okay. I guess you're who you say you are."

"You leave Doris out of this, Polycrates. She's got nothing to do with you. Nothing to say, neither. I thought she made that clear already."

Rosco finally found the switch on the table lamp and glanced at his caller-ID box. He didn't recognize the number, and the prefix wasn't the downtown exchange of Fogram's tavern. Again, he was second-guessing himself as to who the caller truly was. "Hold on a sec, there, Vic . . . This phone's a piece of junk. I'm having trouble hearing you . . . Let me call you back on a different line."

"You can't do that . . . I'm not home."

Rosco jotted the number on a pad of paper. "Well, why don't we let this conversation ride till you get there," he said.

"This can't wait till later. We gotta talk now. I'm in danger here, Polycrates. One man's dead already."

Rosco felt the skin at the back of his neck prickle. What did this man know? "Who would that be?"

"Vauriens. Pepper's brother-in-law. Last night." The voice contained scarcely concealed panic.

"So I heard. Traffic accident . . ."

"Don't count on that 'accident' stuff, pal. Vauriens had the inside dope. I got money says he was set up. I say the body was dumped there."

"There's a witness."

"An old lady. She doesn't know what she saw."

Again, Rosco found himself questioning the caller's identity. The tone and phrasing had elements of Vic's clipped Massachusetts accent—but not enough. "Okay, Vic, what's your theory?"

"Why do you think Pepper kept sending Vauriens checks?"

"Maybe you'd better tell me."

"To keep him quiet, that's why."

"Quiet about what?"

"That's what we need to talk about."

Rosco faked a lazy, disinterested yawn. "Okay by me. I can be at the Admiral in half an hour."

"No way, Polycrates. I'm not showing my face until this mess is cleared up. The Admiral's closed. You don't believe me? Drive by tonight. I'm telling you Vauriens was killed, and I don't want to be the next in line. I know as much as he did, more maybe. You want to meet me or not?"

Rosco considered his options. If the caller *wasn't* Fogram, then whoever it was had zeroed in on the tavern; Vic's life might be in genuine danger. Moe Quick, Rosco thought again; maybe it was Quick. Maybe that was the cause of the explosive reaction over Doris. "I've got to get this straight, Vic. You're saying Pepper was responsible for the hit-and-run?"

A nervous groan ricocheted through the phone line. "Come on, Polycrates; use your head. Who do you think

Genie's life-insurance policy reverts to if Billy shows up dead? Next of kin. That's the way those things are written. Tom Pepper's the big winner here. Just like always."

"I don't buy it, Vic. Pepper needs five million dollars like he needs a new pair of shoes."

"That's where you're wrong, pal. Pepper's into me for seventy-five grand—plus some. And I'm not the only one. He's in hock up to his ears."

Rosco's back jerked straight; he swung his feet onto the floor. "Hold on there . . . You're saying Pepper owes you seventy-five thousand dollars? You and some others?"

The response was an edgy laugh. "You got wax in your ears, buddy?"

Rosco didn't answer; instead, he stared hard at the phone number scribbled on the pad of paper. Who was this man if it wasn't Fogram?

"I'm talking about the G.O.L.D. Fund, Polycrates . . . I put seventy-five Gs into it. I bought Pepper's pitch: 'double your money in six months!' Except when I tried to collect—*nada*. Not a nickel. Something's fishy about the whole damn thing. Now I can't even get my phone calls returned. A month, I've been trying. And I'm not the only one who's getting burned."

The word "burned" set off alarms in Rosco's head. "You're sure about this? There are some heavy-duty organizations invested with Pepper. They would have screamed their heads off if they'd been had."

"CFOs don't like to admit they've been conned by some shark . . . But there's gonna be plenty of wailing soon."

"Why you? Why did you invest with Pepper?"

"What's that supposed to mean? That blue-collar guys like Vic Fogram can't play with the big boys?"

"Seventy-five thousand's a good chunk of change."

The caller took a long exasperated breath. "My old man

left me a piece of property . . . Now, you know what's happening to Newcastle—developers crawling all over it . . . Pop bought the land for five thou. I sold it for three-fifty. That's how come I own the Admiral—with seventy-five Gs to spare."

Rosco grabbed the pad of paper. "You said you have names?"

"I gotta go."

"I need tangibles, Vic. Without tangibles, I've got nothing but the allegations of some guy *claiming* to be Vic Fogram."

The caller hesitated. "The abandoned piers up on Water Street. I'll meet you in an hour in the one furthest north on the river . . ." There was another pause. "My old man had a favorite expression when I was a kid. He used to say: 'I wouldn't trust that *Tom Pepper* further than I could throw him.' A Tom Pepper's a liar in bygone fisherman lingo . . . This is before your boss man was even born."

Rosco started to speak, but the caller cut him off with a sharp: "No beer bottles this time." Then the line went dead.

At six-twenty, Rosco entered the long empty shed of the derelict commercial pier fronting Water Street. A screech of pigeons rose in perturbed flight, raining debris and grubby feathers from overflowing nesting places; the sound the birds made echoed throughout the expanse of steel support columns and cold cinder block walls. Rosco instinctively reached for his .32. If there was one thing he was fairly certain of, it was that meeting a man who *claimed* to be Vic Fogram, and *claimed* to have incriminating information about one of Newcastle's leading citizens, probably wasn't all that safe. Not a "power position," as Pepper would probably have put it.

Rosco waited for several long and silent minutes, listening for the sound of human feet, but all he heard were the sounds of rats scrabbling over the concrete floor and the pigeons returning to the eaves under the corrugated tin roof. Cautiously, he began tracing the perimeter of the vacant space. Five years prior, a developer had purchased the site with the intention of creating a renovation similar to the restaurants and shops in the Front Street area, but the project had stalled and then halted. The result of this aborted refurbishment was that most of the building's flooring had been resecured and the larger gaps in the walls boarded up. When the moneymen decamped, they'd left behind several self-contained officelike structures that now stood scattered about the otherwise empty space like miniature houses in a game of Monopoly.

As soundlessly as he could, Rosco approached each one. Daylight was scarce, and the pier's interior a permanent gray gloom. He peered through grimy windows, but the mini-buildings were also deserted. He waited; something warned him not to say Vic Fogram's name aloud.

Fifteen minutes passed, then twenty. Rosco glanced at his watch more often than necessary. He listened for the sound of a car door but heard only the Newcastle River slopping against the pier's pilings. Twice there was the throaty gurgle of a lobster boat heading out to check pots. He waited another five minutes, then recircled the space; this time he looked for traces of recent human presence. Maybe Fogram—if the caller had been Fogram—had left some type of message.

Nothing.

It was now seven A.M.; Rosco very much regretted a missed second cup of coffee. Insufficient morning caffeine was beginning to make his head ache. He considered heading back down to the deli on the lower end of Water Street, but knew he couldn't risk leaving his post. Damn Fogram, he thought. This information had better be worth it.

Seven-fifteen. Nearly one hour cooling his heels in a building as dank as a walk-in freezer; Rosco was growing truly irritated. He walked the length of the pier again, making as much noise as he wanted. Fogram had better have one terrific excuse, he thought. The man's been nothing but a royal pain.

A third rumble of inboard motor chugged past outside. The noise sounded like a terminally ill patient gasping for breath. *One man's already dead,* Rosco suddenly remembered, then reminded himself that two women were also still missing and presumed dead—and that the entire group had direct links to Edison "Tom" Pepper. He tried to recall Belle's discussion of crossword clues relating to money and investing, but all he could conjure up was that she'd once played the part of Shylock in *The Merchant of Venice*—information that didn't seem particularly apt.

He patrolled the building again, this time examining several barn door–size openings that had originally served as ports of entry for freight-bearing ships. Outside, the narrow wood deck was spongy and rotten. Rosco peered through a number of gaping holes; he half expected to see Vic Fogram semisubmerged within the complex of broken pilings.

No one.

It was now ten minutes before eight. On the off chance that Fogram had changed venues, Rosco decided to quit the building and check messages from his car phone. He trotted down the street to the Jeep and punched in numbers. No messages. He sat in the driver's seat thinking. Pepper, Vauriens, Flack, Fogram, Quick, Colberg: was the connection between the men more convoluted than it appeared? And had one or some or all been involved in setting fire to the *Orion*? If the motive had been kidnapping, where were the abducted women—and why hadn't there been a ransom note? And if, as Belle had suggested, this was an inside job intended to garner publicity, why hadn't the kidnapping template been followed?

As Rosco drove to his office he chewed over the publicity-stunt angle, but eventually discounted it. Fogram was obviously frightened to show his face in public; he honestly believed Vauriens' death was no accident, and if that was true, the likelihood of a publicity stunt incorporating a murder was remote.

While he was unlocking his office door, Rosco heard his fax emit an elongated beep indicating it had just finished receiving a transmission. He grabbed the paper still rolling out of the machine. Imprinted on the flimsy document were two names complete with addresses and phone numbers. Both men were identified as commercial fishermen, and beside each name was the exact dollar figure they had invested with the G.O.L.D. Fund. There was a side note reading, *Monies Unrecovered*.

What Rosco didn't realize was that seven minutes earlier Belle's fax machine had also received a message—a fifth crossword puzzle.

Across

1. Taxis
5. Tiny——
8. WWII battle site
12. Till
13. Penned
15. Bow
16. Oklahoma tribesman
17. Covered with ice
18. Deserve
19. Revenge adage, part 1
22. Radio repairman, maybe
23. Delicious color?
24. Discrimination grp.
25. Hwys, e.g.
27. Swab
30. Revenge adage, part 2
35. Lion portrayer
36. Farm animal
37. Black in Bordeaux
38. Revenge adage, part 3
43. City in Kirghizia
44. "——naughty night to swim in," Shak.
45. Mid East lang.
46. "What's the——?"
47. "Year in——"; eternity
51. Revenge adage, part 4
54. Mean
55. Separate
56. Informer
58. First name in mystery
59. Loud
60. Half a train sound?
61. Playthings
62. Matsue moola
63. Chemical suffixes

Down

1. C.G. noncom
2. Sacrificial place
3. Daniel——
4. It's on the cob
5. "I'll Follow the Sun" Beatles' prediction
6. Road to Rome
7. O.R., e.g.
8. Race
9. Cafeteria Necessity
10. Folk——
11. Possess
13. Bolt tightener
14. Abundant
20. Mongol tent
21. Robin's home
26. Deuce beater
27. Night-light?
28. Auricular
29. Netic lead-in? Var.
30. *The Sun——Rises*
31. New Mexico tribesman
32. Oops!
33. ——Parker, 3-Down portrayer
34. One way to snag a grounder
39. "How would you like——I did that?"
40. Breakfast joint?
41. Talkative
42. Munich mister
46. Capitol roofs
48. "I'm all——"
49. Many a Mormon
50. Spasm
51. Spanish bull
52. Air France destination
53. "The Gold Bug" writer, abbr.
54. Snare
57. Boxing decisions, abbr.

PUZZLE 5

CHAPTER

27

Belle snapped the plastic cap onto her red Bic pen and dropped it into the ceramic crossword mug she reserved for writing instruments. Then she pushed her office chair back from her desk, placed her feet squarely on the floor, and stared at the puzzle she'd been faxed scarcely ten minutes earlier. She'd completed it so quickly that she'd hardly had time to analyze the clues or answers. Now the red ink seemed to jump from the paper like spurting blood. Studying 19- and 30-Across, she murmured, "AN EYE FOR AN EYE, A TOOTH FOR A TOOTH," then followed the adage with its companion quip: "SOON IT'S MY CHANCE TO OFFER A TRUTH . . . Soon," she repeated. "Yes, but how soon?"

She folded her arms across her chest and stared through the window, half seeing her friend the sparrow preen itself in the morning sun. "Soon," she muttered. "When is 'soon'?"

The sparrow ruffled its feathers and cocked its head

undisturbed. Belle dragged her eyes back to the puzzle. "5-Down: TOMORROW MAY RAIN . . . That means there's more to come . . . 'Tomorrow'—or 'soon.' "

She stood, walked to the wall of bookcases, and removed a licorice stick from a clear glass jar, then bit the chewy end while deftly severing a four-inch strip like a cowhand with a length of beef jerky. Her mouth full of sticky black candy, she returned to her desk and began drumming her fingers on the puzzle, gradually focusing on the fax markings on the edge of the paper. The time and date of the transmission were neatly indicated, along with the return fax number—which Belle suddenly recognized as being Papyrus, the monster office-supply store from which the second puzzle had also been faxed.

She grabbed the phone to call the shop, then suddenly reconsidered. No, she decided, this time I'll go out there and talk to a clerk in person, something I should have done in the beginning—despite Rosco's warnings about "weirdos" and "validating aberrant behavior."

It never occurred to her that the action could put her in peril or that a call to Rosco might be wise. In Belle's mind, she was merely embarking on a "fact-finding mission." "Tomorrow" or "soon" were the operative words in the time frame. If she could discover who had sent this latest crossword, then maybe she could anticipate that person's next move. Besides, as she promised herself, there was no need for fear in a public place as huge as Papyrus. Patience, as Rosco had observed, was not one of Belle's virtues.

She grabbed her purse, locked the house, jumped in her car, and pulled into Papyrus's parking lot fifteen minutes later. Business was already booming; a surprising number of cars lined the expansive facade. Belle parked next to a powder-blue Range Rover, then walked to the entrance, where double electronic doors swept open and a gust of refrigerated air pulsed out, revealing the mammoth interior. Every imaginable stationery and office product was on display: neon-colored erasers, sparkly notebook covers, pens and pencils of every hue and type, clipboards, letter paper of every weight, size, and color, reading chairs, lamps, desks that unfolded hidden shelves. If such emporia had existed when Belle was a child, she knew she would have found heaven.

She spotted a young man in a dark green polo shirt embroidered with the store's logo and marched toward him. He was arranging fountain pens in a display case, and quickly locked away the items as Belle approached. She wondered whether his mistrust was store policy or whether she had the words "ulterior motive" stamped across her forehead.

"Can I help you?" he asked.

"Yes, could you direct me to the fax machine?"

"I don't see it."

"Pardon me?"

"Your fax. It has to be the correct size. Some weights of paper we can't handle."

"Oh . . ." Belle looked down at her empty palms, half expecting a sheet of paper to appear. "I didn't bring it with me . . . I just wanted to check on your prices first."

"It depends on the location you're transmitting to."

Belle didn't respond, and after a beat he pointed toward the rear of the store. "In back—at the copy center. Tina handles the faxes."

"Thank you."

Belle turned and walked down a seemingly endless aisle lined with a vast array of envelopes. At the end of the aisle four self-service copy machines faced a long counter behind which stood a tall woman in her late forties with jet-black hair cut in a trendy retro bob. She also wore a green polo shirt.

Belle smiled. "Are you Tina?" she asked.

The succinct reply was a less than promising, "Yes."

"Perhaps you can help me, then," Belle began, although Tina's wooden expression didn't suggest she was in a benevolent mood. "I received a fax from this store at around eight o'clock this morning. Were you working then?"

"I start at seven when the store opens."

"Oh, good. So you were here . . ." Belle smiled again. "You don't happen to remember who sent it, do you?"

Tina's long frame stretched taller and more austere, reminding Belle of time-lapse photography of some exotic botanical specimen—a Venus flytrap or other carnivorous plant. "It is not Papyrus's policy to peruse private faxes or cover sheets for the purpose of obtaining telephone numbers. Our customers rely upon confidentiality and discretion when they bring a document into our emporium . . . Sorry."

Belle doubted the sincerity of the apology; she smiled for a third time. *More flies are trapped with honey,* she thought, expanding her metaphor. "This wasn't actually a letter, Tina; it was a crossword puzzle."

"Oh!" Tina said in new state of awareness and excitement. "You're Annabella Graham. You're the crossword lady at the *Evening Crier*. I do the puzzle every day."

"I'm very glad to hear it," Belle said, attempting to cover her impatience. "So, you do remember who sent the puzzle? The reason I ask is that the crossword was good enough to publish. The *Crier* always pays constructors for their work—but I need a name to accompany the check."

Tina thought for a moment while Belle grinned for a fourth time.

"Well," Tina began, "this is against Papyrus policy, but seeing as how you're trying to do a favor . . . It was Ricky. He also sent one last week, didn't he?"

"Well, someone did. And darn it if that name wasn't omitted, too."

"It was Ricky, all right. A nice kid but kind of dopey, if you get my meaning. I didn't think he had the smarts to make up a crossword puzzle. So he's trying to get them published, huh?"

"That's what I assume, but unfortunately, I haven't been able to contact him. You wouldn't happen to know his last name, would you?"

" 'Fraid not."

"But you know his first name? Even though he's only sent two faxes?"

Tina let out a long laugh. "It's not what you think. He's a kid, like I said . . . comes in the store a lot . . . You know, to get things photocopied for the motel."

"The motel?"

"Sure. Blue Hill Cabins." Tina pointed vaguely toward her right. "It's about a quarter of a mile from the interstate on the old Boston Post Road. There used to be a gas station near the cabins, and some kind of mom-and-pop restaurant that finally went belly-up . . . you know, when the highway built all those fancy rest areas and commercial traffic moved east . . ."

Belle looked blank, and Tina sighed again. "I've lived in this area all my life," Tina continued. "There used to be other places like the Blue Hill—tourist cabins, they called them way back when. They were nice . . . secluded, low-key, kind of quaint . . . vacationers could spend a week there without breaking the bank . . . Newcastle was a different town in those days . . ." Tina's glance finally refocused on the bright lights and aggressive merchandising of the super-store around her. "Anyway, Blue Hill gets their rate sheets printed here—not that much changes in that respect. Ricky's sort of their delivery kid and all-around helper."

"Well, perhaps I'll visit the cabins and see if I can find him."

"Oh, you'll find him all right. Look for a Red Sox hat and he'll be the kid under it. And he is a kid, too . . . kind of small for a guy . . . His puzzles are really good, huh?"

"Remarkable." Belle smiled for a fifth time. "Thanks, Tina, you've been a big help."

She left Tina to her memories, quit the store, climbed into her car, and entered the westbound traffic lane without noticing the blue Range Rover pull out directly behind her.

Exiting the interstate onto an unkempt and sadly empty side road—the remainder of the once-great Boston Post Road—the Blue Hill Cabins' entrance lay several hundred yards on her right. Belle angled into a parking space in front of the office, a small freestanding two-story building that looked as if it had three rooms, a bedroom upstairs, and an eat-in kitchen and office on the first floor. Two neon signs hung in the front window; one said OFFICE, the other VACANCY; both were still lighted. Tina was right; the world had lost all interest in places like the Blue Hill.

Before entering the office, Belle studied the cabins dotted among the trees as if they'd been perched at the edge of a dense, impenetrable forest. Against the invading greenery, the units looked tiny, but she could imagine how spruce and tidy they must once have seemed: a bed-sitting room, a kitchenette, the sound of the wind in the pines at night, the ocean only a few miles away. *Affordable family fun,* the brochures must have advertised. Only two cars were parked in front of the cabins, and they looked as weary as the buildings.

Belle stepped into the empty office. There was a registration area cluttered with papers, a side table holding several magazines, and two folding metal chairs. A small TV sat on the reception desk pointed in the direction of an overstuffed chair. Belle tapped on a plastic button nailed to the desk and a gong sounded in a back room curtained off from the office with a floral-printed sheet. After a long minute a man with a melon-shaped stomach and a poorly fitting toupee emerged from the back. He retrieved a toothpick from a shot glass on the desk, placed it in the corner of his mouth, and eyed Belle up and down.

"Checkin' in, honey?" He gave her a lecherous smile.

"No . . . I'm looking for Ricky."

The man laughed, making his stomach roll from side to side. "Must be Ricky's lucky day . . . a cutie like you lookin' for him . . . Who is it wants him?"

"Ah, well . . . I'm . . . from the school . . . and—"

"Ricky dropped out of school a year ago," he announced.

"Of course . . . I knew that." Belle cleared her throat. "It's just that . . . for that reason . . . well, we like to follow up on the kids who leave us. To see if we can change their minds. I'm sure you know that education is a vital factor in success."

This brought a boisterous belly laugh from the desk clerk. "Yeah, well, I wouldn't say 'success' was a priority for Ricky."

Belle could feel a line of sweat form at her hairline, but she refused to break eye contact with the man. "May I talk to him?"

"Be my guest, honey . . . He's down the road apiece at that doughnut shop near the interstate . . . We used to have a nice little eatery nearby . . . local folks, not a big chain." His hands waved irresolutely in the air. "But progress is progress . . . People like 'brand recognition' nowadays. I can't compete with HoJo and Motel 6." He gave Belle another leer and added, "If anyone can get that bozo to shape up, I guess it'd be a looker like you . . . And, hey, if you ain't doin' nothin' later . . . stop back, okay? We got some vacancies. Take a load off your feet."

"School business doesn't leave me much free time."

"I know how it is."

Belle smiled her sixth fake smile of the morning, then hurried out to her car and drove back toward the interstate and the Whole Earth Doughnut Company, a glossy, glass-facaded building devoted to satisfying the human urge for comfort food. She parked near the shop's east entrance, then realizing her car would be easily visible from the building's interior, decided to leave the windows down. There was something so pleasant about the aroma of sun-baked auto—a last gasp of summer irresponsibility.

The Whole Earth Doughnut Company was awash in the mingled perfumes of cinnamon, sugar, chocolate icing, fruit jam, and coffee—not exactly health food but a good deal more tempting. Behind the counter were an impressive array of three dozen different types of doughnuts, sweet rolls, crullers, and plate-sized spiral confections thick with frosted goo. Belle considered one of the spirals, but instead opted for a time-trusted jelly doughnut as she perused the customers. A retirement-age couple sat at a windowside table, three construction workers hunched over coffee and crullers nearby, and a young man with a Rex Sox cap sat alone at a counter staring moodily through the far window. His confection choice was chocolate-coated and dotted with a plethora of multicolored sprinkles. Belle wondered if this was part of a "nutritious breakfast"; she grabbed her doughnut and walked toward him.

"Are you Ricky?"

"Yeah . . . who are you?"

"I'm the lady you sent the fax to."

"Wow . . . cool . . . How'd you find me here?" Ricky looked around the Whole Earth as though he'd previously considered such a public and impersonal place the ultimate hideout.

"I work for a private detective agency on occasion . . . what you might call a subcontractor . . . We specialize in finding people who wish to remain hidden."

"Cool . . . Subcontractor," Ricky repeated. "Way cool."

Belle found herself affixing another pasted-on smile. "I also happen to be a crossword expert, Ricky." She stressed the word "expert." "Those were very interesting puzzles you faxed me. Were you the constructor?"

"Huh?" He scratched his head and glanced at the construction workers as if they might have secret knowledge of the proper response to females' peculiar questions.

"Did you make up those puzzles?" Belle said, looking for words she thought Ricky might understand. "Did you design them—or write the clues?"

"Who me?"

Belle gritted her teeth and broadened her phony smile. "Of course . . . you."

"No," he admitted after a long moment of silence, "I don't know who made them up."

"I see. Then how did you happen to send them to me?"

A look of panic darted across Ricky's stealthy face. "I'm not gonna get in trouble, am I? Mr. Hacket, over at the motel." He cocked his thumb in the Blue Hill's direction. "He said he'd fire me if I got into any more trouble."

"No, you won't get into trouble." Belle tried to sound reassuring, but in reality she had no idea how much difficulty Ricky might already be facing.

"What'll you give me for telling?"

"Give you . . . ?"

"Yeah. What'll you give me? Some old lady handed me twenty bucks to send them to you. Each time. Twenty bucks. That's a lot of dough. And she paid extra for the faxes, too. So, what'll you give me if I tell you who she is?"

"Some old lady?"

"Yeah."

"How old?"

"Like old . . . you know . . . like my grandma, maybe."

"Where did you meet her?"

"At the motel. Where else?" Ricky suddenly seemed to realize his demand for payment hadn't been properly addressed. "Hey . . . hold on, what're you gonna give me?"

Belle ignored the question. "She's staying at the motel? In which cabin?"

"You gotta give me something first."

Belle opened her purse.

"Nah," he said, "I don't want money."

"What do you want, then?"

He grinned broadly, a swagger beginning in his still-scrawny body. "Come out to my car and I'll tell you."

Belle shook her head, put a twenty-dollar bill on the table, and said, "Just tell me what cabin the old lady's in, Ricky."

"Nah . . . I said too much already. You're not gettin' any more unless you come out to my car."

"What's in your car?"

"You'll see."

Belle thought for a second. "Okay, but just for a minute."

She returned the twenty to her purse and followed him through the shop's west entrance. At the rear of the building, almost hidden by a gigantic Dumpster, stood Ricky's old and rusting gray Honda. The rear window was littered with Grateful Dead stickers. He smiled and said, "This is my ride. Pretty nice, huh? It's a real solid piece of machinery. Just needs some new paint, is all. You're not into the Dead, are you?"

Belle found herself growing increasingly impatient—and nervous, a sensation she didn't like. "Look, Ricky," she said, raising her voice and pulling herself erect as if her physical attitude could overcome his recalcitrance. "I didn't come here to discuss automobiles or attempts at music. What is it you want?"

He chuckled and tried for a come-hither look. "Just a kiss . . . That's all. You're a pretty lady."

"I don't think so."

Despite Belle's authoritative tone, Ricky grabbed her upper arms and squeezed tightly, forcing her against the car. Although no taller than she was, years of wrestling with lawn mowers, saws, and other yard-maintenance equipment had made him a good deal stronger. Belle tried to twist loose, but he held tight.

"That's it, Ricky," she said. "You're in serious trouble now."

Ricky's thumbs released their pressure slightly. "What do you mean?"

"Mr. Hacket hired me."

Ricky leaped back, a horrified expression on his face.

"He wanted me to find out what you were up to. He's not going to be pleased when he hears about this."

"No. Wait. I was just joking around . . . Please . . . You can't tell him . . ."

When Belle didn't answer, Ricky's worried speech rushed forward. "The old lady with the crosswords . . . She's in cabin fifteen. It's the last one on the left—kinda hidden by all the trees . . . Please don't tell Mr. Hacket. He's gonna fire me for sure."

Belle took a minute to make it appear as if she was considering his request.

"Come on, lady," he repeated, "please."

"Okay," Belle acquiesced, "but don't you ever pull a stunt like that again. Not with anyone!"

"I won't. Honest, I won't. I swear." Ricky looked as if he might momentarily begin to cry.

Belle stepped past him and began circling the doughnut shop toward her own car. When she was nearly out of sight, he called out: "Wait a minute, if you're working for Mr. Hacket, how come you didn't ask him where the old lady was."

"I guess I forgot," Belle answered, and disappeared around the corner.

As fortunate as she'd been to outmaneuver Ricky, it had taken time, and more important, it had forced her to leave her car not only unlocked but unattended. As a result, Belle was completely unaware of the shadowy figure who had slipped into the backseat in her absence.

CHAPTER

28

"... I've been trying to reach her since eight-fifteen this morning, Rosco. It simply isn't like Belle not to answer her phone. Especially as she was expecting my call ..."

Sara Briephs' voice emanated concern tinged with a hint of regal impatience. Before responding, Rosco glanced at his watch, then chose his words carefully; the last thing he wanted was to further rile an already perturbed lady.

"I haven't spoken to her today, Sara, but last night she mentioned she'd be home all day working on tomorrow's crossword for the *Crier*. She must be so deep in thought, she can't hear the phone. You know how Belle is."

Sara cleared her throat, then took a purposeful breath. "I see," she began, "so your contact last night was only via the telephone?"

Rosco frowned at the air. Dealing with older people, especially those who adhered to a rigid etiquette, could be

trying. He was about to respond that he and Belle maintained separate—and independent—lives when Sara's
voice continued with a swift:

"I hope you don't think I'm prying, Rosco. I don't mean
to suggest that Belle might have . . . spent the night with
you . . ." Her voice faltered ever so slightly, then charged
ahead in typical Yankee fashion. "Heaven knows, I'm not
accusing you of impropriety . . . or . . . or wantonness . . .
I'm not an old hen, as some people believe; I'm well aware
that relationships develop differently nowadays than they
did when I was young. Intimacy between a modern couple . . . well, no more need be said."

Rosco shook his head, then glanced across his office. He
tried to imagine a young Sara and her swains—an affluent
group from a bygone era whose antics probably ran to
such "crimes" as putting salt in the sugar bowl or hiding a
gentleman caller's hat. "You're not prying, Sara," he said.
"Belle was at her home last night. I was in my apartment."
Then he changed the subject. "Did you speak to her
answering machine? Ask her to pick up the telephone?"

"Absolutely! I've called four times, and each time mentioned that my message was urgent. If she were home, she
would have heard me."

Rosco smiled. He wondered if Belle was fully aware of
the demands involved in her newfound friendship with
Sara. "Perhaps the tape machine was muted so Belle could
work undisturbed."

"Oh, I sincerely doubt that. It's not like her to be so
spineless. The girl has extraordinary powers of concentration."

"I wouldn't worry, Sara. Perhaps, she's at the market
or—"

"For two hours? You know as well as I do that Belle

can't cook anything more complicated than deviled eggs."

Despite himself, Rosco found a sense of unease creeping into his thoughts. "Well," he began, "I'm sure there's a logical—"

"I'd be a good deal more concerned if I were you, Rosco, especially given this G.O.L.D. Fund debacle." Sara's voice cracked suddenly. "Oh, dear," she gasped. "Oh, dear. I didn't intend to tell you yet."

"What about the G.O.L.D. Fund?"

"Oh, dear," Sara repeated. "Oh, my goodness. This is a dreadful dilemma."

Rosco thrummed his fingers on his desktop. "Perhaps you'd better begin at the beginning," he said.

After a long silence, Sara responded, "I don't mean to sound secretive . . . or . . . or as if Belle and I have been scheming behind your back. But my news involves your present employer, Mr. Edison 'Tom' Pepper." She paused again as if ordering her thoughts into organized ranks. "It's simply that I'm afraid your integrity may be compromised if I disclose this information to you . . . You do have a privileged client-employer relationship with Mr. Pepper, do you not?"

Rosco's fingers tapped the desk again. "Yes, Sara, I do. But you know me well enough to realize I'd dissolve my relationship with Mr. Pepper in a second if I believed he'd broken any laws."

"Oh, dear," Sara repeated. "This is why I needed to speak with Belle first. It was the crossword, you see . . . that one she brought to my house . . . the one with all the monetary clues."

Rosco felt another prickle of fear. Vauriens dead, Fogram, Genie, Jamaica missing. "What did you discover, Sara?" he asked.

She pondered the request for the merest split second.

"Your Tom Pepper is nothing more than a high-rolling con man, Rosco. That's the information I needed to share with Belle."

"What—" Rosco began, but Sara cut him off.

"I have now conferred with several old and trusted friends, all of whom had the misfortune to invest in your Mr. Pepper's G.O.L.D. Fund. Although initially reluctant to broach the subject, they eventually overcame their embarrassment. Money is not something we WASPs are comfortable discussing . . . At any rate, the result of my inquiries is this: The G.O.L.D. Fund is a total sham. It's no more than a sophisticated Ponzi scheme—similar to the one perpetrated on the world some eighty years ago by that horrible Charles Ponzi."

Rosco stared into space. "You're certain about this?" he finally asked.

"Do you mean about Mr. Ponzi's fraud or the 'reliability of my sources'—I believe that's the correct term? Is that what you're asking me?"

Rosco hesitated. "Yes, I guess that's what I'm asking."

Sara's reply was frosty. "Neither I nor my friends are in the habit of spreading malicious rumors—"

"I didn't suggest they—"

Sara barreled past the comment. "My friends and I have concluded that Pepper has been using monies from new investors to repay clients with a prior claim: an ever-revolving pool of the naive, the hopeful—or the greedy. Naturally, the scheme relies upon maintaining the strictest secrecy as to investors' identities. It wouldn't do for them to publicly discuss their portfolios' shortcomings—which made my ferreting out of information all the more arduous."

Again, Rosco tried to interrupt; and again, Sara ignored him.

"After a good deal of heated discussion amongst my companions and me, we reached the opinion that it's a matter of weeks, or perhaps even days, before Pepper's entire machine collapses. I needn't remind you, young man, that these people are among Newcastle's wealthiest individuals . . . They sit on the boards of every corporation and charitable institution in this town. How this *nouveau* snake charmer was able to hoodwink them will remain a mystery to me. *I* spotted him as a ne'er-do-well at first meeting . . ."

Suddenly Vic Fogram and his panicked telephone call fell into place. But recognizing the connection between the Red Admiral's owner and the CFOs of Newcastle made Rosco feel a deeper concern for Belle's safety. "Belle was aware of your activities, I take it?" he asked.

"Of course! But, as I mentioned, we thought it wise, given your position with Pepper—"

Rosco groaned in frustration. "I wish you'd had the confidence to share your suspicions with me earlier."

Sara didn't respond for a long and wounded moment. When she spoke, her words sounded surprisingly chagrined. "You don't think this Pepper character would—"

"Pepper's brother-in-law is dead, Sara. His wife is missing, along with Miss Nevisson and a saloon owner who also had invested with him. I don't know what type of crime—or crimes—we're dealing with, but I do know that amateurs and homicides don't mix . . . Now, what exactly were you and Belle planning to do with the G.O.L.D. Fund information?"

"I hope I haven't done anything to put that girl in jeopardy . . ." Tears, or what sounded like tears, clogged Sara's voice.

"I'll find her," Rosco said.

"I know you're crazy about her." The redoubtable lady

paused; Rosco could hear worry slowly give way to pragmatism. "It's high time you two made a stronger commitment to one another."

Rosco shook his head. A quiet smile crept over his face. "I'm working on it, Sara. I'm working on it . . ."

"In my day—"

"Sara!"

Silence again filled the phone line, broken, at length, by Sara's contrite: "Belle's extremely fond of you, you know."

"I know," Rosco answered.

"And she's a perfectly lovely girl."

"I know that, too, Sara."

"I'm not intruding, Rosco. I'm simply stating obvious facts."

"Let's return to your information on Pepper," Rosco answered.

"Oh, I supplied the police department with all my findings," was Sara's airy reply. "That delightful Lieutenant Lever spoke with me."

"What?" Rosco didn't know which statement was more astonishing: Sara's admission that she'd already told Lever—or that she described him as "delightful."

"We had a most erudite conversation."

"With Al?"

"Is there another Lever on the force?"

Rosco shut his eyes tight. He was beginning to think he'd been trapped in an ancient Burns and Allen routine.

"I informed the lieutenant that accusations of fraud could, and would, be backed up in a court of law. I told him that my friends—all leading lights in this city—were more than willing to come forward with evidence. No one will ever accuse Sara Crane Briephs of being an apathetic citizen . . . Albert said he would begin proceedings directly."

Rosco mouthed a nonplussed "Albert?" while Sara's disembodied voice reasserted itself. "Now, the more pressing problem is what has happened to your Belle?"

"I'll drive over there right now."

"I know you don't appreciate me meddling in your affairs, Rosco, but I feel I should also mention that Albert wholeheartedly agrees with me on the subject of Belle's security."

Rosco raised disbelieving eyebrows. "I'm on my way, Sara."

"Good boy," was her lofty response before the line went dead.

Rosco shook his head and muttered, "Albert?" as he punched in Belle's number.

Her answering machine picked up on the first ring, sounding six beeps to indicate she had previous messages. "Belle?" he found himself almost shouting. "Are you there? This is important . . . I have to talk to you . . ." He waited ten more seconds until silence forced the machine to cut him off. He punched in a second number.

In the middle of the first ring a typically harassed voice barked: "Lever."

Rosco's reply was sarcastic. "Hello, *Albert.*"

Lever chortled. "That's some classy old dame, Polly— Crates . . . We had a nice little chitchat about you and your lady friend."

"So I gathered."

"She wants you two to get hitched, she tell you that?"

"I believe Sara might have mentioned it."

Lever's laughter grew.

"Did you bring in Pepper yet, Al? Or have you decided to go into the marriage-brokering business?"

"You never read the sign on my door, Polly—Crates? It says 'homicide,' not 'bunko.' "

"I meant the department, not you personally, Al. Although it wouldn't do you any harm to get up and move around once in a while . . ."

"Temper temper, buddy . . . The information on Pepper went straight to the DA's office as soon as Mrs. Briephs' chauffeur drove it over. The DA started drooling like a wolf over a baby lamb. He loves this stuff. Called a judge—not Lawrence—and got a warrant issued in five minutes flat . . . I'm afraid the DA doesn't think much of your employer."

"*Former* employer, would be more like it . . . So the bunko boys hauled him in?"

"That's the odd part, Polly—Crates. Somebody must have tipped him off . . . The squad car arrived at Pepper's estate forty-five minutes ago, but it seems your boy's flown the coop. Disappeared into thin air."

"What?"

"The butler maintained he hadn't seen his boss since he went out for a drive at around nine o'clock last night. Never came home. The boys searched his house—zippo. We put out an APB, but after twelve hours? Hell, he could be anywhere."

Rosco let out an exasperated sigh.

"It gets worse," Lever said. "Here's another little tidbit we learned this morning . . . The truck that killed Vauriens?"

"Yeah?"

"It turned up at two A.M. in a vacant lot near the interstate . . . Reported stolen three days ago in Brockton . . . Abe Jones dusted it for prints, but there wasn't a single one. Interior *and* exterior—all slick as a whistle."

Rosco let the information sink in. "Do me a favor, will you, Al?"

"What's that?"

"Put out an APB on Belle, too."

"Lost girlfriends, Polly—Crates . . . you know how the saying goes . . . Besides, I don't think Mrs. B would—"

"Mrs. 'B'?" Rosco's tone was incredulous.

"A sweet old lady like that, what else are you going to call her?"

Rosco pulled the phone from his ear and stared at it long and hard. Sweet, he thought, erudite, delightful: what was the world coming to? "Just ask your guys to be on the lookout, Al . . . That's all I'm saying."

"Hey . . . Maybe she ran off with Pepper!" Lever laughed at his own joke.

"You're a very sensitive guy, *Albert*. Anybody ever tell you that?"

"Yeah, as a matter of fact."

"Please don't tell me who."

CHAPTER

29

As Belle buckled her seat belt, she had an eerie sensation; as if the atmosphere inside her car had suddenly shifted. She stared anxiously through the window, expecting to see lightning flickering overhead, while her skin and hair prickled as if affected by a rogue electrical charge. She glanced around the parking area of the Whole Earth Doughnut. Nothing seemed out of the ordinary—another early-autumn New England day on a sunny patch of asphalt near a busy interstate. A Lexus sedan and gray pickup truck arrived bearing two more customers for a midmorning snack. Belle noticed that neither person needed to stock up on extra calories as they waddled toward the entrance. Why is it, she wondered, that we humans reward ourselves with the very foods that most harm our bodies? Why aren't we genetically engineered to yearn for carrot sticks or tofu squares? But the thought only made her wish she could duck in for another sugared treat.

Instead, she turned her key in the ignition and retraced her route to the secluded Blue Hill Cabins. There she circled past the office, searching for cabin fifteen, which she found sequestered within a patch of scruffy trees. Behind the small structure stood a dense woods that spread into the surrounding acreage. As Ricky had suggested, the site was well removed from the other cabins—a perfect place for a stakeout. Belle noted this with satisfaction as she silently repeated the phrase "subcontractor to the Polycrates Agency." She considered her handling of Ricky and his peculiar employer pretty darn professional.

She parked her car facing the motel exit but close enough to cabin fifteen so that she'd be able to get a good look at the old lady who'd given Ricky the two crosswords. She then pulled out a map and slouched down in her seat in imitation of a tourist examining likely spots to visit. If it took all day before the woman showed her face, Belle would wait.

The idea of waiting *patiently* in one place, however, lasted all of eight minutes. Belle checked the clock, drummed her fingers on the dashboard, repositioned the map, checked the clock again, opened and closed the glove compartment, and after an additional seven or eight minutes muttered an exasperated: "This could take forever."

She stepped out of the car and stretched stagily. Not a soul was in sight, and the October chill became noticeably colder as a raft of patchy clouds drifted in to block the sun. Belle shivered and closed her jacket around her neck. For good measure, she stretched again, arching her back slightly as if the muscles had stiffened after a long and arduous drive. A breeze rushed at the neglected trees, sending a noisy shower of autumn leaves scooting over the dry ground. It was the only sound in the deserted place.

Belle's bravado began to desert her. Although she'd

angled her car, preparing it for a hasty departure, she realized she was completely out of sight of the motel office. And if Mr. Hacket were busy watching television—a likely activity—she could scream her head off for a month of Sundays and he'd never hear her cries.

Anxiety made her tap the left front tire of her car with the toe of her shoe. The car was something she knew, and the act of touching it made her feel as if she had a backup, a solid means of escape. Unbidden, Rosco's previous worries flooded her brain, but these she argued away by reminding herself that the operative words were "tomorrow" and "soon." According to the crossword puzzle, no potentially criminal activities could possibly happen today. Belle tended to subscribe to logical, linear thought when it suited her.

She took two steps toward the cabin. A little voice in her head whispered: *Curiosity killed the cat*. This was immediately followed by a remembered quotation from Benjamin Franklin's almanac: "The cat in gloves catches no mice."

Belle wiggled her fingers, smiled smugly, then strode up the dirt path until she reached cabin fifteen and its small stoop fashioned out of graying cedar. Her shoes sounded a hollow *clip-clop* as she mounted the stoop—enough noise to arouse anyone inside. She listened at the door, heard nothing, raised her hand to knock, then stopped short and turned to glance behind her. She had the distinct feeling she was being watched.

Belle left the stoop and studied the woods behind her car. Overhung with bittersweet vines, the trees were in sorry repair; broken limbs lay entwined in the suffocating tendrils whose brilliant orange berries looked like a thousand restive, foxy eyes. Belle decided that nothing larger than a feral cat could be hiding among such a tortuous jungle.

She approached the stoop once more, brought her fist up, rapped three solid times on the paneled door, then immediately jumped back. There was no point in letting some crazed old lady attack her with a broom. Three minutes passed, then five, then seven. The door remained solidly closed. There was no hint of movement inside.

Belle glanced toward cabins fourteen, thirteen, and twelve. Barely visible within the rustic compound, they also appeared vacant. "Okay," she muttered aloud, "this is stupid. I'm alone."

She studied her hands, found they were trembling, and stuffed them in her jeans' pockets as if nonchalance were her middle name and trailing old ladies a harmless pastime. Then she walked to the cabin's front window and tried to peer in. A dusty green shade had been lowered, and although it boasted a large rip, the cabin's interior was too dark to discern. Belle pushed at the window frame, but it didn't budge; peeling yellow paint flaked off on her hands.

She walked to the side of the cabin, where she spotted another locked window, then to the rear, where she found a second door. She tried the handle; the knob turned; the door opened about six inches. An inside chain lock prevented further movement.

Belle brought her face to the opening. "Is anyone home?"

No reply.

She pushed harder on the door, but the chain held fast.

"Hello . . . ? Ma'am . . . ? I have a message from Ricky. The fax didn't go through. He says he needs a second copy of the puzzle."

No response.

"I—" Belle began again, but at that instant she was

snatched by the elbows and slammed face forward against the door.

" 'Something wicked this way comes,' " a voice hissed in her ear. " 'Open, locks, whoever knocks!' "

CHAPTER

30

Pitched forward within her assailant's grasp, Belle could see nothing but the cabin's dark and mildewy siding. Flecked with slimy moss and red circles that she guessed were mold spores, it was an unappetizing sight, and made her suddenly remember the potential harm lurking in such airless and vacant spaces: rabid rodents and poisonous ticks and spiders being her primary concerns. The irony of the situation didn't go unnoticed. Here she was, caught by two brutal hands, and her brain insisted on dredging up information on Lyme disease and the lethal Hanta virus and how its flulike symptoms had finally arrived full-blown in the northeastern United States.

The viselike grip shoved Belle further earthward. "Why were you breaking into my cabin?" This time Belle recognized the voice as female, although definitely not "old," as Ricky had indicated. It also carried a down-home accent that Belle pegged as being Texan or maybe Arizonan.

Again, she thought of the Hanta virus—spawned by this

woman's native land. Belle tried to hold her breath, then pushed backward mightily. But the movement only gained her a few inches; her face was still perilously close to the cabin walls. "I wasn't trying to break in."

Fingers dug into her elbows, finding the nerves and making her hands go limp while the woman's upper body pressed hard against Belle's back. "Right. This was a social call, huh? You're into it deep, sister. Do you want me to march you over to the manager's office and have him call the cops?"

Some small sag in Belle's spine must have indicated her unwillingness to participate in that scenario. It was a reaction her adversary noticed instantly. "He tries to run a nice place," the woman continued in an even tougher tone. "He'll have a fit when he learns stooges like you are trying to filch things from guests."

"I'm not a thief," Belle spluttered. Her fingers were now numb; her chin almost rested on her chest; and the acrid scent of mildew and rotting wood singed her nostrils.

"Well, you're not the dame who cleans. And you're definitely not my fairy godmother. Let's see, lawyer for my loser of a soon-to-be ex-hubby? I don't think so . . . Private dick trying to get the goods on my 'gentlemen acquaintances'? Don't make me laugh." The woman suddenly spun Belle around. She was tall and sinewy, anywhere from forty to fifty plus; an obsession with serious exercise was revealed in a skintight outfit: a powder-blue Lycra top and white stretch jeans tucked into Western-cut aligator-skin boots. The fabric looked as if it had been painted on. But the cowgirl routine was marred by the color of the woman's eyes. They were as gray, translucent, and watchful as a weimaraner's. "All right, I want some answers. Start talking. What brings you here?"

Belle's mind raced through possible replies; her ability

to reinvent her story and think on her feet had been exemplary recently, but she intuited that this opponent was more canny than the lovelorn Ricky or his smarmy boss. Belle decided on truth. "I'm the crossword editor of the *Evening Crier*," she said.

The statement brought no reaction from the woman; as if the information was common knowledge. She only stared; her eyes remaining icy cold. "And that gives you the right to break into this room?"

"I was told to meet someone here," Belle answered.

The woman sneered, but didn't immediately respond. Belle recognized that she was being judged on criteria beyond her control—her relative youth, effortlessly slim figure, and naturally pale blond hair. In comparison, Belle's opponent obviously spent a good deal of time worrying about her figure, and her head boasted a mess of overprocessed curls the color and consistency of scorched hay.

"And who might that 'someone' have been, Snow White?"

"An 'old lady.' " Belle regretted the words the second they left her mouth.

"Nice, cutie. Real nice. Want to dig yourself another grave?"

Belle stammered a reply. "Ricky . . . the boy who works here . . . cutting the grass and everything . . . He told me about the lady . . . She's been sending me crossword puzzles and I . . . well, he must have gotten the cabin number confused . . . If this is your—" But even as she spoke, Belle realized how wrong the statement was. Ricky was dim, but he knew the value of a twenty-dollar bill. Acting as liaison for the mysterious puzzle constructor, he wouldn't have mistaken her room number. Unless . . . Belle felt a chill run up her spine. Was it possible Ricky and his boss were in league with the kidnappers? Was it possible they'd led her into a trap? "You're not Doris Quick, are you?" Belle asked suddenly.

"Who the hell is that?"

"Or Billy Vauriens' girlfriend?"

"Look, Sleeping Beauty, I'm just a dame renting a cabin at this *deluxe* resort for an indefinite period of time. If this Ricky guy said I was 'old,' then he can go to blazes . . . You, too . . ." The steely grip lessened. Belle found her arms hanging free, but her wrists and hands still felt tingly and inert. "A word to the wise."

Something in the woman's tone or speech triggered a vague recollection in Belle. "What did you say?"

The woman began stalking toward the cabin's front entry. "I said you can both go to blazes—"

"No . . . about a 'word to the wise'?" Again, a surge of unpleasant but unnamed associations flooded Belle's brain.

"I thought you said you did crosswords? Don't tell me you've never heard the expression."

Unintentionally, Belle's mind filled with the memory of Jamaica at the Patriot Yacht Club . . . Jamaica flirting with Rosco and later telling Belle he was only a "transitional" mate. "On the rebound with a private dick." Those were the phrases she'd used, and when Genie had protested, Jamaica had responded with: "A word to the wise . . ."

"I thought you puzzle types were brains," the woman continued. "Goes to show ya . . ."

"Someone sent me crosswords," Belle said. "If it wasn't you, then who?" Her thoughts were tumbling over themselves. If this woman hadn't supplied Ricky with the puzzles, what was the connection with cabin fifteen? "Two women disappeared . . . a yachting accident . . . perhaps you heard about it?"

"I'm not from around here, but I'll tell ya something,

sweet pea: types who go 'yachting' don't hold much sympathy for me. And girlies who try to sneak into other folks' rooms don't do no better. I suggest you get outta here, while the gettin's good." The woman continued toward the cabin's front entry. This time it was Belle who grabbed her arm.

"One of them was a well-known actress . . . a TV star . . . I don't care where you're from, you couldn't have missed it."

The woman stopped; a thin smile creased her hardened face. "Oh, yeah . . . now I remember . . . Newcastle, Mass. . . . I didn't put two and two together . . . I seen it on the news . . . Jamaica Nevisson, the star of *Crescent Heights*—"

Belle pressed ahead eagerly. "That's right . . . Jamaica's a big celebrity . . . and we think . . ." She paused; the pronoun "we" sounded weak; it had neither power nor specificity. She altered her tone and opted for a more official approach. "The police believe that Miss Nevisson's high profile may have inspired the crime. A photographer known to be stalking her in L.A. was apprehended here in Newcastle."

The woman's smile grew. Belle recognized the expression: fascination mingled with pride at a peripheral connection to fame. "Far-out . . ." she murmured, then quickly turned suspicious again. "But how does this cabin fit in? Unless they're hiding under the floorboards, I haven't seen anyone other than me using the place."

"That's what I'm trying to discover. I was informed that an 'old lady' had paid to have crossword puzzles sent to me—each of which contained clues concerning the women's disappearance."

"Uh-huh," the woman said. "Let me get this straight . . . You thought you'd find this old broad sitting here, and she'd up and spill the beans? Is that it?" The icy eyes narrowed and the smile froze. "I gotta tell ya, sister. That is one sorry tale."

"It's the truth," Belle said.

"Yeah, and I'm Dolly Parton . . . You got a husband?"

Belle was so surprised by the question that she blurted out a hurried: "I did. Yes. A former husband."

"What happened? He catch you sleeping around—or vice versa?"

"Neither, in actual fact."

The woman snorted. "Right."

While Belle responded with an increasingly prim, "We didn't have that kind of relationship."

"The sex kind, you mean, honey?" She laughed heartily. "You know, Snow White, men will deceive you every chance they get."

Again, Belle had an eerie sense of déjà vu. "Men were deceivers ever"—the quotation that had appeared in the first crossword puzzle. Was it possible this woman was indeed Ricky's "old lady"?

"There's a line from a play that has a similar message," Belle said.

"Oh yeah?" The woman seemed disinterested, although Belle sensed the attitude was a sham.

"The verse begins: 'Sigh no more, ladies, sigh no more / Men were deceivers ever / One foot in sea, and one on shore . . . ' "

The woman's head jerked up, and her eyes darkened with an expression Belle couldn't read. "How do you know this stuff?"

"I told you. I construct crossword puzzles."

"That doesn't mean you can quote all of Shakespeare."

"How did you know it was Shakespeare?" was Belle's response.

"Lucky guess . . . I mean, who else spouts stuff like

that?" The woman stared at Belle. After a moment her voice continued with a level: "We had to read that junk in high school."

"You must have a photographic memory."

"I was good with poems . . . You memorize something when you're young . . ."

Belle returned the woman's inscrutable gaze. "You wouldn't happen to remember the line that begins 'Bait the hook well: this fish will bite . . . '?"

The woman opened her mouth to speak, then seemed to reconsider the response. "Can't say I do."

"Both quotations are found in *Much Ado About Nothing,* and they appeared in a crossword I received in connection with this case—also sent from this mysterious 'old lady.' "

The woman turned her back. "Well, doll, you'd better find her, then."

"I'm guessing I already have," Belle answered easily. "I'm thinking that a sixteen-year-old might consider a woman past forty to be 'old.' "

The woman spun around, her face contorted in rage. "Do I look like an old hag to you? Do I look as if I'm over the hill?"

"What can you tell me about Jamaica and Genie's disappearance?"

"Not a damned thing!"

"Then why did you send those crosswords?"

A rustling in the tangled woods behind the cabins made them both turn toward the sound.

"Damn you!" the woman spat out. "You're not going to ruin this again!" In a single, fluid motion, she grabbed Belle, pulled a snub-nosed .38 from inside one of her tall boots, and buried the muzzle between Belle's shoulder blades. "Walk!" the woman ordered.

CHAPTER

31

The gun barrel felt warm against Belle's back, a fact she found surprising. Metal, she told herself, is usually cold. Cutlery is chilly; the band of my wristwatch is cool when I strap it on each morning. Then she remembered that the gun had been hidden within the woman's boot. It had been prewarmed to body temperature. This process of deduction filled the space of two strides toward the woods and the person hiding there. The next step and a half Belle devoted to queries such as: What did the woman mean by "ruin this again"? If she knows me, why don't I remember her? What roles do Ricky and his boss play? If I break free, will they help me? Or are these three people working together?

It's amazing how fear elongates time, and how it crystallizes reason.

"Dammit! I know you're out there!" the woman shouted as she impelled Belle toward the screen of trees. "I'm going to shoot this one if you don't make an appearance. You wouldn't like that, would you? Little Miss Manners."

Belle remained mute. She studied the thick foliage, thinking that this might well be the last she saw of the earth. She noticed that the bittersweet vines had covered almost every bough and branch, leaping from one woody arm to the next like Tarzan flying through the jungle. Little Miss Manners, she thought, what a sorry epitaph. A choicer phrase inadvertently surfaced: Mark Twain's "Be good and you will be lonesome." I'm not all that proper and ladylike, she wanted to protest, but what would have been the use? Little Miss Manners. At least Sara would approve. But then, Belle realized, Sara would never know.

"I'm not pulling any more punches here," the woman yelled, then slipped her free arm around Belle's neck in a stranglehold while the gun's muzzle continued boring into her spine. "You can bet your life on it this time . . . Now, you show your face or we'll have an 'accident' on our hands, because, in reality, I caught this one trying to break into your cabin."

"Whose cabin?" Belle managed to gasp.

"Shut your trap," the woman ordered before resuming her forest-directed diatribe. "I'm telling you, I'm not waiting any longer. I've been playing too many games as it is."

The woods remained bitterly silent, which only seemed to increase the woman's anxiety. She prodded Belle again. "I'm running out of patience, here, and you know it. And you also know I'm renowned for my temper. You're pushing me to do something I don't want to do."

The continued lack of reply made the woman's voice explode. "Dammit! I knew we should have planned the job better. Too much was left to chance, but that's the way he wanted it . . . 'An accident,' he kept saying . . . We've got to make it look like a tragic, freak occurrence." Her voice rose in pitch; hysteria entered the words. "That fire should have been so easy . . . two women asleep . . . the boat engulfed in flames . . . if they manage to escape in the yacht's tender, they're burned and weakened . . . They can't survive the night, and their battered inflatable finally washes ashore . . . No rescue, no remains . . . The sharks finish the job . . . Such a neat, neat scenario."

Belle felt a tortured sigh ripple through the woman's body. "We didn't count on the damn propane tank blowing, and those bozos extinguishing the blaze before the *Orion* could sink . . . We didn't count on you surviving. How could we have, especially after we'd taken the tender? I told him we should have killed you first, but he wouldn't hear of it, would he? . . . And you, Miss High-and-Mighty-Fancy-Home, Miss Snooty Manners, herself . . . You couldn't leave well enough alone, could you? Had to act like Lady Bountiful . . . Invite me to visit because I was 'so distraught' . . . 'Poor Jamaica,' getting older and uglier . . . Damn you, Genie!"

"Genie?" Belle gasped. "Jamaica?" Despite the gun and the choke hold, she tried to twist her head toward her captor. "Jamaica?" she repeated.

In response, Jamaica rammed her knees into the backs of Belle's almost buckling her. "Shut up!"

" 'False face must hide what false heart doth know.' " The disembodied voice traveled solidly from the woods and through the trees. "Remember that, Jamaica? *Macbeth, The Scottish Play* . . . ? Of course you do. 'Something wicked this way comes.' Right?"

"The quote from the second crossword!" Belle blurted out while Genie moved slowly into view.

"Belle," Genie said in a passionless voice. "It's good to see you again." She leveled hate-filled eyes on her friend, but her tone remained frighteningly serene. "You didn't count on my finding this unsuspecting ally, did you, Jamaica? Neither you nor Tom. When your original plan failed, and I escaped, you assumed rightly I'd be too terrified to go to the police—that I'd believe any exposure would put me at risk . . . After all, Tom owns this town, you must have promised yourselves. 'We merely have to find her . . . The rest will be easy . . .' "

The two women gauged each other. Although Belle continued to be held hostage between them, their enmity was so acute they scarcely noticed her.

"It must have been unpleasant for you two to find me capable of communicating anonymously," Genie added. "I turned the table quite handily, didn't I?"

Jamaica didn't answer, so Genie continued. "Tom, I'm sure, was especially annoyed. His anger can be brutal, can't it, Jamaica? . . . No, I forget, you must have been sequestered elsewhere. You could hardly afford to hole up in my house . . . Perhaps you haven't yet experienced his displays of rage."

"Tom has been nothing but gentle and loving with me, Genie. Very loving. A side you obviously have never seen."

"Give him time," Genie replied. "He'll change. He's a master . . . deceiver."

"It's been almost three years."

"Really? My congratulations on concealing your mutual ardor so long . . . But three years of clandestine meetings is not the same as a marriage . . . I assume that's what you've both been intending—a state of wedded bliss? Were you planning to scoot off to some faraway and deserted island? I'm so sorry to disappoint you. Poor Jamaica—always a bridesmaid, never a bride."

"Damn you, Genie! Damn you for having everything— and for lording it over me every chance you got!" In her frustration and wrath, Jamaica yanked her arm from

Belle's neck. At the same time the hand holding the .38 slipped to her side, leaving Belle suddenly free, but too stunned and nervous to move.

"You're a whore, Jamaica. You always have been."

"At least I give my men some fun!"

"Do you let them try on your wigs while you're going at it, or is that too kinky?"

"Are you asking me about Tom's preferences, Genie? Because I certainly know all about yours. Your husband is a great talker, my dear . . . And dynamite in bed. Though I guess you wouldn't know that."

"Touché, Jamaica—although a trifle vulgar. But that was always your strong point, wasn't it? Lessons learned from the casting couch, no doubt. It's too bad you're no longer young enough to use them."

"Tom doesn't care about age."

Genie smiled. "Doesn't he?" Both Belle and Jamaica felt the shift in intention. Jamaica took a single, belligerent step toward her former friend while Belle began edging slowly to the left. The gun twitched in the actress's dangling hand. "I was waiting for you at Allyn's Point."

"That's because you followed Belle." It wasn't a question; it was a statement, almost as if Genie had arranged the entire situation.

Jamaica heard the innuendo and hesitated while Belle soundlessly inched farther away, moving finally out of Jamaica's reach. "Tom and I knew Belle would lead us to you."

"And *I* knew Belle would lead *me* to *you*. Which she has." Genie's voice remained preternaturally calm. "So I'd say you and Tom are the ones in trouble now. I imagine that will be the police's response as well—especially when I tell them how cleverly you both staged that little *bon voyage* party on the *Orion*: Tom boarding at the last minute, the concerned and caring husband armed with caviar and champagne—"

"Which you lapped up, sweetie pie—"

"At Tom's urging. Looking back, the plan seems painfully obvious. My disingenuous husband with his professed dislike of the sea . . . his hunting cabin—and the trip he suddenly abandoned to spend time with 'us girls' . . ."

"No man would make me get so thoroughly soused I didn't know which end was up—"

"Jamaica, the sensible and wise. That's a new role for you, isn't it?"

"It's better than being falling-down drunk."

Genie clenched her jaw, the only movement in her otherwise passionless face. "Too bad such a marvelous and Machiavellian plan failed."

"It hasn't, honey lamb. It's only been postponed."

"I disagree." Genie took a languid step forward, while as if from the air, a flat black semiautomatic pistol appeared in her hand. Genie aimed at Jamaica's chest. "Belle was *my* unsuspecting lure. She was the one who brought you into the open. Not the other way around. *I'm* the one who's been waiting for *you* . . . And baiting you . . . You've got to be a fool if you don't think I can have Tom back. Old age isn't his bag—excuse the pun."

Genie smiled. Then without drawing a breath or blinking, without a discernible motion passing across her face or through her body, she fired.

Jamaica's hands flew helplessly through the air, clawing at her chest while her legs and torso crumpled to the reddening earth.

" 'An eye for an eye,' " Genie said as she suddenly focused on Belle.

"You must recognize that line from the last crossword I

sent . . . I suppose the sixth puzzle isn't necessary now. A shame, it would have given you a few choice night-mares . . ."

While Genie spoke she casually moved toward Jamaica's inert body, slipped her semiautomatic pistol into her rear pocket, and picked up Jamaica's fallen .38. For the first time Belle noticed she was wearing surgical gloves.

"It seems a pity, Belle . . . You've been such a help . . . But you must realize I can't afford to have a witness . . . It would have been so much easier if Jamaica had done this for me . . . Killing her was easy. You? I'm not so sure."

Belle took a horrified step backward. In her peripheral vision, she scanned the trees, the cabin's rear entrance, the path that disappeared in the direction of the parking area. If she screamed, she'd be shot before the cry left her throat. If she ran, she'd get a bullet in her back. The thought, for some reason, seemed far more terrible than dying face-to-face.

"But you'll be caught, Genie . . . If you kill me, the police will realize it was your gun—"

"Well, no, actually I'll be using Jamaica's gun." Again, a horrifying stillness suffused the tone. "I'm sure you under-stand that I've had ample opportunity to plan this situa-tion . . . You die with a bullet from Jamaica's weapon; I shoot *her* in self-defense when she tries to finish the job she began on the *Orion* . . . That's the story the police will hear. It's simple and foolproof, and half the problem is already solved . . . The only person not in the mix is my darling husband . . . The poor innocent man whose wife's best friend became so insanely jealous she tried to stage a fatal fire at sea. You have to admit my position is admirable—"

"What about the motel manager?" Belle interrupted. "What about other guests?"

"Sad to say, there are no other guests . . . And the manager, as I'm sure you've noticed, is totally deafened by his horrid television set." Again Genie smiled. "I fired two test shots on Friday. Not a soul came to investigate. Even if the noise had been heard, the average apathetic citizen is far too eager to assume the sound is that of a backfiring car rather than risk getting involved . . . You'll be missed, Belle." Genie raised Jamaica's .38 and leveled it at Belle's chest.

"You're right about that, Mrs. Pepper." Rosco's voice boomed forward as he darted around the cabin.

Genie spun toward the sound, but her reaction was too delayed and surprised to fight off the sudden intrusion. Rosco wrenched the .38 from her hand before she had time to fire.

Belle stared at Rosco. "There's a second weapon in her back pocket," she said, then gazed from Jamaica's inert body to Rosco's face. "How did you find me?"

"It wasn't quite as simple as that, Al..." Rosco answered. Although seated in Lever's office directly across from the lieutenant's desk, he was unable to take his eyes off Belle. "If I hadn't caught up with that kid Ricky... well, all I can say is, the outcome would have been anyone's guess." Rosco gazed at Belle, his look part gratitude that she was sitting beside him, and part fear of how close disaster had come.

Belle's expression remained pensive; her hands clasped her elbows as if she were cold. "Poor Jamaica," she said.

Rosco touched her arm; "She and Tom tried to kill Genie, Belle... She had a gun on you, too, remember? I'm not saying she deserved to die, but—"

"I've never witnessed a murder," was Belle's simple response.

Lever reached for his cigarettes, then glanced at Belle and put them away. "It's tough," he said. "It'll take more than a few hours to get over it."

Belle gave him a gentle smile. "You can smoke if you want, Al. It's your office."

"I'm not in the mood . . . Besides, the wife says I should quit."

Rosco stared at his former partner; a wisecrack died on his lips. Maybe Sara was right about the guy, after all; maybe a sensitive soul lurked beneath the irascible-cop exterior. Rosco shook his head in disbelief.

"What about Pepper?" he asked.

"No telling," Lever answered. "But don't worry, we'll pick him up. How long it takes to find him is another story. The bright side is that he's broken a ton of federal laws; the FBI wants him just as bad as we do."

"And Vauriens?"

"Well . . . That situation is still up in the air. Carlyle"—Al turned to Belle—"he's our ME, our medical examiner—Carlyle places time of death well before the supposed hit-and-run—which means the body was actually dumped from the speeding truck rather than hit by it. Cause of death is still listed as a fractured skull . . . But Abe discovered traces of gravel from the truck's cab that can be linked to Pepper's driveway. Whether we can pin a murder charge on Pepper remains to be seen."

"I'm sure Genie was aware of Tom's financial situation," Belle said after a moment. "That fact now seems completely obvious from clues she planted in the crosswords."

"Yeah, but she's not saying a word until her lawyer arrives," Lever replied. "However, that's a moot point as far as homicide is concerned. We have her on murder one, and we don't need her testimony to prosecute Tom on investment fraud—thanks to Mrs. B."

"You don't think there was 'just cause' in Genie's actions?" Belle suddenly asked. "Her husband and his mistress sail her into Buzzards Bay, ply her with champagne while *supposedly* celebrating a pleasant vacation, render her unconscious, set fire to the boat, then abandon her to die a horrible death? If she hadn't been physically fit enough to swim the three miles to shore, she would have drowned."

Rosco took her hand and squeezed it. "I'm sorry you were dragged into this mess."

Belle gazed at him. "That's not your fault . . . It was Genie who targeted me. I was the one who received the cryptics." Again, she was silent. When she spoke, her posture had changed; the dread and horror of the past several hours had slowly begun to ebb.

"Initially, Genie must have been in a traumatized and paranoid state . . . She was reaching out to the only person she felt she could trust. In her confusion, she must have believed clandestine activity was her only choice . . . Don't forget, Rosco, that you were working for her husband. And, no offense to you, Al, but Tom is a rich and powerful man. Genie had no idea who was in his pocket."

Belle leaned forward, the luster restored to her gray eyes. "Everything must have changed at Allyn's Point . . . Genie must have snapped when she recognized Jamaica in her dog-lady disguise. That's when revenge became the guiding motive. Maybe the *sole* motive."

"Why didn't she come forward, then? If she wanted to gun down Jamaica, she had ample opportunity." It was Lever who posed these questions.

"I'd never pretend to understand the complexities of human pathology," Belle answered. "But my guess is that Genie *intended* to make her presence known on Allyn's Point . . . When she saw Jamaica and me together—talking, in fact—she must have wondered if I'd understood the G.O.L.D. Fund references in the puzzles . . . She must have been one scared and angry lady."

"Temporary insanity," Lever mumbled under his breath. "A few years at the Whiting Psychiatric Facility, and Mrs. Pepper walks . . ."

Belle looked at him. "I suppose you're right," she said, then returned her attention to Rosco. "So the two truckers who chartered the fishing boat with Vic Fogram had nothing to do with Pepper or Vauriens?"

"Not a thing."

Belle pursued her lips in thought. "What happens to Fogram and the other G.O.L.D. Fund investors?"

"That's up to the DA," Lever answered. "But from where I sit, I'd say the chances are pretty good they'll recoup a portion of their money—"

" 'The root of all evil,' " Belle said.

Rosco beamed. "I told you she could spout Shakespeare, Al."

"That's the Bible, Polly—Crates," Lever growled. " 'The love of money is the root of all evil.' " He turned to Belle, an atypical grin plastered on his face. "Where did you find this lamebrain, anyway?"

"He found me, Al," was Belle's happy answer while Rosco stroked her fingers and smiled into her eyes.

"I'm not sure 'Mrs. B.' would consider 'lamebrain' an overly 'sensitive' comment, *Albert*," Rosco chortled.

Lever snorted, but his gruff facade had already crumbled. "You know what I'm thinking, Polly—Crates? I'm thinking there's no time like the present." Lever reached into his desk drawer and removed a large business-size envelope. "I almost forgot this, Belle . . . Someone dropped it off. Said it was urgent . . . I guess you'd better open it here in the office—in case there's a problem . . ."

Belle studied the envelope; confusion creased her forehead. "Did you get a description of the person," she asked as she hastily took the envelope, slit it open, and removed a hand-drawn crossword puzzle. Worry, surprise, and bafflement fought with her habitual curiosity. "Was it a man or a woman? Did the delivery predate my encounter with Genie?" She spread the cryptic on Lever's desk, then gazed at the two men, but their expressions remained blank.

"I'll have to check with the duty officer," Lever finally said.

"But I thought the entire situation was wrapped up," Belle responded. "Genie in custody, Flack released . . ."

As she spoke, she plunged her hand into her purse for her trusty red pen. "Circles on diagonal letters," she muttered to herself. "Whoever constructed this must have a truly urgent message."

Her hand raced over the paper. "2-Down: VENOM . . . 5-Down: *Cape* ANN . . . 41-Across: '*Swept* AWAY,' *Wertmuller film* . . . Is this another nautical theme?"

Then her pen suddenly halted. "50-Across: *Polycates, e.g.* I get it. No 'R.' I guess that makes it RLESS . . . Hmm . . . What's going on here? 9-Down: *Rosco's proposal* . . . 20-Down: *Sentiment from Rosco to Belle* . . . What?"

She looked up at Rosco in wonderment and joy. "Yes," she smiled, "Oh, yes."

Across

1. Big initials down under?
4. Lowly fish?
8. Direct distribution company
13. CSA, formerly
14. Agent's share
15. Pool-table covering
16. Literary monogram
17. Mexican mister
18. Mild oaths
19. Brighter
21. Soothsayer
23. Melt ore
24. In song, it's built for two
28. Safety org.
31. Alien messages on the Internet?
32. "Imus in the Morning" claim?
36. Author Bombeck
37. Bunch of badgers
38. German mug
40. 60s happening
41. "Swept———," Wertmuller film
42. Green Mountain, e.g.
44. Iron column
47. Young horse
48. Guarantees
50. Polycates, e.g.
54. 1980 WBC champ
56. Land a fish?
57. "The———Brothers," Aykroyd film
60. Assistants
62. Lexington inst.
63. Pitcher of record, 1951 All-Star game
64. Fortunate
65. Shoe size
66. New———resolution
67. Mailed
68. Monopoly purchase, abbr.

Down

1. Some South Africans
2. Spite
3. Search for water
4. Suds
5. Cape———
6. Portico in ancient Greece
7. Brush
8. Run off with
9. Rosco's proposal
10. Military battle stat.
11. Antiviral drug, abbr.
12. Belle's answer to 9-Down?
14. African fly
20. Sentiment from Rosco to Belle
22. Judo outfit
25. Watches out (for)
26. *The Sky's the———*, Astaire-Leslie film
27. Impetuous ardor
29. Holds
30. Place to find cartoons? abbr.
32. Clark's pal
33. Slanted letters, abbr.
34. Government duty, abbr.
35. Annoy
37. Famed photographer Robert———
39. Cartoon denial
43. Most unique
45. Reliances
46. Cloth end
49. Swedish imports
51. Glass eel
52. Where Kish was
53. Peeper
55. It runs north
56. Break
57. Social reformer Nellie———
58. Love, Scot.
59. "———creek, without a paddle"
61. Lair

POSTSCRIPT PUZZLE

ANSWERS

PUZZLE 1

D	E	L	T	A		B	O	A	T		W	A	R	S
O	R	I	O	N		O	N	C	E		A	L	A	I
A	R	E	Y	O	U	Y	E	T	L	I	V	I	N	G
			L	S	D				N	E	A	T	H	
M	S	R	F	D	S		F	H	L	B		S	S	T
A	T	O	L	L		C	R	E	E	D				
J	A	M	A	I	C	A	I	N	N		O	R	T	
	D	E	C	E	I	V	E	R	S	E	V	E	R	
	I	R	K		G	E	N	I	E	G	E	N	I	E
		H	A	R	D	S		O	N	E	A	L		
B	O	G		E	R	N	S		I	T	S	E	L	F
U	S	U	A	L			F	L	A					
T	H	E	F	I	S	H	W	I	L	L	B	I	T	E
T	E	S	T		Y	A	W	L		K	I	T	E	S
S	A	S	S		S	W	I	M		S	T	O	N	E

PUZZLE 2

R	A	T			H	I	P	S		R	A	F	E	R
I	S	H		M	O	O	R	E		E	R	E	C	T
F	I	E		O	F	W	A	R		R	O	A	M	S
F	A	L	S	E	F	A	C	E	M	U	S	T		
S	N	A	P		A	N	T		O	N	E	U	P	S
		P	E	A		S	I	F	T	S		R	E	O
	S	P	E	W	S		C	I	I		S	E	T	S
	H	I	D	E	W	H	A	T	F	A	L	S	E	
S	I	N	S		I	A	L		S	P	E	C	S	
A	V	G		A	P	P	L	E		A	Z	O		
C	A	S	T	L	E		Y	R	S		A	R	M	S
		H	E	A	R	T	D	O	T	H	K	N	O	W
S	H	O	E	R		A	E	I	O	U		H	O	E
A	U	R	U	M		N	A	C	R	E		E	N	D
S	T	E	P	S		A	D	A	M			R	Y	E

PUZZLE 3

F	A	K	E	D		A	N	N	E	S		E	R	A
I	R	I	S	H		S	O	N	A	R		L	E	T
N	E	W	S	O	N	T	H	E	R	I	A	L	T	O
K	A	I		T	O	R	I				L	E	A	N
		W	E	N	O	T		R	E	V	E	N	G	E
F	A	T	A	L	E	S		O	D	I	C			
I	C	E	R			O	B	I	E		B	A	T
T	H	E	Y	A	R	E	N	O	T	W	O	R	T	H
S	Y	N		C	O	V	E			V	I	V	A
			S	H	O	E		E	A	S	I	E	S	T
M	A	N	B	E	T	R	U	S	T	E	D			
A	M	O	I			S	T	O	A		S	M	S
C	A	N	C	A	T	C	H	H	I	M	O	N	C	E
R	I	O		D	O	N	E	E		E	R	O	D	E
O	N	S		T	O	N	E	R		N	O	W	I	N

PUZZLE 4

¹C	²H	³E	⁴R		⁵L	⁶I	⁷F	⁸E	⁹R		¹⁰C	¹¹C	¹²P
¹³S	A	V	E		¹⁴I	R	A	T	E		¹⁵O	H	I	¹⁶O
¹⁷A	T	E	L	¹⁸E	V	E	N	A	M		¹⁹M	A	X	I
			²⁰E	V	E	N				²¹P	E	R	I	L
	²²G	²³R	E	A	S	E	D		²⁵P	R	A	T	E	S
²⁶A	L	E			²⁷R	²⁸A	O	U	L				
²⁹R	E	H	³⁰A	³¹B		³²T	E	L	L	N	O	O	³³N	³⁴E
³⁶I	N	O	N	A		³⁷R	A	T		³⁸E	N	R	O	L
³⁹A	N	E	N	D	⁴⁰G	A	M	E		⁴¹S	E	I	S	M
		⁴²A	G	A	P	E					⁴³O	A	S
⁴⁴F	⁴⁵I	⁴⁶B	B	E	R		⁴⁷R	⁴⁸O	⁴⁹B	⁵⁰B	⁵¹I	N	G
⁵²I	D	L	E	R		⁵³L	I	O	N				
⁵⁴R	E	A	L		⁵⁵D	⁵⁶E	⁵⁷W	D	R	O	P	⁵⁸I	⁵⁹N	⁶⁰N
⁶¹E	A	R	L		⁶²U	N	W	E	D		⁶³U	T	A	H
	⁶⁴L	E	A		⁶⁵B	E	I	N	S		⁶⁶T	A	E	L

PUZZLE 5

¹C	²A	³B	⁴S	■	■	⁵T	⁶I	⁷M	■	■	⁸S	⁹T	¹⁰L	¹¹O
¹²P	L	O	W	■	¹³W	¹⁴R	O	T	E	■	¹⁵P	R	O	W
¹⁶O	T	O	E	■	¹⁷R	I	M	E	D	■	¹⁸E	A	R	N
■	¹⁹A	N	E	²⁰Y	E	F	O	R	A	²¹N	E	Y	E	■
²²R	E	T	U	N	E	R	■	²³R	E	D				
		²⁴C	R	C	■	²⁵R	²⁶T	E	S	■	²⁷M	²⁸O	²⁹P	
³⁰A	³¹T	³²O	O	T	H	³³F	O	R	A	³⁴T	O	O	T	H
³⁵L	A	H	R	■	■	³⁶E	W	E	■	■	³⁷N	O	I	R
³⁸S	O	O	³⁹N	⁴⁰I	T	S	M	Y	⁴¹C	⁴²H	A	N	C	E
⁴³O	S	H	■	⁴⁴T	I	S	A	■	⁴⁵H	E	B			
		⁴⁶D	I	F	■	⁴⁷Y	⁴⁸E	A	R	■	⁴⁹O	⁵⁰U	T	
	⁵¹T	⁵²O	O	F	F	E	⁵³R	A	T	R	U	T	H	
⁵⁴N	O	R	M	■	⁵⁵A	P	A	R	T	■	⁵⁶N	A	R	⁵⁷K
⁵⁸E	R	L	E	■	⁵⁹N	O	I	S	Y	■	⁶⁰C	H	O	O
⁶¹T	O	Y	S	■	⁶²Y	E	N	■	■	■	⁶³E	N	E	S

POSTSCRIPT PUZZLE
ROSCO'S SUPRISE!